WANT

THE FIGHT CLUB, BOOK FIVE

BECCA JAMESON

ACKNOWLEDGMENTS

To my fans. Thank you for loving my dominant fighters. I appreciate you more than I can express.

PROLOGUE

Sabrina could not tolerate another minute of the intense scrutiny coming from across the room. She glanced up from her uneaten slice of pizza to verify that Professor Bascott was indeed still glaring at her. His expression was hard, his brow furrowed as though he was aggravated.

A chill raced up her spine, not for the first time.

Why was the infuriating man staring at her?

She shivered and squirmed in her seat, narrowing her gaze at Dr. Bascott. Something was different about the way he watched her today, his expression more intense than she remembered. If she didn't know better, she would swear he looked like he wanted to tear her clothes off and fuck her in the middle of the restaurant.

No way.

She shook the feeling from her mind and glanced at her friends.

Her friend Dana continued to yap about some sort of office gossip that meant nothing to Sabrina. Thank God Dana had a willing audience in their other two girlfriends

1

at the table, because Sabrina had done little for the last half hour but monitor the gaze stabbing her from several tables away.

Dr. Bascott had been the bane of her existence for the entire spring semester. The man was unbelievably sexy with fantastic dark hair—shaved very short on the sides and left longer on top—and stunning blue eyes that could nail a woman to the wall and leave her speechless. He was fine to look at all right. Better than fine. He was built, his enormous chest bulging beneath every shirt he wore, and his ass a drool-worthy specimen half the student population ogled without apology—the female half. Or, truth be told, probably some of the male half also.

One literature class. That was all she'd taken at the university. It had been over for two months. She'd finally managed to get Dr. Bascott out of her head—sort of. And here he was at King Pizza, a favorite restaurant and bar among everyone she'd ever met.

Fuck.

Another glance.

Still he stared. Or glared. She couldn't decide which.

And she wasn't certain his look wasn't one of lust instead of aggravation.

Dr. Bascott also sat at a table of friends, most of whom looked like they must go to the same gym as him—or take the same steroids at least. All of whom appeared considerably younger.

She hated how badly she lusted after him. She'd hated it all semester. And she still hated it, sitting in her chair squirming against the pulsing of her pussy and the tightness of breasts that suddenly felt too large for her bra.

The problem was the man was a first-class asshole. He'd done little more than grunt at her like she had the plague for the entire semester. And by the looks of things, he didn't think any more highly of her now than he had then. Right?

Nothing she wrote pleased him. Nothing she said in class pleased him. Hell, she couldn't even please him with correct multiple-choice answers.

She cleared her throat and pushed back from the table. "Bathroom. Be right back." She took a deep breath as she walked from the room to the side hall, holding her head high and trying not to trip and fall.

She didn't exhale until she sequestered herself in the blessedly individual restroom and leaned against the door. She bent forward and set her hands on her knees, as though hyperventilating. She didn't need to pee. She needed to regroup, grow a spine, or at least get the hell out of Dodge so she could resume another two months of waking up panting over that damned exasperating man.

She moaned. That's what was going to happen. Seeing him in her favorite pizza joint had not only ruined her taste for the food there, but also set her back in time.

Unfortunately, she had forgotten to lock the door. It hadn't been the first thing on her mind, especially since she had no intention of using the toilet. She jolted forward as someone opened the door, pushing hard as though it was stuck. Not shocking.

Sabrina righted herself and grabbed for the handle, shocked to find a huge male body in her way, not a woman.

She gasped as Dr. Bascott pushed the door closed and filled her space, stepping around her, turning her, and pinning her against the door. He stared at her hard for several seconds, his brow still furrowed.

And then he smiled.

Sabrina was unable to utter a single sound. That's how shocked she was.

Stunning her further, he set his hands on her shoulders

and lowered his mouth to hers. He didn't hesitate. He met her lips at a slight angle and kissed her. He wasn't slow and gentle about it either. More like a starving man who had waited all evening for a taste, and finally getting his opportunity, ravaged her.

Sabrina melted into the door. Dr. Bascott could kiss. *Holy shit.*

She grabbed onto his biceps, forgetting entirely how pissed she had been two seconds ago with this very man. All thought fled her brain as his tongue slid between her lips, demanding entrance.

She freely gave him what he wanted, opening her mouth and letting him devour her.

He kissed with a high level of urgency, as though the world would self-destruct in a few minutes and they needed to hurry. And then he pressed into her, his hands wandering down from her shoulders to her waist. Without hesitation, he grabbed the hem of her shirt and broke the kiss to tug it over her head. He set it on the vanity next to her and met her gaze.

Sabrina hadn't breathed since he'd entered the room. She licked her lips, but then he was on her again, this time cupping her breasts while he tasted her mouth.

She moaned, and Dr. Bascott swallowed her sound. She could have sworn he smiled against her lips. Her breasts swelled as he squeezed them in his palms. When his thumbs tugged the cups of her bra down to flick over her nipples, she bucked into him.

The only word she could think was *more.*

After burning for this man for so many months, she needed him like she needed her next breath. Even if she was dreaming, she didn't care. It was worth it. For a moment she considered that perhaps she had fallen and hit her head and this was where her mind took her while she lay unconscious on the floor.

Totally worth it.

Her nipples continued to harden under his touch as he pinched them between his thumbs and pointers. And then his hands were gone, and she moaned again, hating the loss of his touch against her breasts.

But only for a second, because suddenly his huge fingers were at her jeans, popping the button and lowering the zipper. His lips trailed from her swollen mouth to nibble a path to her ear. "Stand still," he whispered. "Patience."

She hadn't realized she was squirming, wanting her jeans to disappear faster, needing his cock inside her.

Insanity.

She didn't give a fuck.

Insanity won.

She pressed her hips forward when his thigh landed between her legs, rubbing her pussy against him, burning with arousal.

Dr. Bascott set his teeth on the skin behind her ear and bit down, just enough to get her attention. "Stop."

She froze. Stop what?

He leaned back and met her gaze, his hands on the opening of her jeans. His face was fierce with concentration, his brow furrowed as he reprimanded her. "If you want this… If you want my cock inside you, you'll stop wiggling."

She held herself rigid; her nipples, pressing out of her bra awkwardly, pulsed with the need for more contact. Her pussy flooded at his demand. If she didn't know better, she would swear he was a Dom. But that was so unrealistic…

She had to be dreaming. Only in her dreams would her

perfect man also happen to be a Dom. Real life was never that kind.

She nodded, sucking her lower lip between her teeth.

Without dropping his gaze, Dr. Bascott lowered her jeans, tugging them over her hips until he had to squat to pull them off her feet. She stepped out of her flip-flops to help the process, and when he smoothed his hands back up her body from her calves to her thighs, she shivered.

He lifted his face to meet her gaze as he pulled her panties down next. Her cheeks burned as she watched him stuff her panties in his back pocket. She was essentially naked in front of him. And he was fully clothed.

And then his mouth was on hers again, her hands were lifted in the air above her head, and his thigh was between her legs, forcing them wider.

The instant her soaking pussy and aching clit hit the denim of his jeans, she rose on her tiptoes and moaned louder into his mouth.

Dr. Bascott pulled her lower lip between his teeth and nipped her enough to remind her of her role. *Stand still.* He didn't need to repeat the command.

The need was unbearable, but he didn't make her wait long. Shifting both her wrists to one hand, he used the other to pop his own fly and shimmy the jeans down enough to release his cock.

She could see nothing with his tongue dancing against hers, but she felt his cock bob against her belly as he pulled something from his back pocket. Undoubtedly a condom.

At least he had the sense to use one. In fact, with one free hand, he managed to open the wrapper and push the rubber down his cock, never breaking the kiss.

The air whooshed from her lungs when both his hands reached under her arms to lift her off the ground. She'd read about such a possibility in books, but never considered fucking someone against the wall as a feasible reality.

She'd been wrong. Dr. Bascott was tall and lean and muscular. It was clear he expended no effort hoisting her off the ground and forcing her to hover above his cock.

"Please," she mumbled. She was so wet and needy. She wasn't above begging.

"Ask for it."

"Please, Sir. I need your cock inside me." She grabbed his shoulders and dug her nails into his skin. She flinched when she realized she'd called him Sir.

He made no indication he noticed. "That's my girl." As soon as he finished speaking, he thrust into her, lowering her body at the same time he bucked forward to bring his cock into her to the hilt.

Sabrina inhaled sharply. So full. God, his cock was huge. And he knew how to use it. If only he would move...

No one had ever fucked her like this. No one had ever entered her without preparing her pussy first. Hell, no one had ever taken her at all before she'd dated them for at least a month.

This wasn't a man she was dating. He wasn't someone she even liked five minutes ago. And now his cock was buried in her, and all she could think about was how badly she wanted him to pick up the pace. So badly she almost missed the look on his face that attested to his lack of control.

The always stoic Dr. Bascott was closer to orgasm than he would like.

Just as quickly as he'd entered her, he lifted her up and let his cock slide out about halfway before thrusting back home.

Sabrina whimpered. She gripped his shoulders so hard there would be marks. She didn't care. She had never needed to come this badly in her life. "Please," she begged.

"Greedy girl," he admonished. But he didn't stop fucking her hard and fast against the bathroom door. Faster. Harder. Deeper. It seemed like he would split her in two. She willed him to do just that. Her orgasm was so close her vision blurred.

Dr. Bascott cocked his hips forward slightly, making her clit rub against him with each stroke.

That was all she needed. She tipped her head back. Her mouth fell open, but no sound came out. So close...

"Come for me, baby."

She obeyed, her orgasm ripping through her body, pulsing with the pent-up need she'd carried for months.

She moaned. One of his palms landed across her mouth as he released her hip. His cock remained buried deep inside her. "Shhh. Too loud, baby."

It took several deep breaths before she floated back down to Earth and realized he came at the same time she did. She'd been so engrossed in her own orgasm, she only caught the tail end of his pulsing cock inside her. That's how violently her pussy had grasped him.

She blinked and licked her lips as Dr. Bascott released her mouth and lifted her off his cock. He steadied her on the floor and then turned around to dispose of the condom.

Without saying a word, he put her clothes back on her, straightening her bra and pulling her shirt over her head first, and then leaning down to tap her legs one at a time until he had her jeans back in place also. He kept her panties.

Externally, she assumed she was back to rights.

Internally, she was a hurricane. What the hell just happened?

Dr. Bascott finally leaned into her against the door. He gripped her chin, kissed her thoroughly but briefly, and then eased her away from the door. Before she knew what happened, he was gone.

Eyes wide, mouth open, she glanced around the room and met her gaze in the mirror. "Holy shit." She turned on the faucet and splashed cold water on her cheeks. She was barely composed, and definitely shaking, when she opened the bathroom door.

Thank fuck no one stood outside the room waiting. She'd have died on the spot.

The first place her gaze landed when she stepped back into the main room was Dr. Bascott's table. He was gone. In fact, his entire party was gone. A family of six now occupied the space.

Sabrina made her way back to her friends. Surprisingly, neither of them mentioned her prolonged absence. She was relieved there was no interrogation. The last thing she needed was the third degree. In fact, she grabbed her purse from the table without sitting.

"You okay, Sabrina?" Dana asked.

"Yeah. My stomach's a little upset. I'm gonna go ahead and go." Sabrina nodded toward the entrance, backing that way.

"Oh. Okay. Well, get some rest. I'll call you."

Sabrina turned and left without another word. She knew her minutes were numbered before she would break down in a shivering pile of tears.

Because what happened in that restroom wasn't a simple fuck against the door. Nope. It was a total act of domination, and Sabrina recognized she'd been in a sub space that was going to leave her in tears and then wrung out before she could drive herself home.

If she could just make it to her car…

She walked out the front door, half expecting the man who had rocked her world to be standing in the parking lot. But her wish was not granted. Dr. Bascott was indeed gone.

Whatever aftercare Sabrina needed, she was going to have to administer it to herself.

∼

Angelica Hudson glared her own brand of dagger at the restroom door. She'd watched the play-by-play for the last hour. She saw how Professor Bascott looked at that bitch. She'd watched the exchange of looks until both parties were sequestered in the fucking restroom of King Pizza—fucking. She had no doubt.

"That skanky-ass ho," she mumbled under her breath as she watched Dr. Bascott exit the bathroom first, looking like nothing untoward had occurred. Instead of heading back into the main section of the restaurant, he turned in the other direction and headed out the back door.

It took a few more minutes for Sabrina to exit. She looked far worse than Dr. Bascott had.

Angelica stiffened. *Yep.* They had definitely fucked like bunnies in the goddamn bathroom.

After working her tail off to get Dr. Bascott to notice her for months, Angelica was pissed. *That fucking bitch thinks she can waltz in here and bat her little eyes and lure him into her web?*

"Ang? Girl, where are you?"

Angelica jerked her gaze back to her friend Renee and forced a smile. "Right here."

"Nope. You're about a hundred miles from here. And you look like you want to kill someone." Renee twisted around to see what might be behind her.

Nothing was there of course. Sabrina was walking toward the front door, looking like her legs would only hold her upright for a limited number of steps.

Renee turned back and lifted her slice of pizza. "You haven't eaten a bite yet," she said around her full mouth, nodding at the entire pie on the table missing only the one piece Renee currently enjoyed. "You said you were starving."

Yeah, I was. Before that ho came in and sat down across the room as though she were a magnet for sexy older men.

What the hell did Dr. Bascott see in her? She was small and skinny with no boobs to speak of.

Angelica sat up straighter. *Unlike me.* She glanced down at herself. Women envied her body, and men lusted after it. She knew she had the entire package, all the right curves with huge boobs, full lips, and gorgeous long black hair. Why on earth Dr. Bascott preferred that bitch was beyond her. The woman didn't even put forth any effort.

Angelica, on the other hand, had worked that scene forever. She had no intention of accepting this development without a fight.

She watched as Sabrina stopped outside the glass front of the restaurant and leaned against the window.

"I have to go," Angelica announced, standing.

Renee's mouth fell open. "Now? We haven't even started."

"Yeah, I don't feel so well." She grabbed her stomach. "I'll catch you later. Sorry." Angelica reached into her purse, pulled out a few bills, and laid them on the table next to Renee to cover her part of the meal.

"Okay. Be careful. Hope you feel better," Renee stammered at Angelica's back as she walked away.

Sabrina was climbing in her car when Angelica stepped outside. She drove a red Honda Accord with a bumper sticker on the back that read:

EDITORS DO IT WITH PUNCTUATION!

What the hell did that mean? "What a geek."

CHAPTER 1

Two months later...

"Oh. My. God." Conner's entire body stiffened as his gaze landed on Sabrina Duluth's sexy ass. An ass that was barely covered by the short black skirt she wore. In fact, *covered* might have been a stretch. He was pretty sure he could actually see the bottom of each cheek every time she took another step away from him.

Zane sat next to him at the bar, twisting his head around to follow Conner's gaze. "What? Oh, wow. Sweet. I think she's with someone though."

Conner adjusted his cock. Two seconds ago, it had been perfectly flaccid. Now, holy mother of God.

Zane turned back to face him. "Conner?"

"I know her," he muttered.

"You do? I've never seen her here before."

"Me neither."

"Where do you know her from?"

"She was in my British literature class last semester."

"Wait. Don't tell me she's the hot chick you mentioned a few times?"

"The very one." Conner continued to watch her back, craning his neck to see where she headed. He'd spoken of her months ago. He had not, however, mentioned the incident in King Pizza. Even though Zane had been there —hell, all six guys from The Fight Club had been there— he'd left them to follow her to the restroom. In a moment of insanity, he'd literally fucked the woman against the bathroom door. He couldn't believe he'd done it even eight weeks later. He'd barely stopped thinking about her every hour of every day. He'd whittled it down to perhaps only at night…and a few times a day. That's how sweet she'd been. He'd forced himself not to hunt her down for all these weeks to get another taste of her own brand of heaven.

What he had not done was burn her out of his system by fucking her in the bathroom. He'd told himself the entire semester she was way too innocent for the likes of him, and he'd used that motto to keep her at arm's length, going so far as to treat her harsher than the other students, just so there would be no misunderstanding.

Until the afternoon at King Pizza. When he saw her squirming in her seat unable to take her gaze off him, he needed to have her. Like a drug, he was lured to her.

And like an idiot, he took her. She held his entire life in her hands now. She could ruin him if she wanted. Fucking a student was strictly forbidden.

That pissed him off. Even though it was entirely his fault.

And here she was in Extreme. A BDSM club. One of the top clubs in the Vegas area. A club where *he* was a member. *Not* her. And he wanted things to stay that way.

Deep down, he'd known she was submissive after that incident. Even if *she* hadn't known, he had. She was way too young to dabble in BDSM, however. Way too young for him. And way *way* too young to be hanging out at Extreme.

The woman was off limits. He hadn't seen her on campus this semester, but that didn't mean she wasn't taking classes in other departments. He was an asshole of the largest variety.

And here she was walking through his life again. *In my fucking club.*

Zane chuckled, completely oblivious to Conner's plight, both the physical and emotional plights he fought. "What luck. She's into BDSM." He paused. "Although, again, it seems she's with that guy who has his hand on her back."

Conner stood, scooting his stool back several inches. He didn't have the first clue what he intended to do, but sit on his ass and watch her wasn't an option. Hell, it hadn't been an option the last time he'd seen her either. Thus the restroom incident.

The woman pulled him in like a magnet.

"Conner." Zane grabbed his arm. "You better think about this, dude. Now doesn't look like a good time to approach her." Zane had no idea what Conner was so worked up about. He was misinterpreting Conner's haste, probably assuming lust drove Conner to react.

Although, on the one hand, that was true. The lust Conner felt for Sabrina Duluth made his cock hard and his blood pump. And if he thought his cock had been stiff for her sweet ass two months ago at King Pizza, after having a taste of her, his cock was solid steel this time.

Conner seethed. He'd had his eye on Sabrina Duluth for the entire spring semester. Fraternizing with a student was more than prohibited. Besides the fact it was against university policy, it was entirely unethical. Conner would never cross that line. Never. But then he had. He wanted to scream for his foolishness over the summer. All she'd have to do was turn him in, and he'd be fired on the spot.

It had been a rough several months with Sabrina's cute ass sitting in the second row of his class three times a week. It had been a rougher two months since he'd had her.

At thirty-eight, Conner was far too old for her. He'd never once in all his years of teaching considered dating a student. Until January. He'd scampered from the classroom more times than he could count to avoid making eye contact with Sabrina or revealing the hard-on he inevitably got each time she spoke in class.

He closed his eyes for a moment and gripped the edge of the bar. He could picture her licking her lips before she asked a question, her timid hand held in the air. The way she tossed her long brown curls over her shoulder.

The first day he saw her, he did a double take and swallowed his tongue. Assuming she was an eighteen-year-old freshman, he'd chastised himself repeatedly. As time went by, he began to doubt she was actually *that* young. She didn't giggle with the other girls in class. It didn't seem she knew anyone, nor did she take the opportunity to get to know them.

It would have been easier to ignore her if she'd been in her teens. But Sabrina was undoubtedly a woman, not a girl. Way too young for him, but old enough not to feel like some sort of pervert when he lusted after her.

"Conner. Let's think this through."

Conner opened his eyes to meet Zane's gaze. "You're right." He sat back down, but stared across the room where Sabrina disappeared down the side hall. "Shit. Do you think she's doing a scene?"

"It's possible. Or watching one."

The hall she'd turned down had a series of three-sided rooms where Doms and subs could play while other patrons watched. The idea crawled up Conner's spine and made him stiffen his neck. He moaned.

"Does she know you're into her?"

"Of course not." Conner furrowed his brow. "I haven't seen her for months. I've never been so relieved for a class to end." That wasn't entirely true. He had seen her—once. But that didn't mean she knew he was into her.

"Okay, then it really isn't reasonable for you to stomp up to her and go all caveman. She's with a guy. You're going to have to handle this another time."

Conner took a deep breath. "I have no business handling this *ever*. She's a student."

"It's a new year. She's not in your class anymore, right?"

"Yeah, but that doesn't mean she's not going to show up in one of my other classes someday. If she's an English major, there's a good chance I'll have her again. I still can't approach her. It's totally against school policy to date a student, even if she isn't in my class." He cringed, listening to his own lecture.

Zane leaned forward, blocking the spot where Conner's gaze wandered again. Zane's grin was huge.

Conner startled. "What?" He shook his head to clear it. There was no way he was ever going to have that woman again.

"Want me to see where she went?" Zane asked, ignoring Conner's rhetorical question.

"No." Conner stood again. He didn't say anything to Zane as he walked away, heading in the direction his sexy student had traveled. He wouldn't confront her. That would be beyond uncomfortable. He just wanted to know where she went. Another glimpse of her wouldn't hurt anything. She would never know. And then he'd leave the club. Obviously tonight wasn't a good night for him to be at Extreme.

Hell, if she started coming to the club often, he'd never be able to return.

Sauntering slowly down the viewing hall, Conner scanned in every direction, unsure if he would find Sabrina watching or participating. If he found her inside one of the rooms with that other Dom's hands on her... Hell, he didn't know what he might do.

Nothing, you asshole. You don't own her. And you have a moral obligation to completely ignore her.

Suddenly, he stopped dead in his tracks. There she was. He couldn't breathe. For one thing, the hint of perfect ass he'd seen peeking out from under her skirt was completely in his line of sight. She was positioned on a spanking bench, her smooth white cheeks exposed with her skirt pushed up to her lower back. He could make out the distinct tan line that split her ass from her thighs.

She wore a thin, lacy, black thong that barely covered her pussy. With her legs spread on the pads of the bench, she left little to the imagination.

Conner's gaze darted to the man dominating her as he set his hands on Sabrina's ass and massaged her cheeks. Conner didn't know him, though he'd seen him at Extreme before. He was closer to Conner's age than Sabrina's. He was built and tall, though not as built or as tall as Conner, but few people were.

When the first spank landed on Sabrina's ass, Conner flinched—not because he was averse to watching a woman get her ass swatted but because he had a deep clawing urge to yank this particular Dom off Sabrina and take over the scene.

He wouldn't, of course. But he fisted his hands at his sides and forced himself to remain still.

Conner's reaction was nothing compared to Sabrina's. The little minx moaned. Pink rose up on her smooth cheek as she squeezed her knees against the padded sides of the bench.

The second swat landed on the other cheek. The Dom was good. His blows were perfect. He wasn't a regular at Extreme, but Conner could see he was very familiar with the lifestyle and undoubtedly belonged to another club. He had experience. The evidence was on the perfectly pinkened ass of Ms. Duluth.

The man stepped between Sabrina's legs and molded his palms to her butt, massaging the sting.

Conner almost groaned. It had been years since he'd reacted like this to a woman. He'd had the hots for her for so long his balls ached. Seeing her with another Dom didn't make him feel warm and fuzzy. Even though he couldn't have her for himself, it smarted.

The Dom stepped back and resumed the role playing, landing several more strikes on Sabrina's ass and thighs until they were a gorgeous rosy color.

After another round of soothing touches to Sabrina's inflamed skin, the guy stepped around and leaned down to say something in Sabrina's ear.

She nodded. Her thick brown hair fell across her cheek, and the man tucked it behind her ear.

The Dom eased back.

Sabrina had turned her face in Conner's direction, however. And the second the Dom stepped out from Conner's line of sight, her gaze met his.

Conner inhaled sharply. He hadn't meant for her to see him. He was caught. He froze.

Her gaze widened. Her mouth opened. The Dom at her ass didn't notice.

Conner finally had the sense to spin around and walk

away. He turned the corner toward the main section of the club, taking deep breaths.

Shit.

Sabrina was under his skin. How the hell had that happened? He'd been a member of Extreme for years. He'd done hundreds of scenes with many different women. He'd even dated a few. Never had he had a reaction to a submissive like this. His cock was hard, and his heart pounded.

When he could manage to control his legs again, he ambled back toward the bar. Zane was no longer around. Thank God. The last thing he wanted to do was chat about what he'd seen.

"Water," he said to the bartender, who nodded and handed him a bottle.

The club didn't serve alcohol. If they had, Conner would have asked for the entire bottle of something stiff and taken about a dozen shots to get the image of Sabrina's fine ass out of his head.

"Fuck," he muttered under his breath. He needed air.

Conner headed for the entrance, which was at the back of the building, spilling into the parking lot instead of the street. The arrangement allowed people to come and go from Extreme without encountering the general public between their cars and the door. Many patrons arrived and left severely underdressed.

As soon as Conner stepped outside, he nodded at the guard, Frank, and leaned against the side of the building, several yards away from the door. He was supposed to meet up with Rafe and Mason later. He hated to bail on them and hoped if he hid for a while, he could avoid Sabrina and catch his friends outside when they arrived.

It was with this idea in mind that he took several deep

breaths, crossed his legs at the ankles, and let his head fall back to rest against the wall.

~

Sabrina couldn't breathe.

Doug continued to mold his hands to her burning rear cheeks, but she hadn't breathed for so long she wasn't sure she remembered how. He was an attentive Dom. He knew something was up, and he circled back toward her face and kneeled in front of her. "You okay, Sabrina?"

She stared at him for several moments, blinking. Her mind could only process the sexy Dr. Bascott, who had made eye contact with her and then fled as if the place were on fire. She had seen him correctly, right? She knew she had. After a semester of lusting after every aspect of that man, she would know him anywhere. Hell, even if all she saw was his hand or his elbow, she would know him. That's how much time she'd spent staring at his every feature for four months.

That would have been enough to cause her to pause. But after he busted into that restroom two months ago and fucked her against the door, her last brain cell had been sucked out. She was ruined for other men. Hell, she was ruined for other Doms.

Doug was a nice guy. More than nice. She wanted to feel something for him. In fact, she'd worked hard for the last month of seeing him to make that happen.

Professor Bascott shattered that hard work in two point five seconds.

Before the incident at King Pizza, she never acted on her lust for the sexy professor. She wasn't stupid. Besides, she assumed there was surely a Mrs. Bascott, even though the man didn't wear a wedding ring. At the very least, he had to have a girlfriend. That's how fucking sexy he was.

He didn't look like a British literature professor—whatever a British literature professor was supposed to look like. He looked more like a bodybuilder. But the man was passionate about his literature, and he knew it well.

The only thing that dampened his good looks was his attitude. Although he clearly enjoyed teaching and loved his job, he treated her with a certain level of distain the entire semester. She didn't think she imagined it. He never spoke to the other students with quite the same level of frustration. It didn't make him less sexy, however. And she hated that fact even more.

Sabrina blinked in an effort to dislodge herself from her wandering mind and return to the present. It was impossible. The scene was ruined.

"Sabrina," Doug repeated.

She licked her lips. "Sorry. I spaced." What was she supposed to say? *I just saw the man of my dreams, and he turned around and hightailed out of the room as though I'd bitten him.*

Doug set a hand on her shoulder. He stroked her cheek with his thumb. Suddenly she had very little interest in him. This was the first time she'd come with him to this particular club, and she wasn't sure if she thoroughly regretted the decision or wanted to thank Doug.

Nope. She was sure. Regret. Now she would have images of Dr. Bascott filling her brain for weeks again. She'd finally gotten to the point where she didn't think of him every other minute since the last time she'd seen him. It was almost October, for heaven's sake. She needed to shake Dr. Bascott and move on.

The unexpected made her head spin. "I'm sorry, Sir. I

seem to have broken the scene. Can we try it again another night?"

"Of course, hon." Doug smoothed her skirt back over her butt and helped her stand. He held her hand as she steadied herself. "You feel okay?"

She scrunched her face. The perfect excuse. "Just a headache. Thought it would go away. Guess it's distracting me."

He pulled her in close and hugged her against his chest. Her ass stung where her skirt swayed against her exposed cheeks, but she hadn't slipped into a subspace that required recovery. What she needed was to get the hell out of Extreme quickly before she saw Dr. Bascott again and made a fool of herself.

She lifted her face. "If you don't mind, I think I'll call it a night." Thank God they'd arrived in separate cars. The last thing she needed was to sit in awkward silence with Doug on the way back to her condo.

"Okay, hon. You sure you're all right?"

"Yeah. Call me tomorrow?"

"Of course." Doug squeezed her closer and planted a kiss on the top of her head. He turned toward the hall, still holding her hand. "I'll walk you to the door."

"Thanks, Doug." She squeezed his hand, silently thanking God Doug was so nice and easygoing. She felt like a bitch for leaving him like this and practically lying about it at the same time.

At the entrance, Doug kissed her softly on the lips and held her face tipped back to stare into her eyes. "You sure you're okay?"

"Yeah. I'll be fine."

"I'll call you tomorrow."

She smiled and headed out the door.

The man who worked at the entrance nodded. Frank.

He introduced himself when she arrived. "You need help getting to your car?"

"Nope. It's close. You'll be able to see me from here." She could spot her dark red Honda Accord in the second row of the parking lot.

She turned to step in that direction when she noticed movement out of her peripheral vision. Her automatic response was to glance that way. She was a smart girl. It wasn't prudent to ignore her surroundings in a dark parking lot late at night.

Her breath caught for the second time. Dr. Bascott. She couldn't see his face in the shadows, but she would know his stance anywhere. And now that she'd turned to face him, she had no choice but to acknowledge their acquaintance. She cleared her throat and took several steps toward him, her head held high.

Before she could say a word, he beat her. "Aren't you kinda young for this sort of thing, Ms. Duluth?"

Sabrina gasped. "Pardon?"

His voice was gruff, accusatory. "Which word didn't you understand?"

Jesus. The nerve. Was there any reason for him to be such an ass? They were both adults. So they'd run into each other at a local club. That wasn't a crime. No need to be an ass about it. It wasn't her fault he'd fucked her in a pizza restaurant bathroom. If he regretted it, that was on him.

She was on the defensive immediately, however. There was no way to avoid it. She wasn't a woman used to being stepped on. Sure, she dabbled in BDSM. She had for several years. But she was smart enough to know the power was all hers. If she chose to give herself over to a Dom for an evening of fun, it was her decision.

"How old do you think I am?"

Dr. Bascott chuckled. "Too young for a fetish club."

"Is that so? Isn't the age requirement eighteen?"

"Yep. But that's way too young in my opinion. No one that age knows themselves well enough to practice submission, or dominance for that matter."

"Huh." She set her hands on her hips and glared at him. She was close enough now to make out the edges of his face, but she couldn't read his expression. He stood in the shadow of the building. She was aware the reverse wasn't true. He could see her fine. The outside light hit her in the face, making her squint. "I guess as long as I'm eighteen, I should be able to make my own choices with regard to where I hang out and with whom."

"With whom?" He chuckled again. "I never saw you fraternize with anyone in class. You don't sound like a college student. Even an English major has worse grammar at your age."

She cocked her hip to one side, fighting the urge to slap him. She lowered her voice, glancing around to make sure no one could hear her. Frank wasn't paying any attention. "I wasn't too young for you to fuck in a public bathroom. But now I'm too young to frequent a club you happen to attend?" She didn't hesitate before she continued. "Not that it's any of your business, but I'm twenty-six, and I'm pretty sure I'm capable of making up my own mind about how I spend my evenings."

"Twenty-six?" He righted himself, pushing off from the wall and stepping into the light. "Fuck," he muttered under his breath.

What did that mean? "Listen, obviously it pisses you off to no end that I would dare to appear at the same club as you. Don't worry. I won't return. I don't know why you need to be such an asshole about it. It's hardly my fault you were here tonight."

"Good. As long as we agree on one thing."

"Seriously? That's all you have to say? You're an ass."

He flinched, his eyes going wide. "You shouldn't cuss. It's unbecoming."

"Fuck you. You spend the entire semester being a complete dick to me, without speaking more than a few words, you fuck me in a restaurant, and then you run into me at a club and wig out like you own the planet and my presence anywhere near your vicinity is appalling. I do live in this city. I can assure you I'll probably run into you from time to time. It happens. I eat at restaurants, drink coffee, grocery shop. It's life."

Dr. Bascott stepped closer. "I wasn't an ass to you all semester." He winced. He had been, and he knew it.

She hesitated and then rolled her eyes. "Oh, come on. Even the other students wondered why you acted like I had the plague."

He winced again, but didn't comment on her observation. Instead, he changed the subject. "Who was that Dom you were with? He's too old for you."

"Are you fucking kidding me? You have some nerve. Why do you care who the hell I sub for? Or fuck for that matter? You don't even like me." Her voice rose, and she fought to control her emotions. She could feel her cheeks heat with fury. He might be a sexy god, but that didn't mean she liked who he was on the inside. "Like I said, it's none of your fucking business. I'll choose my Doms, thank you. Although I'll be lucky if Doug ever calls me again after the way you disrupted my scene."

Dr. Bascott chuckled. "Me? I didn't do shit. If you got distracted, that's on you."

She gasped. He was right. Still an ass. But right.

"What are you, jealous?" The words slipped out unbidden before she could filter her response. He acted like a jealous teenager, though.

26

He shook his head and took another step toward her. Only a few feet separated them now. "I don't date students. And why would I care who you fuck?"

The way he said fuck was so harsh, she stepped back. "You shouldn't." She turned away from him and took two steps toward her car, hoping her legs would carry her that far before she lost her ability to command her muscles to move. She twisted to look back over her shoulder as she walked away. "I'm not a student anymore, big guy. I was only taking that one class." She bit her lip as she strode away, head held high, wondering why the hell she bothered to tell him that.

She was surprised he hadn't known before he thrust his cock into her. He could get fired for fraternizing with a student. Just thinking about what they'd done that day made her pussy cream all over again.

As if it hadn't been wet and waiting to do it again for two months.

∼

Conner watched Sabrina's sexy backside as she strode toward her car without looking back. God, she was hot. Smokin' hot. Her ass swayed as she walked, and he wondered if it was intentional. She tossed her hair over her shoulders. And she was not eighteen, but twenty-six. Still too young for the likes of him, but not a teenager. And not a student.

"Fuck," he muttered.

He watched her get into her car and drive away before he turned around and headed back inside. He'd intended to leave. But whoever Doug was, he decided he needed to have words with the man.

Sabrina Duluth was under his skin. He never wanted to

see her again, but he sure didn't want her coming to Extreme. This was his territory. She and her Dom could go elsewhere.

Nope, he wasn't fond of that idea either. He didn't want to think about her with the man she'd been with this evening. Notably she hadn't left with Doug, but after the weird confrontation Conner had with her, she'd probably been unnerved by the Dom and called the evening off early.

Good.

Oh, yeah. He was a world-class asshole. He didn't want her for himself. And the Dom she was with needed to lay off also. Both of them were too old for her anyway.

Keep telling yourself that, Conner.

It didn't take long to find Doug sitting at the bar with a soda in his hand. After all, his date had fled the building.

Conner sidled up next to the guy, his gaze roaming up and down the man's body. He was tall. Not as tall as Conner's six four, but almost. In either case, they both towered over Sabrina's tiny frame. She was at least a foot shorter than Conner. Maybe five two. Doug wasn't nearly as built as Conner, but few men who didn't fight MMA on the side were.

"Sorry, man," Conner said as he took the stool next to Doug.

Doug furrowed his brow. "For what?"

Suddenly it occurred to Conner that perhaps Sabrina hadn't mentioned to her date why she was leaving. "I saw your date leave. I might have had something to do with that."

"What?" Doug twisted his body to face Conner.

"She saw me watching your scene. I know her. I think she was stunned." That sounded polite enough.

"Ah." Doug took a drink of his soda. "I wondered what

her deal was. One second she was all in, and the next she was...well, all out." He smiled. "Has she subbed for you before?"

"Oh. Hell no. Nothing like that. I'm way too old for her."

Doug flinched. "You can't be older than me."

Conner swallowed hard. Doug was right. He was probably older. Open mouth. Insert foot. "Maybe, but I don't Dom for women that young."

"She's twenty-six. I know she looks much younger, but trust me, I asked for her driver's license the first night we met." Doug laughed. "I didn't believe it myself."

Conner forced a smile. He hadn't actually been sure what to believe when Sabrina announced the same thing outside.

"So, how do you know her?"

"She took a class at the university last semester. I was the professor."

"Ah, she mentioned that class. Said the teacher was a dick." Doug didn't drop Conner's gaze. The man had some balls.

Conner didn't doubt Sabrina said that about him, considering what she insinuated outside, but it smarted.

"Yeah, well..." *What, dude?*

"You want her." Doug grinned. He didn't phrase the statement as a question.

"Of course not."

"You do. And you're fucking jealous she was here with me."

Doug was astute. Conner couldn't really dispute this claim. It was spot on. "Maybe. Look, I'd appreciate it if you'd back off."

"From Sabrina? Fuck no. That woman is sexy and funny, and she makes my cock hard every time I'm near

29

her. If you hadn't shown up and fucked up my scene, I would have finally had her in my bed tonight." Doug stood, leaving his can on the counter. "Not a goddamn chance in hell I'm giving her up without a fight." He glanced up and down Conner's body. "You may outweigh me by several pounds, but I can take you in other areas, especially since she thinks you're an ass."

Doug had a point. Again.

Conner didn't know why he was posturing with this guy. He hadn't come over here to play cave man. But something had changed. And he was no longer quite so certain Sabrina wasn't someone he wanted to get to know better.

It pleased him immensely to find out she'd never slept with Doug.

Doug turned around and walked away. In a few seconds, he headed for the door, never glancing back at Conner.

Doug had one thing on Conner. That was for sure. He had Sabrina's phone number and address. Conner had neither. "Fuck me."

As if he didn't have enough on his mind, the second Doug left, someone else took his place at the bar, her hand sliding down Conner's back with a precision that told Conner exactly who he would face when he twisted toward the stool next to him.

Sure enough, there she was. In the flesh.

"Hello, Conner." Her syrupy sweet voice grated on his nerves with those two words. When he didn't respond to her, she stuck out her bottom lip and put on her pouty face. "What? No smile? No hey, Missy, how are ya?" She flipped her fake blonde hair over her shoulder and batted her blue eyes.

What the hell he'd ever seen in her, he didn't know, but

she was officially on his last nerve. "Not in the mood, Missy. Got a lot on my mind."

Missy leaned into him, pressing her enormous fake tits against his forearm. She ran her hand up his biceps and gave him more of her syrupy voice. "Bet I can help you forget your troubles."

Her touch did nothing for him. He wondered how it ever had. Instead of making him desire her, her fingers on his arm made him wince. He'd gotten a bigger hard-on for the feisty woman in the parking lot who did nothing but throw obscenities at him than Missy. Of course, Sabrina's cute little frame was more his type anyway. But when she cocked her hip to one side and took him to task... "Not tonight, Missy." *Not ever.*

Conner hadn't done a scene with Missy in months. And he never intended to again. The woman had ulterior motives. He was sure of it. She didn't just want *his* hands on her body, she wanted *her* hands in his wallet. And contrary to what she believed, his wallet wasn't that exciting.

Missy knew he was a fighter on the side. She'd made it clear she found that sexy. The trouble was she didn't believe he was strictly amateur. No matter how many times he explained that he made no money fighting and never intended to, she didn't buy that truth. She'd giggle. *"Nobody fights like you do for no money."*

Trouble with her theory was she was wrong.

Conner fought. He had for over half his life. He did it for the exercise, the exhilaration, the thrill of the win. He'd turned down many attempts to get him to go pro over the years because he valued his brain and his professional work over having his head beat in week after week until he became a vegetable.

Not that amateur fighting was significantly safer, but it

was an improvement. And he only fought in competition every few weeks. Giving up his academic life as a professor to tour the world getting pummeled had never been an option.

He'd also received numerous offers over the years to fight with the underground. He had absolutely no interest in that. But no matter how many times he explained that to the local Russian mob king, Anton Yenin, the man continued to hound him.

Missy pouted again. "Ah, honey…" She danced her fingers up and down his arm.

It was all he could do to keep from jerking away from her. There was no need to hurt her feelings. Just because he didn't care for her style didn't mean he needed to cause a scene. Although, he wondered why he bothered. How was it he could go head to head with Sabrina in the parking lot and not with Missy in the club?

Because Missy doesn't mean shit to you. She isn't worth the effort.

"Bet I can take your mind off whatever's bothering you." She moved her hand from his biceps to his thigh and squeezed, letting her fingers inch closer to his cock.

Conner stiffened. He really didn't want her hands on him. The only hands he wanted on him were Sabrina's, and that wasn't going to happen, but it didn't change where his mind was. He set his hand over Missy's and lifted it off his leg. He needed to make himself clearer. Grasping her fingers a bit too tight, he looked her in the eye. "Missy, it isn't happening between us. We did a few scenes. It was fun. I'm not interested."

She gasped as though he'd slapped her.

"Sorry, but I need you to understand how I feel." She sure wasn't taking any hints.

"You'll regret this, Conner Bascott." She jerked her hand

from his and jumped down from the stool to turn on her heels and stomp away.

Good. He was exhausted. The last thing he needed was a fight with another woman.

Conner glanced around. He was too pissed to stay at the club. Rafe and Mason were not there yet. Even though they had planned to hang out, Conner decided he was in no frame of mind to be good company. He nodded at the bartender, stepped off the stool, and headed for the door.

The sooner he got home and climbed into bed, the better. His track record sucked for the night.

CHAPTER 2

On Monday, Conner was in a mood. Nothing he did chased Sabrina Duluth from his mind. He wanted her worse than he had for months. Maybe if he had never seen her again, he'd have been able to shake her from his dreams. But now that she'd come to Extreme, she'd given him a lot to think about. She was submissive, old enough to not be considered jailbait, *and* no longer enrolled at the university.

He thought he might sleep better knowing he hadn't committed a serious infraction by fucking her that day in King Pizza. The idea had haunted him for the two months since the incident. Whatever the fuck he was thinking that day, he didn't know. But sticking his cock in the woman in a public restaurant had been the dumbest decision he ever made in his life. *If* she'd still been enrolled, *if* she'd wanted to turn him in for harassment, *if* someone had seen them…

He shivered at all the thoughts that had circulated in his head since that insane moment of complete stupidity on his part. He could have easily thrown away his career for a quick fuck with a woman he didn't really know just because he had the hots for her. More than the hots.

He was relatively certain no one saw them meet in the bathroom, but there was always the possibility. Now it didn't matter what anyone saw. He could fuck her anywhere he wanted. There was no law against dating *former* students.

Relief was short-lived, however. He had too damn many things on his plate to take a moment to breathe. The weekend had been spent grading papers and recording scores. Monday was hectic. His only break was a student-free office hour. He wasn't shocked. After an exam, most students didn't have a lot of questions.

As he pulled into the gym parking lot later that evening, the last thing he wanted to do was go head–to-head with Anton Yenin. The man stood next to his car, leaning against the shiny chrome, his feet crossed at the ankles, his arms crossed over his chest.

"Yenin," Conner said, exasperated. He wanted to get inside, change, and beat the hell out of a punching bag. He did *not* want to have a verbal dual with Yenin.

"Bascott." The man's voice penetrated Conner's system, making him groan inwardly. Was it too much to ask for one evening of peace?

"What do you need, Yenin?"

"A fighter." Anton pushed from the car and stood upright. The man had a fucking limo with a driver. Everything about him screamed dirty money.

"I've told you a thousand times, not interested." Conner kept walking past Yenin.

Anton stepped in his path and halted him with a hand to his chest. "Need you. Big fight this weekend. Need to win. It's important."

Conner growled. "Anton, it's always important. And the answer is still no."

Yenin pursed his lips and firmed the pressure on Conner's chest. "Trying to ask nicely, bro."

"I'm not your bro." Conner stepped back a pace, narrowing his gaze. "And I'm not fighting for you."

"I have ways of forcing you to comply. It would be to your advantage to join my team willingly."

Conner stiffened and stood firm. He was a head taller than Yenin. Larger too. And Yenin was soft. Conner didn't have a weak spot on his body. "Are you threatening me, Anton?" he growled.

Anton shrugged. "Never said that."

"Sounded to me like you were threatening me." Conner stepped closer, glaring down at Yenin. "Let me repeat myself. I. Am. Not. Fighting. For. You. Ever."

"We'll see."

"Fuck you. You have nothing to threaten me with. I'm clean. I only play above the law. Now get the fuck out of my way so I can get to my workout." Conner pushed past Anton, shoving the man to the side as he took several long paces to the rear entrance.

He didn't look back, though he was aware Yenin could shoot him in the back if he wanted. But it wouldn't do the man any good. He still wouldn't have the fighter he seemed desperate for. And he'd have a shit ton of problems shooting a man in the back in the early evening in a public place.

No. That wasn't Yenin's style. The man had other means of getting what he wanted.

As soon as Conner was inside, he leaned against the wall and took a deep breath. "Fuck." He seriously hoped Yenin had been bluffing and full of hot air. The man did seem inordinately desperate, but surely he wouldn't stoop so low as to blackmail Conner to get what he wanted.

Could this day get any worse?

Conner shivered at the thought. At this point, nothing would surprise him.

∼

Ah, but his day could get worse.

Two hours at the gym sparring with Zane and then lifting with Rafe only managed to take the edge off his frustration.

Both men asked him a series of questions he wasn't prepared to answer. Zane wanted to know what happened with the student whose ass he'd been ogling before following her down the hall. Rafe found this beyond fascinating and decided the reason for Conner's disappearance Friday night must have had something to do with the sexy ass under the short skirt.

Both men were right. And Conner had no intention of satisfying either of them. For one, he had nothing to say since Sabrina Duluth unceremoniously put him in his place and stomped away without looking back. And two, Conner wasn't interested in a rehash of how the woman had spoken to him in the parking lot, both stiffening his cock to the point of pain while making him itch to spank her until she lost the same attitude that made him hard in the first place.

Instead of facing the two other members of The Fight Club currently at the gym, Conner provided them with nothing more than a series of grunts and pretended to be interested in lifting weights and not talking. It wasn't far from the truth. Ordinarily he would be glad to chat with the other guys while they lifted, but after the weekend and then day he'd had, he didn't have the energy.

When he finally got home, he grabbed a beer from the fridge and leaned against the kitchen counter to listen to his messages.

He pressed *Play* on the machine while he took a long swig of his beer.

The voice on the machine made him grit his teeth. "Fuck me." It would never end. He was stuck in hell.

"Conner. Darling. You're avoiding me." She giggled, a totally ridiculous sound coming from the mouth of a grown woman. Someone who should be completely professional.

Dr. Tina Chang.

Everything about her made him cringe. She was a faculty member. Ironically, considering her name was Tina, she was Chinese, and she was the head of the foreign language department. She had also been hot for him for several years. She pestered him endlessly. She was one of the few people from work who knew he frequented a BDSM club. She came there with a friend one time years ago and hadn't ceased throwing the night in Conner's face every chance she got.

The fact that he belonged to Extreme wasn't exactly a deep hidden secret. It also wasn't something he advertised at work. It wasn't against any rules. And it certainly wasn't against the law. However, for everyone's sake, it was easier for Conner to keep his private life just that. Private.

Unfortunately for Conner, he got a little tipsy at a faculty party last year and was blindsided when Tina backed him into a dark corner and stuck her tongue down his mouth. She'd had him in her sights ever since.

He tried to ignore her rambling on his machine. It wasn't the first time she'd left him a message at his home.

What he really wanted to do was enjoy his beer, take a long hot shower, and drop into bed to thoughts of Sabrina. Not Yenin, and certainly not Tina Chang.

"...so I need you for this. It's Saturday night. Six o'clock. I'll pick you up..."

What the fuck? Conner jumped to attention and rewound the machine to listen more closely. That crazy woman was trying to strong arm him into accompanying him to some sort of family function? Was she crazy? Again, what the fuck?

Her sing-songy voice kept coming. "We don't have to stay long, but I told my mom I was dating you, and she's hounding me to make a public appearance. I wouldn't ask if it weren't important. Okay?"

What? Why on earth would that woman tell her mother she was dating him? One kiss almost a year ago and she thought she owned him. Fucking Jesus Christ.

Conner tipped his beer back and downed the rest of the bottle without coming up for air.

When he finished, he slammed the bottle on the counter and yanked open the fridge to grab another. He didn't have enough beer in the house to sedate him enough to keep him from throwing something across the room.

He popped the top on the second bottle and pulled his cell from his pocket. With great haste, he texted Dr. Chang.

Tina, so sorry. I already have plans for Saturday night. Can't help you out.

He didn't give a fuck what plan he came up with for Saturday, or none at all, he wasn't going anywhere with that woman. Having his nails removed from their beds one at a time would be better.

Yes, indeed, his day could get worse...

39

CHAPTER 3

Sabrina sat seething in the parking lot of the university. She was still so pissed after a week of anger she couldn't control her emotions.

Goddamn that infuriating man and his interference in her life.

When Doug called her Sunday morning and asked her to dinner, she readily agreed. Anything to chase Dr. Bascott out of her head. It hadn't worked, however. She spent the entire meal making comparisons and causing Doug to come up short in every category, with the exception of his pleasantness.

She was shocked beyond measure when Doug casually mentioned his run-in with her professor after she left the club Friday night. The audacity of the asshole to suggest that Doug step aside.

Really? She couldn't believe how low he would stoop. And why? She understood on some level he was into her. She even convinced herself over the last several days the reason he'd been a dick to her all semester and then acted like a royal jackass at Extreme were both tactics he used to keep her at arm's length, when in reality he was into her. Why then did he so easily fuck her *one* time and then leave immediately, never contacting her again?

This knowledge didn't do her a bit of good. But it was enough to cause her to check into his schedule for the fall semester, plant herself in the parking lot she knew from experience he used, and lie in wait for him to emerge from the literature building.

She didn't have a clue what she intended to do when she saw him, but she was fired up anyway.

She wiped her palms on her jeans for the tenth time and gulped when Dr. Bascott came around the corner. He didn't glance up as he walked to his car. His head was buried in his phone. It was a wonder he didn't get hit by someone on his way across two aisles. She considered volunteering to be the one to hit him.

Sabrina froze. She couldn't get herself to exit the car. What the hell would she say? She had no intentions of railing on him in the parking lot of the university.

Instead, she decided to follow him. It seemed like an excellent choice. Then she would know where he lived. At least she'd be that much closer to facing the object of her frustration.

The man was infuriating. She was both hot and cold for him, and it pissed her off he had this effect on her. Damn him.

As he pulled out of his spot, she started her car. Soon, she was following him out of the parking lot and down the street like a first-class stalker.

They drove for several miles to the outskirts of town.

Where the hell is he going?

She'd assumed he lived nearby. Most of the professors owned or rented homes in the surrounding area. It was easy to get to work. And the neighborhood was nice.

Either Dr. Bascott didn't live in town, or he wasn't going straight home.

Shit.

Sabrina had serious doubts about her decision to stalk Dr. Bascott as soon as she pulled into the parking lot of an arena. The marquee indicated there was an amateur MMA fight occurring.

What the hell had she gotten herself into? She parked near Conner and watched as he exited his mid-life-crisis, deep blue Mustang GT. He got out, popped the trunk, and heaved a large gym bag out of the car. Without noticing her, he swung the bag over his shoulder and turned toward the arena.

Sabrina was stunned. She watched his ass as he walked away. He wore perfect-fitting khaki pants and a maroon polo. He had been dressed similarly every time she saw him last semester. And those damn pants fit him so fantastically…

He didn't go in the front entrance, which made her more curious. Instead he rounded the side of the building and disappeared.

Taking a deep breath, Sabrina removed her seatbelt and stepped out of the car. She had no idea what she intended to do, but she'd come this far, and curiosity ate a hole in her. Did he work at the arena in the evenings? Maybe he was a bouncer. He was certainly built for such a job, but why would he need the extra job? She figured university professors were paid well enough to enjoy life.

Sabrina entered the front of the building, paid the admission fee, and then made her way into the crowded stadium. She'd never been to a fight of any sort, and the scene that greeted her was shocking. The arena was large, but packed. It was loud too. Everyone was screaming, though she couldn't discern a single word. Her gaze rose from the throng of spectators to the fenced area in the center of the room.

Two fighters were in the middle of a match, or whatever it was called. The spectators were on their feet, shouting at the two sweaty men who wore only shorts and gloves. They seemed engaged in a choreographed dance, hopping around each other.

Until one of them threw a punch and knocked the other to his knees. The crowd screamed louder.

Sabrina glanced around the room. There was no way in hell she would ever find Conner in this throng. Whatever his role was in this sport, she doubted she would glean anything tonight. She didn't think he was there to watch. If he had been, surely he would have entered through the front door.

Maybe he was a referee... *Or, maybe he's a fighter...*

She giggled to herself at the thought. He certainly had the body for it, but she couldn't picture him inside the strange cage thingy throwing punches, or getting punched, by night while discussing all the most famous British authors by day. Too incongruent. Not to mention his interest in BDSM. The man was a total conundrum.

She wandered down an aisle, determined to get closer to the action. As long as she was there and had paid admission, she decided she might as well see what all the hype was about. There were obviously hundreds of people who found this sport fascinating. And according to the sign out front, this was an amateur fight. She cringed, wondering what a professional match looked like. Anything more intense than this was unimaginable.

As she maneuvered between the spectators to get closer, one fight ended and another began. She was glad for once she was small enough to wiggle between people, but she was also short, which put her at an extreme disadvantage since everyone was standing. Not for the first time in her life, she glanced at all the seats and wondered why people didn't use them. If everyone would just sit, they could all see. Instead, the happenings of the world were only witnessed by tall people.

At least she was dressed appropriately. Jeans and a tank top were worn by most of the women in attendance, and there were many. Perhaps half the spectators were women. They were as excited about the competition as the men.

Suddenly, the room filled with the booming sound of the announcer describing the next two men to fight. She caught the majority of what they said as she squeezed into a small spot near the fence. Why she'd found it necessary to weasel her way to the center of the action she would never know.

"...In the red corner, we have Rider 'The Enforcer' Henderson. Weighing in at one eighty-two..." The crowd cheered so loud she couldn't hear the rest of the description. "...and in the blue corner, we have Gage 'The Ranger' Holland..." Again the cheering covered the announcer's voice. The entire room vibrated from the loud speakers and the stomping spectators.

Two women wormed their way next to Sabrina. They were smiling broadly and giggling.

One of them, the one with long blonde curls, bonked into Sabrina and turned to apologize. "So sorry." Her deep green eyes widened as she steadied herself by grabbing Sabrina's arm. "It's so crowded in here."

Sabrina smiled. "No problem."

"Who are you here to see?" the woman asked.

"Oh, uh, no one in particular."

The blonde glanced around. "Are you alone? You just came to watch fighting by yourself?"

Sabrina had to admit it was a bit strange, but it wasn't

as though she could tell this stranger the real reason she was there. *Yeah, I'm stalking my lit professor from last semester. He's a Dom, and I saw him enter the arena. I'm just hanging out hoping to see what he's doing here.*

The other woman leaned forward to address Sabrina. She was shorter, closer to Sabrina's height. She had blonde hair also, the soft curls making her look younger than she probably was. "Don't mind Kayla. She's new." She reached out a hand. "I'm Emily, by the way. Do you come to these often?"

Sabrina took her hand. How had she managed to make friends in this crowded, noisy arena? "Sabrina. And I've never been to a fight before."

Kayla looked shocked. But she twisted her head around when a bell sounded. It obviously indicated the start of the match. "Go, Gage," she shouted, cupping her hands over her mouth.

Emily nudged Kayla's hip with her own playfully and followed the shouting with her own. "Yay, Rider. You got this."

Sabrina gasped. "You know them? Both of them?"

Kayla smiled and nodded, but she didn't take her gaze off the action. "Yep. Sometimes they fight each other. It's damn fun."

Emily added, "For the one who wins."

Craziness.

Sabrina focused on the fight. The men were evenly matched. They were almost the same size. Huge. And they both had muscles that made her drool. Sabrina had never considered herself a tattoo gal, but the tats on these guys were amazing.

As the two men fought, their bodies quickly covered in sweat, Emily and Kayla shouted over each other. It was all in good fun, as evidenced from the smiles on their faces and the way they kept teasing each other with a gentle shove.

Sabrina had no idea what the rules were, but there weren't many it seemed. It was a combination of wrestling and boxing as far as she could tell.

The announcer kept a running litany of what was happening, but it sounded like a jumble of kicks and punches and holds. After a few minutes, the bell sounded again, and both men went to their corner.

"They get a break?" Sabrina asked.

"Yep." Emily glanced at her. "One minute. Always seems like five seconds, though."

"How many rounds are there?"

"Three," Emily continued. "Unless one of them takes the other down beforehand. Which isn't likely to occur between Rider and Gage. They're pretty evenly matched. Rider's a cop. Gage is a K-9 trainer. They don't mess around."

"I see."

"Now, the next guy up after them is another story. He's never been knocked out. You're in for a real treat. He's amazing to watch. His opponent won't have a chance."

Sabrina didn't have any idea why she found this so invigorating, but she was actually getting into it. "Awesome."

Sure enough, the match between Rider and Gage was close. Too close to call. When it ended, the referee had to let the announcer know who had the most points. Gage was declared the winner, but Rider didn't look too torn up about it. They left the room razzing each other.

"'The Gladiator' is next," Kayla said. "The crowd is always wild for him. As soon as he comes out, we won't be able to hear ourselves think."

It didn't take long before the volume in the room rose

to a new level. Sabrina lifted onto her tiptoes to see what all the hoopla was about.

And then she swayed forward, almost falling on her face before she could stop herself.

Emily grabbed her arm to steady her. "Careful."

Sabrina swallowed over her shock, not wanting these two women to find out she actually knew this "Gladiator," as they called him. Her face heated. Stunned, she took a few steps forward, as though drawn to Dr. Bascott by a magnetic pull.

Holy mother of God, he was gorgeous. He'd made her panties damp and her voice squeak so many times over the last nine months, she couldn't count them. But this was an entirely different level of hot.

Sabrina's mouth was dry. She couldn't even lick her lips. They were parted. Hell, she was panting. Her nipples pressed into the lace of her bra, making them feel suddenly too large. And there was no describing the knot of lust in the pit of her stomach that made her pussy pulse.

Dr. Bascott. My, oh my, are you a pile of surprises. First BDSM. Now MMA.

The man was ripped. Huge. Even bigger than she'd thought. Or perhaps that was just the impression she had with his shirt off, wearing nothing but thin shorts. His chest was scattered with a dusting of hair that made her want to plant her hands on his pecs and squeeze.

And then there was his tattoo. She couldn't swallow. She understood why they called him "The Gladiator." His right shoulder and pec were covered with the intricate design of some sort of leather armor. Absolutely stunning and gorgeous. Making the superhuman man more out of this world.

She swallowed. *Get a grip on yourself.*

"...And in the blue corner, we have, Conner 'The Gladiator' Bascott..."

She thought she might faint. He had that much of a pull on her.

"You okay?" Emily asked.

She nodded. She couldn't bring herself to tear her gaze off Dr. Bascott, her professor slash Dom slash fighter slash one-time lover. He'd never taken his shirt off that day at King Pizza. If he had, she might have collapsed into a pile of goo on the bathroom floor.

"I know he's hot. Warned you." Kayla giggled.

"You did." Sabrina licked her lips again. She still didn't glance in the direction of Kayla and Emily.

Before the fight began, the two men took the center of the cage and bounced on their feet. By some strange aligning of the planets, Conner's gaze landed on Sabrina. The shock on his face was palpable. His eyes widened, and he hesitated long enough to make both Emily and Kayla turn in her direction.

Sabrina could feel their gazes. The heat in her face increased. She knew she was beet red. Just as quickly, Conner jerked his gaze back to his opponent as the bell sounded.

"Do you know him?" Emily asked.

"Yeah."

"Why didn't you say something?" Kayla asked.

"I didn't know he was a fighter. I had no idea he was 'The Gladiator' you spoke of."

"Really? It's a coincidence?" Emily's voice rose over the crowd.

Sabrina didn't take her gaze off Conner. "Sort of." No way was she going to tell these two she'd followed him here.

The shorter man swung at Conner, landing a punch to Conner's cheek.

Sabrina winced.

"Shit. You have him flustered." Kayla stepped closer, aligning herself with Sabrina. "I've never once seen him off his game like this."

Sabrina cringed. If she thought the man was an ass in class and at the club, she couldn't imagine how much his asshole-ishness would increase if her presence broke his concentration.

Although a part of her secretly felt a surge of pleasure she had such an effect on him. Served him right.

After several tense moments, Conner found his groove. He straightened his spine and took control of the match. The crowd roared. His opponent backed up several paces until he hit the fence.

Conner spun around and kicked the guy high on his biceps. The man stumbled but didn't go down.

Sabrina held her breath. Her heart pounded in her chest. She'd never been so invigorated by anything in her life. Her best submissive scenes did not compare to this. Conner Bascott screamed virility. And she had never wanted him more than she did right then.

When the bell sounded, ending the first round, Conner headed for the corner farthest from Sabrina. Just as well. She felt a twinge of guilt for her presence. Like the girls had said, the minute was far too short. It didn't seem that Conner had caught his breath when the bell sounded to begin the second round. His heaving chest was nothing compared to the other guy's, however.

The man had a fierce look on his face, but it didn't match his ability to deflect Conner's advances. Suddenly, Conner circled behind his opponent and grabbed him in a chokehold.

Sabrina gasped.

"Don't worry. He won't hurt him," Emily said. "Not permanently, anyway."

The man's knees buckled when Conner swept out a foot. They both went to the ground, Conner on top, straddling the man's chest and holding him down by the neck with his forearm. The referee circled the action, taking in every angle.

Sabrina hoped his main goal was to ensure no one got killed. That seemed imminently possible.

"Conner is well known for his ability to pin a man to the ground," Kayla said.

Suddenly, the man tapped the floor, Conner leaped to his feet, and the crowd went wild.

Emily and Kayla jumped up and down, screaming along with the rest of the spectators.

Sabrina stood rooted to her spot, staring at Conner's fucking hot body and wondering how in the hell she was going to explain herself.

She flinched when Conner turned toward her and made eye contact. His face was hard. He gave no indication of his mood, but he did glance to the side at Emily and Kayla and furrow his brow. And then he was gone, his back to her as he left the cage.

"Come on." Emily grabbed Sabrina's arm and tugged her through the crowd.

"Where're we going?"

"To wait for the guys to come out of the locker room."

Sabrina gasped for a breath of air to no avail. It seemed the room was suddenly devoid of oxygen.

When they stepped into the lobby, the two women regaled Sabrina with ten thousand questions about how she knew Conner. Where did she meet him? How long had she known him? Was she attracted to him? Wasn't he the sexiest man ever?

Sabrina dodged most of their questions easily since they piled them on so fast neither Kayla nor Emily paused long enough for Sabrina to answer.

She did manage to piece together more details about Conner. For one thing, he seemed to be a member of some sort of fight club. Kayla's and Emily's men were also members. There were six in all, and if she wasn't mistaken, Sabrina was pretty sure, from reading between the lines, all six men were also Doms. Interesting.

∼

Conner couldn't believe his eyes. What the hell was Sabrina doing at the arena? Not just *at* the arena, but front and center, *and* seemingly chatting it up with Kayla and Emily.

He lost his concentration for several moments, his mind racing to the woman standing next to the cage. He could feel her gaze boring into him. He'd never once in all the years he'd been fighting, found himself distracted by a woman, or anyone for that matter.

This wasn't good.

She was under his skin. Had been for a week. Or perhaps months, but definitely worse in the last week.

Luckily, he pulled himself together and managed to put an end to his fight by the second round. Now what? Would she be waiting outside the locker room with the other women?

He didn't say a word to Gage or Rider while they showered and dressed for the evening. The plan had been to head to Extreme next.

Conner took a deep breath and followed his friends out of the locker room.

And there she stood, for once looking timid and chagrined.

Conner glanced at the four other people staring at him and made a quick decision to drag Sabrina out of the arena before saying a word. He wasn't about to confront her in front of everyone. Hell, he didn't have the first notion what to say. He narrowed his gaze on her and wrapped his hand around her biceps to lead her away from the crowd.

Sabrina had the good sense to keep her mouth shut too. Neither of them spoke a word as Conner marched her out the front door and straight to his car. He didn't release her arm until he leaned her against the passenger side with a hard stare, hoping to convey that he intended for her to remain where he left her.

He rounded to pop the trunk and dropped his bag in, slamming it shut harder than necessary. With his fob, he unlocked the car, and without making eye contact with Sabrina, yanked the passenger door open. He nodded for her to get inside and waited until she was seated before shutting the door and rounding the hood.

As soon as they were closed off from the world, he took a deep breath and let it out slowly. He wasn't sure it was wise to look at her. The woman could be hell on wheels most of the time, but he didn't know how to interpret this new facet of her personality.

Her scent filled his car, which infuriated him. He had no idea why he was so pissed, but he needed to get a grip before he said something he couldn't take back. He closed his eyes and breathed in her floral shampoo and the faint scent of her perfume. From the thorough look he'd had before the fight started, he knew she wore a tight, pink tank top that revealed enough to entice any man. Her jeans fit her ass to perfection.

He knew from staring at the ground as they'd walked to the car she had on pink flip-flops that matched her shirt, and her dainty toes were also painted the same shade.

His cock was rock hard. He held himself in check to keep from spinning toward her and yanking her mouth to his. He needed to rein in his aggravation, realizing he was mad at himself for allowing any woman to get the best of him. And she most certainly had gotten the best of him, considering she'd hunted him down while he'd had no clue how to find her.

"I followed you," she blurted.

"What?" He turned to face her, confused.

"From the university. I followed you here." She held her head up and kept her face devoid of anything discernable, but her hands were fisted in her lap.

"Why?"

She shrugged. "I was pissed. I wanted to confront you, but not on school property."

"I appreciate that." He frowned at her.

"You ruined a perfectly good relationship with the Dom I was with."

"That Doug guy? He wasn't right for you." Inside he was secretly happy to hear this news.

"Really? How the hell would you know? You got one glimpse of our scene, and suddenly you're an expert on everything?"

"Yep." He knew he was being an ass, but he couldn't stop himself. For his own personal sanity, he needed to put an end to this thing between them. She was twelve years younger than him. And even if he could overlook that small detail, he hated the way she made him lose all brain cells in her presence. Nope. The idea of seeing her ever again was a bad one.

Even if that did make him an asshole for also ruining the relationship she was in.

Sabrina lifted her arms and crossed them under her breasts.

His gaze roamed from her face to her nipples, which were beaded beneath her shirt and bra. He licked his lips, fighting the urge to rip her shirt off and see them again. The edge of her dark pink lace bra stuck out the top of her tank top, making him nearly groan.

She was small. Tiny. And her breasts were also small. He was a boob man, but not in the same sense of most men. He loved the female chest, no matter the size. And frankly, dainty women with small breasts made him harder than huge boobs any day.

He remembered the pink tips, small but hard. The image was burned into his brain forever.

When she spoke again, he jerked his gaze up to her face. "Doug is a perfect gentleman, both inside and outside the club. I *liked* him. Who do you think you are waltzing into my life and threatening my date for no reason at all?"

He focused on the word *liked* and its past tense, fighting a grin. Apparently even without her phone number and address, Conner would win the prize. Hell, she'd come to him. He hadn't had to hunt her down through less than reputable means. The only personal information he had on her was an email address. He'd made no decision to hunt her down her yet. Even though the woman had his cock in her grip, he had spent the week trying to talk himself out of contacting her.

Sure, twenty-six was far better than eighteen. But still, that made him twelve years older than her. What sort of life experiences had she had? Questions had kept him up at night, tossing and turning as he pictured her submitting to Doug. How long had she been a submissive? If she could so readily bend over for a public spanking, she had to have some experience. She wasn't a newbie.

In seven days, he hadn't shaken her from his system. He wanted her more now than he had last weekend. He decided to push. "Yeah. I'm sure you did *like* him. But he didn't make your panties wet and your nipples bead like they are now, did he?" It was a bold move on his part, and he turned to face her more fully, leaning his left forearm on the steering wheel.

Sabrina blinked. Her mouth fell open, and she tightened her arms around her middle, which only made her breasts stand out more, her sexy nipples more prominent. "Are you always this cocky?"

"Yep." Conner leaned closer. "He's too old for you."

Sabrina's eyes widened. If actual flames could have come from her ears, they would have. "Are you fucking kidding me?"

"Nope." He had to fight to keep from grinning. "And don't cuss. Like I said the other night, I don't like to hear those words coming out of your mouth." He wanted to bring this woman to her knees and teach her a lesson about disobeying him. His hands twitched at the desire.

"And like I said last time, fuck you. I'll bet Doug is fucking younger than you. Who the hell do you fucking think you are?"

Conner laughed. "You aren't a very good submissive, are you?" Her feistiness only made him harder. He wanted to drag her across his lap for her blatant defiance, yank her sexy jeans over her sexier ass, and spank her foul language out of her until she begged him to fuck her in the sweetest words he'd ever heard.

"I don't know. Why don't you ask Doug? He seemed to

find me perfectly demure. You, on the other hand, bring out the worst in me."

"Are you still seeing him?"

"None of your fucking business, asshole." Now she was goading him. He seriously doubted she talked like that normally.

Conner lurched forward and took her chin in his hand, forcing her to meet his gaze. "I do not let my submissives cuss, Sabrina. I don't like it. Save that foul mouth of yours for someone else. You're far too pretty to have that shit spewing out of your lips."

"Good thing it doesn't *fucking* matter what the *fuck* you think, since I'm not one of *your* submissives." She yanked her chin free and leaned against the door. Two seconds later, she surprised him again by jerking the door open and climbing out of his Mustang. Before he could comment, she leaned in to meet his gaze. "Nice knowing you." She slammed the passenger door shut and walked away.

Conner watched her through the rearview mirror as she waltzed across the parking lot to a car nearby and climbed inside. She held her head high the entire time, never once glancing back. He smiled as she started the engine of her cute little red Honda and drove away. Oh yeah. She was totally his. There was no denying that anymore. Whatever notion he'd had of shaking her vanished under her sharp tongue. He was going to love training her to obey him.

And she was going to love submitting to him even more.

She was his.

He chuckled when it occurred to him he was right back where he started, however. No address. No phone number.

But he knew she was into him. Nobody gave a man that level of shit without wanting him to fuck her hard. In addition, she'd followed him to the arena. She could just as easily have smoothed things over with Doug and been out at another club with him. Instead, she'd spent her Friday night stalking Conner and getting in his face.

Sexy as hell.

He moaned, wondering how long it would be before he would see her again. Without waiting for him in the parking lot of the university again or hanging around Extreme, she didn't have any more information about him than he had about her.

He wasn't concerned. She'd come around. Or he'd find her.

There was always that email address…

CHAPTER 4

The beginning of Conner's second workweek since Sabrina came back into his world was busy. Besides the usual classes he taught, midterms to grade, and office hours to hold, he got called into the dean's office on Monday afternoon.

After his second class, he trudged to the building two doors down from him, wondering what the hell this meeting was all about. He'd never once been called to meet with the dean in all his years teaching.

The receptionist smiled and nodded at the closed door. "Go on in. They're waiting for you."

They? Conner adjusted his tie and entered Dean Sheffield's office.

Dr. Sheffield stood from the mahogany table next to the window as Conner stepped inside. "Dr. Bascott. Please, have a seat." The woman didn't smile as she lifted her gaze. Two men sat around the table. They both glanced up uncomfortably. Conner knew them in passing.

Shit. This couldn't be good. What sort of "fuck me" sign had he been wearing attached to his back lately?

Conner took a deep breath and made his way to the empty chair.

Dr. Sheffield held a stack of papers in her hand and tapped them on the table as if they needed to be straightened as Conner took his seat.

"Is something wrong?" Conner glanced at the two men flanking Dr. Sheffield before aiming his gaze straight at the dean.

"I sincerely hope not, Dr. Bascott. But we do have reason to be concerned."

Conner furrowed his brow. "Go on…"

Dr. Sheffield introduced the other two men as members of the ethics committee while Conner nodded and held his breath.

"We've received some disturbing emails in the last few days concerning your possible involvement with a student here at the university."

Conner stopped breathing. "What?" He gripped the edge of the table with both hands. His head spun.

Dr. Sheffield continued. "These are printouts of the emails we received over the weekend."

Conner lifted the pages, but he kept his gaze on Dr. Sheffield for several seconds before lowering his face. When he did, he was stunned. Three emails—their contents printed out on the pages in front of him. Each email was similar and sent to a different faculty member, not just Dean Sheffield, but the university president and the head of the language department as well, Tina Chang. Oh, great. Now he would have to speak to Tina also.

Conner's hands shook as he read the lines indicating he was involved with a student, had been meeting with her secretly, and should be investigated.

When Conner lifted his gaze, he found Dr. Sheffield frowning. "Who did these come from?"

"We have no idea, Dr. Bascott. We were hoping you could tell us."

"Of course not. These're lies. I have never, nor will I ever be involved with a student here." *And thank God I'm not lying.*

Dr. Sheffield let out a long breath. "That's about as I expected."

"What? That I would deny these allegations? Hell yes, I will deny this shit. It's not true." Conner tried to control his volume, but it was tough. Who the fuck would do this to him? He sat up straight and set the pages on the table in front of him, tapping the top one with a finger. "Can't anyone trace these? It's a university for Christ's sake. The place must be filled with dozens of people who could hack this address and get more information on the sender." He tried to chuckle, but came up short. Hell, the most qualified hackers around were probably students.

"Not yet." Dr. Sheffield nodded at the printouts.

Conner dipped his head and tried to catch his breath and control his emotions.

"I'm going to have to ask you some hard questions, Dr. Bascott. It's policy. You understand."

"Of course."

"Is there any validity to these emails?"

The two other men in the room squirmed in their seats. They were both younger than Conner. Before this incident, they had both looked up to him. Now they appeared uncertain. Conner couldn't blame them, but he was still pissed. Who the hell would do this?

Conner shook his head. "Nope. Not one word is true."

"So, you aren't dating a student."

"I am *not*."

"You've never had any relations with a student?"

"Never."

"And you can't think of any reason someone would suspect you were or try to frame you?"

"No." Conner pursed his lips and thought back on everything that had happened in his twisted life for the past ten days.

Sabrina.

If anyone saw him with Sabrina, it was a long shot. One quick conversation outside Extreme where the only witness was Frank and one argument in his car outside the arena Friday night. The chances of someone witnessing that were slim. As far as he knew there weren't many students who were aware he was an MMA fighter. It wasn't a secret, but he didn't publicize it, either.

If these allegations had come up before he'd encountered Sabrina at Extreme, he would have shit a brick. It would have been extremely farfetched for someone to have seen him interact with her two months ago at King Pizza. But he still would have pissed his pants worrying about it, since at the time he didn't realize she was not a student any longer.

But after last week, he knew Sabrina was not only significantly older than he'd suspected, but also no longer a student. He'd broken no rules. Not even his own.

How the fuck could this be happening to him within days of running into Sabrina Duluth, though? Was it a coincidence? There was the distinct possibility this had nothing to do with Sabrina at all. If someone wanted to frame him for his supposed involvement with a student, why pick someone who wasn't enrolled? That made no sense at all.

And there was no way Conner was going to drag Sabrina into this mess. She'd done nothing wrong. Besides, there was nothing to drag her into. Involvement with her made him guilty of nothing.

He still didn't intend to mention her name.

"Dr. Bascott, this is very unfortunate."

"Yes, it is." Conner sat up straighter and stacked the pages. "May I keep these?"

"Of course. We have copies. Look them over. See if anything rings a bell."

"I will." He made eye contact with the two men at the table and then lifted his gaze to the dean. She was all business. Her face was impassive. Her perfectly fitted gray suit was wrinkle free. Her hair was pulled back in a bun, not one lock out of place. "Dr. Sheffield, I give you my word these allegations are unfounded. I know you have to follow up on this, and I understand you need my cooperation, but you'll never find anything because there isn't anything to find. I have never at any point done anything inappropriate with a student in all my years of teaching. Not now. Not ever." He was beating this over the head, but he wanted to be sure everyone in the room was clear.

"Do you have any students in any of your classes that are perhaps doing poorly, failing, or seem angry with you?"

"Not that I'm aware of. No." Conner shook his head. "Hell, I haven't even seen a student during my office hours this past week. I'm as perplexed as you."

Dr. Sheffield pursed her lips. "I hear you. And I'm terribly sorry about all this. It's my job and the job of the ethics committee to ensure these allegations are untrue. While we investigate, please be sure you're engaged in absolutely nothing unseemly."

"Of course." It occurred to Conner that being a member of the BDSM community could be seen as unbecoming to someone. He rarely saw anyone he knew at Extreme, but that didn't mean someone hadn't seen him. He'd run into Tina Chang there one time, but she wasn't a regular.

Perhaps another teacher? Or even a student? Someone who wanted to hurt him? It made little sense. If someone wanted to damage his career simply because he enjoyed a little kink on the side, why not come right out and say so instead of twisting it into false involvement with a student?

What about Tina? It was insane to think she would do something like this to him. But was it a coincidence he'd turned her down for Saturday night and now this? Ridiculous fake allegations? He couldn't imagine her stooping so low, but it would be ingenious to send the false allegations to the dean, the president, and herself. *Shit.* Would she try to get him fired over a rejection to date her? If so, she was crazier than he thought.

Conner stood. "If I think of anything, I'll let you know. In the meantime, I'd appreciate if this didn't leave this room. I have a stellar reputation at this university. I love my job. I would hate to be dragged through the trenches over a bunch of lies."

"You have our word. The other recipients of the email know better also." Dr. Sheffield stood, as did the other gentlemen. "Without any specifics, I'm not inclined to take this seriously. If whoever this is wants to nail you to the wall, it makes no sense why they haven't come right out and told us who the mystery student is you're supposedly involved with. That, and the fact your reputation on this campus is completely unblemished, leaves me with no choice but to assume your innocence. I'm on your side in this, Dr. Bascott. Please don't prove me wrong."

Conner nodded and left the room.

He fumed all the way to his office. There wasn't a single thing he could think of that would cause someone to frame him for something so serious. Crazy.

He was late for his slotted office hours, and as soon as

he rounded the corner he found a student standing outside his office.

Angelica Hudson. She pushed off the wall and righted herself as he approached, pasting a big smile on her face. "Dr. Bascott. I was afraid I had my days and times mixed up."

"Nope. Sorry. I was in a meeting." He unlocked the door, trying to muster the energy to speak to this undergrad. He'd had her in class last semester, and this semester she was in another of his classes. It wasn't unusual. If she was an English major, it would be expected.

At the moment, he was in no mood to speak to anyone. But that wasn't Ms. Hudson's problem.

He rounded his desk. "Please, have a seat. What can I do for you?"

She bounced as she walked. Hell, she bounced as she sat.

He imagined she was quite popular. She seemed very friendly, almost too friendly most of the time in class. She flirted mercilessly with at least two of the male students before and after class.

When she leaned forward to open her backpack, her shirt gaped open, showing way too much cleavage. But hell, he wasn't the fashion police. And what did he care? He certainly wasn't interested in her. She was probably nineteen at best and not his type at all physically. It occurred to him that it would be nice if someone pointed out that her shirt was too small and too low, but it wasn't going to be him.

"I was hoping you could take a look at my outline for the next paper we're doing. I'm worried I haven't hit all the points you suggested." She held out a printed piece of paper.

She wasn't the best student in his class. She wasn't the

worst either, but he didn't usually get mediocre undergrads in his office to go over their potential outlines for a paper that wasn't due for another two weeks.

He narrowed his gaze at the page in front of him, not looking at it. Instead he let his mind run rampant in another direction. Absurd, really. He was losing his mind if he thought this bubbly student had anything to do with him being framed for inappropriate behavior. Surely it was simply his recent encounter with the dean that had him on edge and paranoid.

Angelica Hudson was no more likely to be framing him for dating a student than the pope.

"So, what do you think?"

Conner jerked his gaze up to glance at her. He hadn't actually read a word of her outline yet.

She leaned over his desk with her arms crossed loosely on the surface, causing her enormous breasts to push up and forward. A boob guy would find her delightful. Conner was not a guy who enjoyed large breasts.

"This is a good start. I don't know what you're worried about. I'm sure it will be fine. Start the research, and if you have any questions, come back and see me." He handed the paper back to her. It could have been the lyrics to a nursery rhyme for all he knew or cared right then.

It wasn't like him to so blatantly dismiss a student, but his mind was preoccupied. He promised himself he would give her more of his undivided attention in a few days. He glanced at his watch. "I'm so sorry, Ms. Hudson. I have another appointment I need to get to. Why don't you get the paper started and come back next Monday, and I'll take another look."

She smiled and took the page back from him with a syrupy sweet grin that made him cringe for no good reason. "Of course. Thanks for your time. I'll get to work on this and stop back by." She flipped her long black hair over her shoulder as she stood. Flirtatiously? Surely not.

Jesus, Conner. Get a grip.

Moments after Angelica left his office, someone else knocked on the open door and stepped inside. Tina Chang. Of course.

Her brow was furrowed, and she shut the door behind her.

"What's this crazy accusation about you dating a student, Conner?" She cut straight to the chase and plopped down in the chair Angelica had vacated.

He leaned back, in no mood to have this chat, or any chat, with Tina. "I don't know. But it isn't true, of course." He watched her closely, hoping her face would divulge something.

Her shoulders slumped. "Well, thank God. I'd hate for you to get in trouble for something you didn't do." Was that sarcasm in her voice?

Conner didn't move.

Tina tapped the desk. "I really needed you Saturday. It would have been nice if you could have done me that favor." She pouted. A grown woman with a PhD pouting— and possibly blackmailing him. *Fuck.*

He hesitated. Was it a coincidence she combined these two issues in one sitting? Either she was extremely stupid or very very smart. Or clueless. "I already had plans. And Tina, we are not dating. You really shouldn't lead your family members to believe that."

"I know." She trailed a finger along his desk, her voice lowering. "Is it because you practice BDSM? I could give that a try, you know. I've been to your club once. It wasn't too bad."

He sat forward. "No. I'm not interested in you that way, Tina." Lord. The woman was desperate.

She lifted her head and narrowed her gaze. "You seemed interested enough when your tongue was in my mouth."

Jesus. That was so long ago. And besides, it was her tongue in his mouth, not the other way around. "I'm sorry if you felt misled. I was tipsy. So were you."

She pouted again. "Well, think about it, Conner. We could make a good couple. If you gave us a chance." She turned and left the office, not saying another word.

Was that a threat?

He shook his head and gathered the papers on his desk that needed attention at home that evening. First, he needed to go to the gym and blow off steam.

What a day.

CHAPTER 5

Sabrina stared at her computer screen, wishing she could concentrate on her work. She had deadlines to meet. Freelance editors did not get paid unless they actually returned the editing to the client.

She blinked, trying to focus. Even two cups of coffee did nothing to help her stay on task.

It had been five days since her run-in with Conner. Five very long days. And nights.

She hadn't slept well. Conner's words kept running through her head over and over like a broken record.

He didn't make your panties wet and your nipples bead like they are now, did he?

Infuriating man.

He'd laid no claim on her for himself, and yet he'd made it perfectly clear he didn't like her seeing Doug. She didn't get the feeling he knew Doug or enough about the man to warn her off him for some reason. Nope. Conner Bascott had simply destroyed that relationship with no motive.

Unless he did have a motive, and that motive was to

have Sabrina for himself. If that was the case, however, then why act like such an ass?

And she had to admit, if she stepped back, Conner had not been responsible for the demise of her relationship with Doug. Not even close. Sabrina alone held the blame. She was the one who stopped their scene when she could no longer give it her entire attention. She was the one who turned down Doug's suggestion they go out again after dinner last Sunday. She was the one who ignored his calls until she finally broke down on Tuesday and answered the phone to break things off with him.

She couldn't pin any of that on Conner.

But oh how she tried. Damn him for shaking up her perfectly good life accepting the status quo.

He thought she was too young. *Ha*.

She had more experience with submission than most of the women who belonged to his club. It was by sheer coincidence she'd never been to Extreme. She'd been a member of another club across town for several years.

Sabrina had known she was submissive since she was about fourteen, more than twelve years ago, when she discovered the *Story of O* at a neighbor's house where she babysat. Needless to say, she sat for that family happily dozens of times, slowly devouring every bit of the book after the kids went to bed.

It wasn't that she was a masochist. In fact, she'd learned over the course of several years she didn't care much for the harsher elements of BDSM, but she knew she was submissive without a doubt from the moment she'd entered her first club at eighteen and submitted to a well-established Dom who agreed to take her under his wing and introduce her to his world.

That first Dom had been twice her age, almost forty, which *was* significant for someone her age at the time. But she'd always considered herself an old soul and wasn't bothered by the man's age or the looks people gave them.

In the end, she'd fallen hard for him and his style of domination, and he'd broken her heart when he ended things about six months into the relationship. She shouldn't have been surprised. He'd told her from the beginning he enjoyed training women, but had no desire to engage in anything permanent. The moment she told him how she felt about him, he broke things off.

For a while she'd been lost, but she was a strong person. She threw herself into her studies and stayed away from relationships until she graduated from college.

Editing had fallen into her lap by accident. One of her professors noticed her affinity for good grammar and punctuation and encouraged her to make some money on the side editing for other students. That decision had changed her life.

Her degree in political science was immediately stuffed in a back corner when she graduated. By then she had enough clients who needed editing work that she gave up her plans for law school in order to follow her new dream.

When she moved on from student essays to editing for romance authors, her life was complete. The idea of getting paid to read novels all day made her the happiest person alive. Under most circumstances, she couldn't wait to get up in the morning, pour her coffee, and sit at her computer to immerse herself in fantasy.

Until this week.

Again, damn that man and his ability to leak into her every thought while she was supposed to be working.

Sabrina stood and paced the room for several long strides so she could loosen up and straighten out her head. A slight ping told her she had a new email. Why she kept the volume on, she had no idea. It was annoying as hell. Especially on days when she received far too many emails.

She sat in her ergonomic chair, the one she'd invested a fortune in, and opened the browser.

And then she froze.

Dr. Conner Bascott.

Shit.

She hadn't decided yet if she wanted him to contact her with every ounce of her being or if she wanted to throw hot lava on him and walk away. And there he was.

With shaky fingers, she opened the email, totally aware of the way her heart pounded to read his every word, no matter what he might have to say.

> *Sabrina,*
>> *Lunch. King Pizza. Noon tomorrow.*
>> *Conner*

Sabrina stared at the message forever. Short and... weird. Demanding while being soft at the same time. After all, he used his first name. And hers. He'd never used his first name with her. She'd known it from his university bio, but she'd always called him Dr. Bascott or Professor Bascott.

What made the infuriating man think she was available for lunch tomorrow?

She considered stomping up and down and pulling her hair out.

Damn him.

Her emotions were all over the place—as usual where Dr. Bascott was concerned. She wanted to both throttle the man and fuck him again at the same time.

So bossy—which she loved and hated. In eight years she had never been with a Dom who was as blatantly controlling as Conner Bascott. Nor had she been with a Dom who made her panties wet every time she thought about him.

And lately that was all the time.

She needed to work.

She closed the email without answering it and opened the manuscript she was supposed to be editing.

Focus.

Think about the email tomorrow.

~

At eleven fifty on Thursday morning, Sabrina sat in her car staring at the entrance to King Pizza. Really? Did the man have to pick this spot of all places? What was he trying to say?

She'd gone back and forth ten times trying to decide if she should show up or not. She had not responded to his email. *Let him wonder.*

Even at this late hour, she was still uncertain about facing Conner and what she might say. The majority of her uncertainty stemmed from the fact she couldn't imagine what *he* might say first. And she seriously doubted she would have the first or last word.

She considered entering the restaurant late, but thought better of it. If he was the sort of Dom she suspected he was, he wouldn't tolerate tardiness.

Taking a deep breath, she stepped from the car into the October Vegas sun. It was warm out. She smoothed her hands down her T-shirt and smiled to herself. She had intentionally not dressed well. Jeans and the standard white tee were as far as she'd been willing to go this morning. Defiant? Yes. But the idea of putting a lot of effort into her appearance for this meeting made her cringe. She didn't want to play that card and make him think she cared prematurely.

She wasn't altogether sure she *did* care yet. Depended on the next several minutes.

When she entered the crowded pizza joint, she scanned the room. She didn't see him.

For the first time in twenty-four hours, it occurred to her he might not be there since she didn't answer him. That possibility hadn't really entered her mind.

She stood tall and confident, focusing on her hands to avoid wringing them together or fisting them at her sides. The last thing she wanted was to appear weak.

Weak had never described her. Not in any aspect of her life and not with any Dom. Until Conner. The blasted man brought out a strange side of her—one she hadn't known existed.

He caused her to feel discomposed. Apprehensive. And she hated it.

"Just one?" a waitress questioned as Sabrina lifted onto her toes and glanced around again.

"Umm." She turned to the bleach-blonde, older woman, unsure how to respond. "I'm meeting someone. Though we may have gotten our signals crossed."

The woman smiled. "You want me to seat you? Or would you rather wait?"

Sabrina considered her options and decided standing in the doorway waiting for Conner to show was wimpy. Nope. She needed to sit in order to avoid fidgeting. Hell, she needed a glass of wine ASAP to calm her nerves no matter what the day's outcome was. "I'll sit. Thanks."

"Follow me." The woman nodded toward the room at large and turned.

Sabrina trailed behind, trying to avoid looking around again. If he were there, she'd have spotted him.

"This okay?" the kind woman asked. She glanced at the door. "Your friend should be able to easily spot you from here."

"It's fine. Thanks." Sabrina passed the waitress and sat on the opposite side of the booth so she could see the front door.

"You want me to get you a drink while you wait?"

"Please. The house Merlot would be perfect."

The blonde tapped the table. "Be right back."

The kind woman smiled and then walked away.

Sabrina did her best to sit still. It was rare in her twenty-six years, but whenever she found herself in an uncomfortable situation, she always had trouble staying calm.

Now was definitely one of those times.

The sweet waitress returned with her wine. "Anything else?"

"No. Thanks. I'll look over the menu. If he doesn't show, I'll just enjoy lunch alone." Sabrina smiled at the woman to ensure her she wasn't a flight risk as far as eating and taking up space was concerned.

"Okay. I'll check with you in a few. Take your time."

There was no need to look at the menu. She knew it by heart. She'd been to King Pizza dozens of times. If Conner stood her up, she'd order a salad. If he showed...she probably wouldn't be able to swallow.

The best course of action was to pretend to look over the menu. Sitting up straight, she sipped her wine and leaned her face toward the plastic-coated list of pizzas, toppings, pastas, and salads.

At ten after twelve, she began to doubt he would arrive.

Interesting. Was he testing her? Or did he not show because she never responded? Probably the latter.

However, on her behalf, he didn't asked for a response. He simply presented her with a demand.

She kept half an eye on the front door. No Conner Bascott.

Her wine glass was half empty when a hand landed on her shoulder and gripped it before she lifted her gaze and Conner released her to slide onto the bench across from her.

She took another fortifying sip and swallowed.

"Do I make you nervous, Ms. Duluth?"

He did. "No, Sir." She flinched. Why had she chosen to call him Sir without him requesting it? She wished she could suck the word back as soon as it left her lips and refer to him as Professor or Dr. Bascott or even Conner. Anything but Sir. It presumed too much.

He smiled and set his elbows on the table, narrowing his gaze at her. "You're a crappy liar, Sabrina."

She knew that. In fact, even though she'd been born and raised in Vegas, she'd never gambled. Not with money anyway. She didn't respond.

"Let's start over."

Where? Nine months ago, before he'd acted like she had the plague for the entire semester? Two months ago when he'd fucked her in the bathroom of this very establishment? Two weeks ago when she'd shown up at Extreme? Last Friday when they'd fought in his car?

"You're a crappy liar, baby." His voice was lower. The way he said *baby* made her panties wet.

Oh. That. So they were going back thirty seconds to start over. She swallowed again and nodded. "Always have been."

He smiled. "That's better. I don't tolerate lying."

She didn't move, except to grip her pussy tight and

BECCA JAMESON

squeeze her legs together. Otherwise, she didn't even blink above the table.

Holy shit.

He had her number.

The waitress returned. "He showed up. You didn't have your days mixed up after all." She beamed, and Sabrina turned to see her smiling broadly. "Can I get you a drink?" she asked, meeting Conner's gaze.

"Iced tea, please. No sugar."

"Got it." The blonde turned and walked away.

Sabrina's face flamed.

Conner lifted an eyebrow. "You lied to the waitress too?"

Sabrina stared at him, and then she swallowed the last of the wine and set the glass on the table, glancing up to see if the sweet woman who had currently gotten her in trouble was still around.

"That's enough wine, baby. It's noon. And you drove here."

What the hell? Now he was going to tell her what to drink?

She squeezed her legs tighter, fighting the opposing sensations between her body's traitorous reactions to him and her brain telling her to run away fast and never look back.

Her body won.

For now.

"You're squirming," he stated.

She wasn't. Was she?

She set her hands on her thighs under the table and squeezed, hoping to keep her legs from bouncing up and down if that was in fact the cause of his observation. She'd been known to shake her legs under the table. A nervous habit.

"Look at me."

She jerked her gaze back to him, kicking herself for her instant reaction.

He smiled. "Now we're getting somewhere."

Where? Where are we getting? As far as Sabrina could tell, the only place she was "getting" was aroused and frustrated. And how had the tables turned on her so abruptly? The last two times she'd been in his presence had gone poorly. Now this?

"You didn't respond to my email."

She licked her lips. She needed to speak. "You didn't require a response."

"Touché."

"It looked like nothing more than a demand to me."

His smile grew wider. "And you followed my directive. I like that."

She needed to keep her mouth shut.

"Tell me something."

"Yes?"

"Is it true you only took that one class at the university last semester?"

"Of course." She furrowed her brow. "Why?"

He stared at her. "So you aren't currently enrolled in any classes?"

She shook her head. "No. Why?"

"It's unethical for a teacher to date a student."

"Of course." Her voice dipped lower as she spoke. He was simply covering his bases. That was reasonable. He should. She didn't want to get him into any trouble. He may be an infuriating man, but she had no intention of doing anything to threaten his career.

"Why did you follow me Friday night?" He startled her with this new line of questioning.

Hadn't they already covered this ground? "I was angry."

"Why did you follow me, Sabrina?"

She hesitated. He was astute.

"Baby," he lowered his voice. "Why. Did. You. Follow. Me?"

She bit the inside of her cheek and then met his gaze. "Curiosity."

"That's better." He gave her one of his smiles, the kind that melted her a little. "Are you always this nervous?"

Damn his questions. "No."

"I didn't think so."

He sat back a few inches when the waitress returned with his tea and a water. "Do you need a few minutes?" she asked, pulling a pad of paper out of her apron.

Conner shifted his gaze to the woman. "What are your specials today?"

The woman easily rattled off some sort of pasta dish while Sabrina kept her gaze on Conner. The last thing she had any interest in was food.

"Perfect. We'll have two of those."

Sabrina flinched. *Did he just order for me?*

God.

The man was so exasperating.

"Where were we?" he asked, ignoring the fact he'd made a decision for her without knowing the first thing about her likes and dislikes. Hell, he didn't even know if she had an allergy. "Oh, right. I make you nervous," he stated.

"You do not," she lied.

He narrowed his gaze again.

She bit her lip. *Fuck.*

Half of her wanted to run from the restaurant. Who cared if King Pizza was the best in town? She could live without pizza for the rest of her life. Easy.

"Baby, our progress is very slow here." He shook his

head in dismay. "Do we have to go back to the lying? Why is it so difficult to admit what you're feeling?"

"Has anyone ever told you you're irritating?"

He chuckled. "Many times. In fact, several in the last few days."

"Well, they weren't kidding. Do you always sit down with a woman and start a conversation with a series of demands?"

He leaned closer. "Only when I know it's what she wants and needs."

She couldn't breathe. Damn it. "Shit." She turned her gaze to the table.

"What did I say about cussing?"

She pursed her lips together and met his gaze again. "Dr. Bascott, I don't remember agreeing to any sort of arrangement between us that limits what I can and can't say."

"You didn't have too, Ms. Duluth. Your agreement is obvious by your body language and the look on your face. Deny it?"

She didn't move an inch to respond. *Shit*. Again.

"I cuss, Sir."

"Not anymore."

"It's not something I can stop on a dime," she retorted. "Especially when I'm so frustrated."

"You'll find a way, or you'll find it difficult to sit." His words were pointed, and his gaze dug deep.

Sabrina almost moaned. How humiliating? She squeezed her legs for the third time. Tighter. To no avail. Her pussy soaked her jeans, and her clit begged to be released from the denim confines.

"Understood?"

She found herself nodding. "Yes, Sir."

"How long have you been a submissive?"

"Eight years."

"Since you turned eighteen?" He looked stunned.

"Yes."

He paused. "That's awfully young."

"I didn't see it that way."

His brow furrowed. "Did you have a Dom?"

"I did. He was the perfect teacher. I was devastated when he broke things off."

Conner inhaled deeply. "How old was he?"

Sabrina hesitated, gnawing on her cheek again.

"Answer me, baby."

"Forty."

"Fuck. Are you serious? That's almost illegal."

"Almost, but not quite." *Why does he get to cuss?*

Conner closed his eyes, clearly fighting his furious response to the information. She couldn't quite imagine why. "He took advantage of you, baby."

"He didn't. I was a willing participant. More than that. Eager. And besides, after a few months when I realized I had fallen for him, he broke things off. I was hurt."

"Well, at least he had the good sense to let you go. Are you crazy? He could have been a predator. You could have been seriously hurt."

She frowned. "He was a member of the club I belong to. I didn't pick him up on a street corner."

Conner shook his head. "Doesn't matter. Do you think just because some guy is a member of a club, he's on the up and up?"

"Of course not, but I did my homework." That wasn't entirely true. She'd met Sir Jacob soon after she'd been old enough to enter the club and hadn't really looked back once until he dumped her.

"Riiight." Conner rolled his eyes.

Sabrina was saved from more of his interrogation by the arrival of their food.

Conner sat back to give the waitress space to set their plates down. "Be careful. The plates are hot. Can I get you anything else?"

"No. Thank you. We're fine." Conner smiled at her, making her smile back. Who wouldn't? He was the sexiest man in the room, probably all of Vegas.

As soon as the waitress left, Conner started his interrogation again. "How many Doms have you been with since then?"

"A few."

"That's vague, baby."

She blew out a breath, wiping her hands on her jeans. She'd yet to glance down at their plates. "Enough to know what I like."

The smile that spread across his face was huge.

She'd given him the wrong impression. Or had she?

"Eat your lunch, Sabrina." He tipped his gaze to his food and grabbed a fork.

For the first time, Sabrina glanced down. It smelled delicious and it looked even better. And she wanted to throw a tantrum right there for Conner's ability to select her meal.

Nevertheless, she had no desire to act like a brat and give him any fuel to torment her with. It would be easier to ignore this slight and just eat her food.

The first bite was divine, some sort of chicken dish with a white wine sauce and corkscrew pasta. Thank God she didn't have to manhandle long noodles into submission.

They ate in silence for several minutes.

When Conner chuckled, Sabrina lifted her brows. "Something funny?"

"You."

"What'd I do?"

"Do you always moan like that when you eat?"

She froze. "I do not."

He chuckled louder. "Don't get me wrong. I love that you enjoy your food, but that little noise is making my cock press uncomfortably against my pants."

At first she was shocked, but then she realized nothing with Conner should shock her anymore. So she decided to goad him instead. On the next bite, she moaned intentionally around the fork as she slid it from her mouth. She let her eyes drift halfway closed and gripped the edge of the table, her head thrown back and her chest thrust forward as she gave a short *When Harry Met Sally* rendition.

Conner dropped his fork with a clank.

She struggled to swallow the bite, wondering if she'd gone too far. And wondering if she cared.

"Are you always going to test me like this?"

"Probably." She reached for his ice tea, taking a long drink while he held her gaze. When she set the glass back down, she wasn't sure she hadn't pushed him too far.

His gaze was piercing, his lips pursed. He gritted out his next words. "I'm sure you think you're cute. Hell, even I think you're cute. But trust me when I say there will always be consequences for your actions, even when we aren't in an appropriate location for those consequences at the time. Am I understood?" His assumption that their relationship as a Dom and sub was a foregone conclusion both infuriated her and made her want to kneel at his feet.

Sabrina nearly choked. Oh, yeah. She'd gone too far. *Shit*.

"Words, Sabrina."

"Yes, Sir," she muttered, suddenly far more humble than

she would like. She didn't know Conner well enough to presume what his idea of punishment might entail.

Just as suddenly, he picked up his fork. "Finish your lunch, baby. I have a class this afternoon."

She nodded, unsure if she could swallow the rest. Luckily, she was still hungry, and she didn't think it would be prudent to defy him again right then. Perhaps if she toned down the sass a bit, he might go easy on her later.

That was what she wanted, right?

She managed to eat the rest of the meal without giving the professor any reason to reprimand her further. As she set her fork down, she lifted her gaze to find him leaning back, his gaze on her.

He was smiling. "What do you do, Sabrina?"

"Excuse me?"

"For work."

"Oh." She relaxed. "I'm an editor."

He lifted an eyebrow. "For the paper?"

"No, books."

"Proofreading?" He said that one word with a bit of disdain.

"No. Content edits. I'm a freelance editor."

"Really? Huh." He seemed surprised.

"What's so strange about that?"

He shrugged. "Nothing. I guess that explains your excellent writing and grammar."

Now she was shocked. "You think my writing is good?" He had given no indication of that the entire semester.

"Of course. Some of the best I've ever seen."

Then why did you ride my ass for four months?

He chuckled. "You didn't think I cared much for you, did you?"

"I thought I was the scum beneath your shoes you couldn't manage to avoid stepping in." She gave him a fake smile, keeping her voice level as though she'd announced it would be a sunny day.

Now he laughed. "Good."

She flinched.

He leaned closer, setting his elbows on the table again. "Didn't want anyone in the classroom to realize how fucking hard I was for you."

Sabrina stopped breathing. She grabbed the edge of the table.

He grinned. "Including you."

"Why?" She swallowed. "I mean why the charade? You could have just talked to me."

"Really? And said what?" He altered his voice to make a fake speech. "Hey, Ms. Duluth, may I speak to you a moment after class? Yeah, I just wanted you to know that I totally want to dominate you. How about when you're done with school, you get down on your knees and suck my cock like a good girl?"

Her shock gradually slid away until she giggled. "I see what you mean."

He lowered his voice. "You aren't a student anymore."

"Nope."

"Still not sure what to do with you. You're so young." He held up a hand before she could contest this repeated territory. "I get it. And I'll agree you do seem more mature than your twenty-six years. That helps. And you have experience as a submissive. That also helps. Although I do wonder who the hell trained you, seeing as your mouth runs you in a ditch most times you open it."

She smiled smugly. "Only with you. No one else ever complained." She crossed her arms over her chest.

"If you agree to be mine, Sabrina, you'll have some relearning to do. If you think you can run roughshod over me like you may have gotten away with in the past, you're mistaken." He didn't give her a chance to respond before he continued. "And put your arms at your sides, baby. Don't cross them like that. You aren't to close yourself off from me."

Sabrina sucked in a sharp breath and dropped her arms to her thighs.

"The plain T-shirt and jeans are a hoot by the way. I'm sure you thought hard about what to wear that would be the least attractive. You missed the mark, however. The white tee is snug enough for me to enjoy your chest and the lace of your bra. I can even see your nipples puckering under the material." His gaze lowered to her breasts. "And those jeans are fucking tight and sexy as hell." He smirked.

"How would you know?"

"I watched you all the way from your car to this booth, baby."

She jerked her eyes wide. "You were already here?"

"Yep."

"You hid and watched me?"

"Yep." He continued as if that revelation weren't the least bit odd. "In the future, unless I give you permission, no jeans or pants when you're with me. Understood?"

Her mouth fell open. Was he serious?

"I like to know your pussy is open to me. I don't like to struggle to get to the prize. I almost came in my pants the last time I attempted to get to your cunt in this restaurant."

Sabrina bit her lip. So many emotions slammed into her at once. He was so cocky and dominant. He was also right. She'd never subbed for anyone remotely like him before. No man had ever spoken to her like that. And she'd never heard someone use the word *cunt*. Shock was too mild a word for how she felt.

"I know you're overwhelmed. That's to be understood." He slid from the booth and stood, leaning over until his lips were right next to her ear. "Think about it, Sabrina. Has your pussy ever been this wet? Have you ever needed to come so badly with any other Dom?" He didn't wait for her to respond. And she couldn't have with his lips driving a shiver down her neck. He slid a folded piece of paper into her hand and pressed it against her palm. "This is my number. Text me your address. I'll be there tomorrow night at seven. That gives you a full day to think about submitting to me."

What? So, if I text him, that's my consent. And If I don't... Who was she kidding?

He stood. "I'll pay the bill on my way out. Leave whenever you're ready." With that, he turned and walked to the front.

Sabrina sat frozen while he handed a credit card to the waitress and took care of lunch. She continued to watch as he turned toward the front door without glancing back.

As he reached to open the glass door, it swung in and a cute girl Sabrina remembered from her class last semester stepped inside. Angela or something...

Sabrina watched as the girl ran a hand through her long, thick black hair and flipped it behind her. She smiled too broadly and batted her eyes. She spoke to Conner as though they were long lost friends. She was flirting. It made Sabrina cringe.

What the hell? Are you jealous?

The girl was maybe nineteen at the most. If Conner thought Sabrina was young, he would think that co-ed was a baby. But Lord was she ever gorgeous. She had the entire package—hair to die for, fantastic bronzed skin, boobs any model would be happy to show off, a narrow waist, and an ass most men turned around to watch go by.

The girl tipped her head back and laughed hard at

something Conner said. Conner's expression from the side was one of shock. He stepped back a pace.

Good.

Sabrina needed to kick the ugly green monster out the door. The man had fucked her in the restroom of this very restaurant. So take that, Ms. Cleavage.

Finally Conner left, nodding at the girl as he went.

Sabrina stared long and hard at the entrance before she finally shook herself out of her stupor. "Fuck," she muttered, a new shiver racing down her spine at the expletive he hated. His ass was fine. He was the entire package.

Before she knew it, the girl from class walked right toward Sabrina's table. When she reached Sabrina, she paused. If Sabrina wasn't mistaken, she would swear the girl narrowed her gaze in disgust before she pasted on a sickly sweet smile. "Hey. Sofie, right? Weren't you in my lit class last semester?"

"Sabrina. Yes."

"Right. Sabrina." She looked like she was going to say something else, but then decided not to. "Well, gotta run. Have a nice lunch." She bounced away, heading deeper into the restaurant. Weird.

∼

Angelica couldn't believe it.

Interesting day. She saw Sabrina's car in the parking lot as she pulled in. Perfect opportunity to get some retaliation and wipe some of that glass-half-full expression off the bitch's face.

Running into Professor Bascott was even better. Finding out he'd undoubtedly been dining with that bitch from class again was epic.

Feeling lighter than she had in days, she headed straight for the restroom and locked the door—the very same bathroom she knew good and well Dr. Bascott had fucked that skinny bitch in over the summer.

What the hell did he see in her? She was mousy and annoying. Who liked a know-it-all? Sabrina sat at the front of the class all semester with her hand raised and a ready answer to just about anything.

Hell, Dr. Bascott never gave that bitch the time of day all semester. In fact, he seemed downright annoyed by her most days.

Nope. She was certain the man didn't like a know-it-all. Then why the hell was he dallying with the flat-chested waif now?

Angelica used the facilities and washed her hands. As she reached for a paper towel, she stared at herself in the mirror. She was having a great hair day. She lowered her gaze and plumped up her ample chest. Yep, her cleavage was smokin' today also.

She hadn't made great strides with Dr. Bascott on Monday, but after working on her paper this coming weekend, she intended to show up during his office hours again. He was bound to notice her sooner or later.

In the meantime, she had more important things to deal with. Namely, her plans for Saturday night. Leo... She'd met him at a club a few weeks ago and things had really been heating up between them. He was sexy as hell and totally into her. She intended to make a move on him this weekend and put that damn professor out of her mind.

CHAPTER 6

The following day was long for Conner. No day had ever been that long. He had confidence Sabrina would come through for him. But waiting to see her again was a challenge. He'd left the restaurant so hard, he thought his dick would explode out of his pants.

The woman was hell on wheels, and he loved it. He was so going to enjoy bringing her to her knees and training her to do his bidding the way he liked.

And the mouth on her. Oh Lord. For as much as he hated hearing her cuss, at the same time he loved how feisty and determined she was.

She was an editor? Who made a living editing books? He hadn't even asked her what type of books. But he couldn't imagine she made much money. He didn't know anyone who edited and earned enough to survive on.

He did his best to ignore the feeling of impending doom that haunted him day in and day out worrying about the person who was trying to frame him. He'd come up with no feasible explanation. If he'd been asked to make a list of his enemies, it would have been lengthy, especially lately. He seemed to have managed to piss off a slew of people in the last few weeks.

As expected, Sabrina didn't text her address until six thirty. The imp.

When he pulled up to her house at seven, he was shocked to find not an apartment or condo, but an actual house. Maybe she had roommates.

His cock was already hard before he got to the front door. As he knocked, he adjusted himself, shaking his head at how the woman affected him.

It took several seconds for Sabrina to answer. But when she did, Conner couldn't decide whether to laugh or scream.

The woman wore jeans and T-shirt again. He wasn't kidding. She looked hot in anything. The denim hugged her hips perfectly and curved around her ass in a way that made any man drool. He could definitely see the outline of her bra beneath the plain tee. And like yesterday, her nipples made an impression.

She stepped back to allow him entrance, her face unreadable, but he decided on cocky. Determined. Strong. All characteristics he loved and hated at the same time.

"I see you decided not to heed my advice about the jeans," he stated as she shut the door behind him.

She shrugged. "This is what I wore all day. Didn't see a good reason to change. And besides, you gave me no indication as to what we might be doing this evening."

"Going over my expectations again apparently." He stepped farther into the room and looked around.

Every surface was covered with books. Even the couch had a book on it, open and upside down to hold her spot.

"Can I get you something to drink?" she asked.

He picked up a novel from her coffee table and lifted his gaze. "Do you have a beer?"

"Of course." She shuffled through the room into the adjoining kitchen.

While she was gone, he examined the book in his hand. A romance novel. He set the book back down to grab another. The same. He tipped his head to one side to stare at the spines of dozens of books. Romance. All of them.

A beer appeared in his line of sight. "This okay?"

"Perfect." He took the bottle and lifted it to his lips. He was going to need a few of them.

Sabrina also held a beer. She plopped onto the couch and crossed her legs under her while she drank. Lord, she was cute.

"You read all this shit?" he asked.

Sabrina pursed her lips and narrowed her gaze. "Excuse me?"

He waved his free hand through the air, indicating all the literature in her living room. "Smut. Sex. Whatever you want to call it."

She lifted one brow, challenging him. God he loved sparring with her. "I don't just read it. I edit it."

Now he tipped his head back and laughed. She edited trashy romance?

"What's so goddamn funny?"

Still chuckling, he met her gaze. "Language, Sabrina. Watch it."

"Thanks, but no thanks. I'm good with my language. Now what's so funny?"

He took another look around. Her house was a home. Lived in. Loved. Warm and inviting. "You have roommates?"

"No. Why would I have roommates?"

"Some sort of inheritance?"

"Dr. Bascott. Are you insinuating I couldn't possibly make enough money as an editor to afford to live my life?"

"Nope. Not insinuating anything. Flat out stating the facts."

She jumped to her feet and set her beer on the corner of the coffee table. He'd hit a nerve.

"So it's true, then."

"What's true?"

"You *are* an asshole all the time. It's not a part-time gig."

He laughed again. "I've been called worse."

"Why?"

"How should I know? People must not like how brusque I can be. Never have held my tongue well. Ask my mom."

"No. I mean, why are you an asshole? I don't frankly care how many people agree with me."

He stepped closer, thankful she held her ground and didn't back away. She was way shorter than him, but she tipped her head back and met his gaze, hands on her hips. "Actually, it's mostly just you. I mean, I do tend to speak my mind, but I'm harder on you than other people."

"Why?" The word came out softer. She'd lost some of her anger.

He took a deep breath. "Because I want you so badly I can't sleep. And I've fought that need for nine months."

She tucked her lower lip between her teeth. He reached to cup her face with one hand and grazed her lip with his thumb, tugging it away from getting mauled. She opened her mouth when he did so and tipped her head into his palm.

Damn, she was so fucking sexy. And so submissive when she let herself slip into the role. Now if only he could get her to submit to him more fully.

She repeated the same question again. "Why?" This time her voice was deeper, breathy.

"Thought you were too young. Too innocent."

"I'm not. And you know that now. Yet you're still an asshole."

He chuckled.

"You have a new excuse?" She crossed her arms over her chest like she had at lunch, cocking one hip to the side and putting all her weight on one leg.

"Now? Hmmm..." *Good question.* Conner set his beer next to Sabrina's without having to do more than lean down a few inches. Then he wrapped his hands around her wrists under her breasts and tugged them free. "Please don't cross your arms. It closes you off in more ways than one. I don't like to feel alienated from you."

"Then don't talk to me like I'm a stupid child, Dr. Bascott."

"I think we can lose the formality, Sabrina. Conner. Or Sir when you're subbing for me. Stop calling me Dr. Bascott."

"Okay, Conner then. Stop changing the subject." Her hands hung at her sides, fisted, but at least not crossed.

Conner couldn't help himself. He cupped her face with both hands and leaned down to kiss her. He intended a quick peck, but after his initial taste, reminding him of the last and only time he had her mouth, he couldn't keep from slanting his head and deepening the kiss. He licked the seam of her lips, and when she opened for him, he dipped inside her mouth.

Instantly he heard a moan. And it was his. The woman had his balls. And this was why he busted her ass all the time. He hated that she held his balls. He knew he would do anything for her. Even tolerate her sharp tongue, her cussing, and her need for trashy romance.

She tasted of mint and beer. He moaned again. She may not have changed clothes for him, but she had brushed her teeth.

When her hands landed on his forearms and gripped him, he knew she was as lost as he was in the kiss. He needed to pull back. If he didn't, he'd end up fucking her in the living room, probably on the coffee table, before they'd had a proper conversation about what he expected from her.

Conner reluctantly broke the kiss, setting his forehead against hers, noting her eyes were glazed and she swayed slightly.

Thank God she seemed as affected as him.

"Your stalling tactics are amazing," she muttered.

"If I keep kissing you, can we forgo conversation?"

"Probably, but I'm not sure it's a good idea."

He released her and stepped back enough to put a foot of space between them. "You're right." He ran a hand over his short-cropped hair. "Sit, baby." He pointed at the couch where she'd been before.

"So bossy," she mumbled as she resumed her spot, reaching for her beer to take another sip.

"Having trouble making a distinction between dominating you and not."

"I see."

He began to pace. He needed to move. If he didn't, he would combust. "Okay, so first of all, I don't mean to be an ass. Partly your mouth brings it out in me."

"Don't blame it on me, Conner."

He stopped pacing to meet her gaze and nodded. *Just say it.* "You scare the fuck out of me."

She flinched, her eyes wide, her mouth open for a moment before she spoke. "What? Why?"

"That's how bad I want you. Never craved a woman like I do you. Thought I would have worked it out of my system in the bathroom that day. Didn't happen. You turn me inside out. You're like a drug. That makes me defensive."

Her eyes bugged out.

"Tell me you're mine." He needed her to say it. It was too soon. It was also not soon enough.

She licked her lips. "Conner…"

"Baby, you know this is going to happen between us. We have chemistry. I realize we have two thousand details to work through, and I'll readily admit, I come with a shit ton of baggage, but I'd like to take them one at a time after you admit you're mine."

She nodded. Thank fuck.

"Say the words, baby." His chest pounded.

"I'm yours, Sir."

He let his shoulders slump several inches. Relief washed through him at her words. It wasn't that he expected anything different. But until she admitted he made her world spin, he couldn't move on.

Conner took a long stride to get right in front of her. He kneeled at the edge of the couch, pulled her legs apart so he was nestled between them, and grabbed her shoulders. "You won't regret it, baby. I swear." She humbled him. She made a light shine in the murky darkness that had entered his world lately.

She nodded again. Uncertainty lurked in the corners of her eyes, but he watched her chest heave, and she shivered beneath his touch. He hoped those were signs that she felt something similar to what he experienced around her. He was banking on it.

Fuck the details. They could discuss the particulars later. "Now, can I fuck you first and talk after?" He needed her so badly, his cock ached.

"Please, Sir."

"Excellent." He closed the space between them and kissed her mouth, this time with restraint, pulling back after a few seconds. "Take these jeans off for me, baby. Sexy as they are on you, I'm betting they're much sexier on the floor."

She shivered. "Okay."

He tucked his hands under her arms and lifted her, switching their positions so she stood facing him and he sat in her spot on the couch. He nodded. "Now, baby. Strip for me."

He leaned back. It was either that or fall.

Sabrina took a step away and pulled her tee over her head first. Her lacy bra was the only thing left blocking the view of her nipples. She was so petite, and her breasts matched her stature. He loved them. Wanted to feel his palms completely covering them.

Her hands shook as she popped the button on her jeans, lowered the zipper, and then wiggled her hips back and forth as she tugged them down her legs. Her sexy feet were bare, and she stepped on one leg of the jeans and then the other to pull the denim free of her body.

She fought the need to fidget under his scrutiny. He watched her battle, her face tight, her hands fisted.

"The rest, baby," he whispered. "I didn't get a good look at you the first time. I want to see all of you now."

"Conner..." She glanced around the room, pausing at the window.

He knew what she was thinking, but the blinds were closed. "No one's going to see you."

She turned back to face him.

"Take off your bra and panties, baby." This time he spoke with more authority, although it still sounded slightly desperate to his ears. And hell, that was how he felt. Desperate. Needy.

Sabrina lowered her gaze to the floor as she popped the

clasp on her bra and let the lace fall down her arms to drop it on the floor.

He remembered those tits. So pink and sexy. Her chest was flushed with embarrassment. Also a good sign. He wanted her to be somewhat more demure when she subbed for him than her usual feisty self.

When she lowered her panties to the floor, keeping her legs too close together, he swallowed a moan. "So sexy, baby."

She shivered as though cold, not meeting his gaze. "So uneven, Sir."

He chuckled. "True. But I'm the Dom here, yes?"

"Yes, Sir."

"So, it stands to reason I'll take off my clothes when I'm ready, right?"

"Yes, Sir."

"Turn around, baby."

She almost stepped on her own feet as she did his bidding. When her back was to him, he inhaled sharply. Her ass was so firm and round. He loved the faint tan lines he remembered seeing when she'd been spanked by Doug at Extreme.

"Do you enjoy spanking, Sabrina?"

She nodded.

"Words, baby."

"I do, Sir. With the right Dom."

"You trust me?"

"Yes, Sir. Irrationally."

"That's okay. That trust will build with time. Turn around. Look at me."

She spun back to face him.

"For now I need you to know that I'll never hurt you, at least nothing more than the sting of my palm. I would never leave a permanent mark on your body. I would never speak to you in anger while you're submitting to me. When we play, your safety, comfort, and arousal are my top priorities."

"Okay."

"I will push your boundaries, but only with your permission and trust. Is *red* a good safe word for you? Or would you prefer another?"

"Red is fine, Sir."

"Use it."

"Okay."

"I'm not even going to address all the times you've smarted off to me lately or the number of blatantly defiant acts you've taken to rile me up. But I am going to spank your sweet ass for wearing those jeans tonight after I expressly prohibited it. I'm going to go out on a limb here and assume you knew this would happen and intentionally egged me on."

She flinched.

"That's what I thought." He sat straighter and scooted to the edge of the couch. "Come here, baby."

She shuffled closer.

He spread his knees, needing to touch her before he punished her. Grabbing her wrists, he pulled her between his legs and then released her to set his palms on her hips. God, she was tiny.

His thumbs spanned so wide, he easily grazed the upper swell of her pussy. She was clean-shaved. He loved it. Couldn't wait to run his tongue over her smooth skin.

Conner trailed his hands up to cup her breasts. She arched into him, her nipples pebbling further when he stroked his thumbs over the tips. Her head tipped back as though he'd thrust deep inside her instead of just caressing her breasts. "So responsive, baby. Love that."

His pants were too tight. They had been even before he

arrived, but since entering her home, he was close to losing it. He needed to tamp down the craving for a while longer. Until he pinkened her ass with his hand, he wasn't going to take her.

Releasing her breasts, he directed her around to his side and angled her over his lap. "Lie across my knees, baby."

She did as he instructed without a word. Her breaths were rapid as she landed over his thighs, reaching out her hands to brace herself on the floor.

Conner held her lower back firmly. She didn't need to balance herself with her hands or her feet. He would never let her fall. He smoothed his free hand over her fine ass and massaged the firm flesh. "Sexiest ass on the planet, baby."

She didn't acknowledge him.

Finally, he lifted his hand and swatted her with enough force to make her gasp. He repeated the action on the other side, pressing into the small of her back to hold her steady. "That's my girl. I love the pink of your cheeks now. I'm going to cover them with my handprints. You'll stay still while I do so."

"Yes, Sir." Her voice was desperate, squeaky.

His cock pressed into her hip, pleading with him. He spanked her two more times, lower, where her cheeks met her thighs.

She spread her legs wider without being told.

"Such a needy little sub."

"Yes, Sir." Her head fell forward to hang between her arms.

"Are you wet, baby?" He smoothed his hand over her ass as he spoke.

"Yes, Sir."

He reached between her legs and stroked one finger through her folds.

Sabrina stiffened and moaned, spreading her legs farther.

"Not yet, baby. You don't come until I say so. Got it?"

"Yes, Sir."

He spanked her again without warning. And then three more swats, alternating between cheeks. She was good and pink by then, and eight was enough for this first time. Plus, he feared she would come without any help if he didn't let her reach her release soon.

Conner thrust two fingers into her pussy until his palm flattened against her, his thumb against her rear hole.

"Oh, God." She lifted her chest off him and gripped his thigh with both hands. "Sir, I can't…"

"I know, baby." He thrust again.

She moaned louder. "Conner…"

Music to his ears.

"Give it to me, baby. Come. Now."

She shattered around the fingers still buried inside her. He hadn't even touched her clit.

Oh yeah, Sabrina Duluth was his.

CHAPTER 7

Sabrina gasped for oxygen. Her mind was so scrambled she couldn't form words.

Her pussy still gripped his fingers, and he left them inside her.

When the tremors finally subsided, he began to move again, stroking her G-spot and driving her back to full arousal in seconds.

Her legs shook. "Conner. Oh, God."

"Just feel, baby."

"I can't…" She was too sensitive. Even her clit, which hadn't been touched yet, felt tender.

"Oh, baby. You can. And you will. You'll learn to come for me so many times you'll lose count."

She flinched at those words. Her face heated. God, how she wanted that. Was it possible? No Dom had ever taken her that far, as much as she'd willed it to happen. Wasn't that the stuff of her romance novels? In real life, people didn't actually have multiple orgasms until they collapsed, right?

Conner's damn fingers kept stroking, slow and steady

until the pressure built. He paused his movement inside her pussy to press against her rear hole again. "Has anyone taken this tight bud, baby?"

"No." She moaned. She'd never even thought about it. But suddenly she knew it was Conner's. She would let him fuck her there if he asked.

He massaged the entrance. "That makes me so hot, baby," he muttered. "This hole is mine, Sabrina." His voice was rough. She liked it.

His hand disappeared, and he grabbed her hips. Before she knew it, she was on her feet, swaying too much to stand.

Conner didn't release her, though. He was sensitive to her plight. He stood in front of her and then swung her up into his arms. "Bedroom?"

"Down the hall. On the right." She met his gaze, wishing he would hurry.

His strides were wide. In moments they were in her room. She'd at least made her bed, knowing, or hoping, this would be their ultimate destination this evening.

When Conner set her on her feet, he dragged his hands up her body to cup her face again. She loved the way he did that, meeting her gaze and forcing her to meet his. "Take my clothes off, baby."

She nodded.

Conner released her.

Her hands shook as she tugged his shirt over his head and dropped it. Damn he was built. She trailed a finger along the edge of his tattoo and leaned in to taste his skin, licking a line across his nipple.

"Baby…"

Good. She affected him too. Maybe not as much, but close.

"Jeans, Sabrina."

She set her forehead on his pecs and watched as she reached for his button, popping it quickly and then lowering the zipper. His cock sprang free. Commando.

"Take them off, baby." He wove his hands into her hair as he spoke.

The strands dragged through his fingers as she lowered herself to her knees and tugged the denim over his hips. She pulled both his shoes off and then his jeans, one leg at a time when he lifted his feet. Lastly his socks.

When she lifted her face, his cock bobbed in front of her lips. Without hesitating, she licked a line from the base to the tip. He hadn't given her permission to do it, but she didn't think about anything except the need to taste him.

He moaned and set his hands on her shoulders, gripping hard, but before he could stop her, she sucked his thick cock into her mouth.

"Oh, God, baby…" His thighs shook when she gripped them. Good.

Heaven. His cock was larger than any she'd had before, but then so was the rest of him. And she longed to have him inside her, but first this. She sucked him harder. Deep throating a man wasn't something she'd ever excelled at. But apparently she'd never been with the right man.

Conner did something to her that scared the fuck out of her. He made her want on a whole new level. She wanted to please him. She wanted everything from him.

He didn't stop her. Surprising.

"So good, baby. So good…" His voice trailed off as he spoke.

In a moment, he stiffened, his fingers digging into her shoulders. She didn't care about the slight pain. She loved it. It told her how much he enjoyed her mouth.

When he thrust forward, she knew he was there. His come splashed against her throat, and she swallowed, learning the taste of him and relishing the closeness. As his body relaxed, she continued to suckle him. His cock remained surprisingly stiff.

Eventually he pulled out of her mouth and lifted her by the arms to stand in front of him. He cupped her cheeks and lowered his mouth to hers, devouring her like a starving man, obviously undaunted by his flavor on her tongue.

Without releasing her mouth, he backed her up until her thighs hit the bed. He lifted her onto the mattress and scooted her back while crawling up to straddle her, never ending the kiss.

Conner Bascott was divine. She trembled beneath him, wanting his cock inside her while knowing it would be a while before she had him. He would need to recover. She prayed it wouldn't take long.

Straddling her hips, his hands wandered to her breasts. He squeezed them gently and then pinched her nipples.

Finally he broke free of her lips. He was breathing heavily, and his eyes were glassy. "Fuck. You're the sweetest woman I've ever held in my arms." He grinned crookedly. "When you aren't fighting me, that is. Now that I know what it takes to keep your sharp tongue occupied..." He scooted down her body and lifted one knee to plant between hers. "Spread for me, baby."

She widened her thighs as he climbed between them.

"Good girl. See how easy it is to please me?"

She rolled her eyes. "Cocky bastard."

He chuckled again, the sound music to her ears. God, how she loved this side of him.

He resumed toying with her breasts and nipples, making her glance down and wince slightly at the vision. She was not well endowed. Conner didn't seem to notice or care. In fact, he made her feel more beautiful than she'd ever felt in her life.

As if he read her mind, Conner blew across her nipple and spoke. "Love these, baby. So gorgeous. Perfect." He punctuated his words with a slight squeeze to both globes at once.

She lifted her chest off the bed.

"That's it, baby. So responsive." He leaned over her and licked one nipple before sucking it into his mouth.

Sabrina gripped his shoulders. "Sir…" It felt so good. He worshiped her body, switching to the other nipple before trailing kisses down her belly until he reached her clit.

Conner flattened himself between her legs, pulled the hood up to expose her nub, and flicked his tongue over the swollen flesh.

She made a sound she didn't recognize. It came from deep inside and shocked her.

He didn't relent. Instead he sucked her clit into his mouth and lapped at it with the flat of his tongue.

"Oh, God." She squeezed her eyes closed, trying to stave off the impending orgasm.

She didn't have to fight too long. Just before she reached the cliff, he released her to lower his mouth until his tongue trailed between her lower lips and then dipped inside. "So fucking sweet. Like honey." He went back to work, fucking her with his tongue and moaning around her entrance, so the vibrations shook her body and drove her need to new heights. She'd come on his lap minutes ago. That seemed like a distant memory now.

"Conner, please…"

Suddenly he was gone, sliding away from her, making her eyes widen with the shock. Two seconds later he was back, ripping a condom open with his teeth. "You on the pill, baby?"

"Yes." She reached for him.

"Get tested. I will too. Hate these things." And then he was over her, rolling the rubber down his length and then landing on her body, his elbows planted on both sides of her head. His cock was lodged at her entrance. "You ready for me?"

"Oh. God. Honestly. Conner. Please. Sir…" When she said that last word, out of breath and lifting her hips up to meet his cock, he thrust into her.

A low groan rumbled through him. He held himself steady deep inside her.

She breathed around the intrusion, having forgotten how full she would feel with him buried inside. He knocked her breath away.

"Jesus." He set his forehead against hers. "Forgot."

Ah, so it wasn't just her.

"Tightest, sweetest pussy ever." He pulled out and then pressed home again on a grunt. "I'll never get enough of it." Again. "So wet for me, baby." He reached for her face with his hands on both sides and stroked her temples.

Sabrina met his intense gaze.

"You're mine, baby."

She blinked at him, unable to think about anything other than his cock and how damn good it felt.

"Say it, baby. You're mine."

She licked her lips, trying to get her mouth to move to form the words he asked her to repeat for the second time tonight. "Yours, Sir. I'm yours." She'd made that decision before texting him this evening, knowing full well a text to Dr. Conner Bascott was the same as consenting to be his submissive.

"That's right, baby. Mine." He picked up the pace, thrusting faster, seemingly deeper with each pass.

She grabbed onto his waist and held on for her life

while he plunged into her. So damn perfect. She never wanted it to end.

But there was no way to keep her orgasm at bay. She needed release. As much as she wished she could hold on to this moment forever, she was too close to hold back.

"Come, baby."

That was all it took. She tipped her head back, opened her mouth, and moaned loudly through the pulsing of her pussy around his cock.

Conner continued to fuck her, harder maybe.

As her orgasm subsided, she met his gaze. In seconds, she found herself climbing the mountain again, the base of Conner's cock rubbing her clit with each pass.

"That's it, baby. Let it rise again. Give it to me."

She couldn't believe this was happening. She'd already come twice. A third was unimaginable, especially so soon after the others, but like waves in the ocean, the pressure built again.

Conner gritted his teeth. He'd also come recently. How could he be ready again? Was he as turned on as she was?

"So close, baby. Give it to me again, Sabrina. Now."

At his words, she let herself go, a deeper orgasm sweeping through her, taking her by surprise and tilting the world on its axis. This release came from inside her instead of her clit. Her pussy gripped his cock so hard she felt the muscles working to milk him.

Conner must have felt the same thing, because seconds after her, he thrust to the hilt and held steady, exposing more of his neck as he lifted his face toward the ceiling and groaned through his release.

Sabrina could barely see, her vision blurry, probably from all the blood in her body congregating in her pussy.

Conner collapsed, sliding to her side at the last second to avoid crushing her.

She turned toward him. Or rather, he tugged her alongside him as he fell, keeping her chest close to his side, not letting any space get between them.

He breathed heavily for long minutes, shifting to meet her gaze and not speaking for so long she thought perhaps he never would. "I'm ruined."

She smiled. If he was saying what she thought he meant, she was glad to have helped.

"Mine," he repeated, making himself clear. He pulled her closer and kissed her forehead. His eyes were closed when he leaned back against her pillow.

Sabrina shut her eyes too, thinking to rest them...

~

It was dark in the room when Sabrina blinked awake, confused and warmer than usual. She glanced around, realizing there was a hard male body pressed against her.

A quick assessment of her memory flooded her with all the events of the evening. She inhaled deeply of Conner's scent and smiled into his chest. It didn't appear either of them had moved an inch since they'd worn themselves out. The covers were smashed to the foot of the bed, but Sabrina wasn't as cold as she would have expected. The heater next to her warmed her entire body.

"Mmm, I can feel you thinking," a deep rumbling voice said from next to her.

She smiled against his chest, unwilling to move.

"Share?"

"Sated. Happy. Complete." God, had she really said that? It was too soon. They hadn't even negotiated anything yet.

She stiffened. What if all they had between them was lust and they were completely incompatible otherwise? It was possible. Especially considering how often they fought when they weren't fucking.

"Hey. Those were sweet words, baby." Conner reached for her chin and tipped her face up. In the dim light coming from the hall, he met her gaze. "Now you're thinking too hard. Relax. I know this is crazy. Crazy good, though. The details will work themselves out."

"Will they?"

"Yep. Trust me." He kissed her nose. "No way will I allow any other outcome. You're too fucking awesome."

"You aren't so bad yourself, when you aren't bossing me around."

"Get used to it, baby."

She stiffened further. "How about we discuss that?"

"We will. Don't worry."

"You say that as though *you* will do the discussing, and *I* will do the listening." Was she reading too much into his few words? She pushed off him to sit upright.

He let her right herself, but didn't stop touching her. "I'm not an asshole."

"Really?" She wasn't kidding when she asked that. "I'm hoping you can prove that."

"I can." He pulled himself up beside her and took her lips in a passionate kiss, melting her resolve. "Shower?"

"Sounds fantastic." Her muscles ached. Her skin felt sticky. She needed to use the bathroom too. "Give me a second?"

"Of course, baby. Yell when you have the water warm."

She eased off the bed, grateful he understood her need for a moment of privacy. She was sorer than she'd expected. As she padded across the room and entered the attached bath, every muscle complained.

She flipped on the water without turning on the light

and used the toilet. When she was ready to climb in, she leaned back out the door. "Coming?"

"Yep." Conner was on her in an instant, striding across the room so fast it seemed incongruent with his recent deep sleep. He wrapped his arms around her and backed her up toward the shower.

As though he'd been to her house dozens of times and knew every intricate detail, he opened the glass door and helped her over the ledge to back her into the stream of water. He closed the door behind him without glancing back.

His hands were everywhere at once, angling her under the warmth and tipping her head back to wet her hair. He grabbed her shampoo, and without saying a word, massaged it into her scalp until she was sure she'd died and gone to heaven. He kept working until he had her entire body clean and supple, even stroking his fingers between her legs, but not lingering long enough to get her too worked up.

When he finished, he opened the door and helped her out. "Dry off while I finish, baby."

She stared at his back, the glorious tattoo across his right shoulder as he lifted his arms to wash his hair, and then the rest of his body. She reached for her towel at some point, but held it in front of her, in no way sure what it was for.

She startled when the water shut off and Conner stepped out next to her. He chuckled. "You didn't dry off."

She glanced down. *Shit.* The word made her flinch. She was glad she hadn't broken the moment by uttering it out loud. No telling what he might do if she started cussing right now. Would he be disappointed in her when she cussed and reprimand her verbally? Or would he take her over his knee and make her come? The first option made her wince. She wasn't at all sure she could stop cussing so easily. But she hated to disappoint him. It was a new sensation, but it slammed through her like a lightning bolt.

Shit, she thought again. The last thing she needed was for Conner to turn her into someone she was not. Or someone she didn't want to be.

"You're thinking too hard again." He took her towel from her and dried her off, wrapping it around her hair when he finished and twisting it until he had it satisfactorily settled on top of her head. Next, he grabbed another towel from the rack, dried himself, and wrapped the terry cloth around his waist. "Come on." He took her hand and led her from the room. "We need food."

Her stomach growled at the reminder. "What time is it?" She twisted around as they entered the bedroom to glimpse the clock on her nightstand. Eleven thirty. Was that all?

"Early still," Conner commented. "And you made me hungry." He unwrapped her hair, patted it until it was only damp, and draped the towel over a chair. And then he led her to the kitchen, holding her hand and leaving her trailing along behind him. "You have stuff for sandwiches?"

"Yes." She glanced down at her naked body. He hadn't said she could put anything on. It was slightly unnerving, but she didn't say a word.

"Perfect." When he stepped into the kitchen, he flipped on the light above the stove and turned to grab Sabrina by the waist.

Before she knew what he had in mind, she was lifted into the air and settled on the counter. "Conner," she admonished.

He chuckled. "I'll make sandwiches. You sit there and look pretty." He stepped away and reached for the fridge handle. As he opened the door, the room flooded with more light. He surveyed the situation and grabbed an armload of items, kicking the door closed as he returned. The makings of sandwiches were dropped unceremoniously on the counter next to her.

"I could help."

"You could spread your legs."

She jolted.

Conner tapped the closest one, telling her he was serious.

She opened her thighs several inches as he tore into the package of turkey and then reached for the bread. "Wider, baby. I want to be able to see your pussy."

She gasped, but did as he said.

"Better," he said without looking. His attention seemed riveted to the task of making sandwiches, but he clearly had eyes in the side of his head and the back too. "You like mayonnaise or mustard, baby?"

"Mustard, please."

He was efficient. In no time she held a sandwich and took a bite. It tasted fantastic. It was just bread, cheese, and lunch meat, but she was hungry, and the way Conner took care of her made her feel and sense things on a whole new level. The way he settled between her legs to eat heightened her awareness of how he affected her body.

As though she hadn't had the best sex of her life all evening, her pussy gripped, wetness pooling between her legs. She ate, but gradually the taste slipped away until she wasn't aware of anything but the way Conner looked at her and how he made her body sing under his gaze.

When they finished, Conner put everything away and hefted her off the counter.

She wrapped her legs around his waist when she realized he wasn't going to set her down. Instead he carried her back to bed and tossed her unceremoniously on the mattress.

She giggled. "What was that for?"

He climbed up alongside her and propped pillows up against the headboard to lean against them. "Come here, baby." He patted the spot next to him, and she crawled to his side, wishing the towel he wore had somehow fallen away.

He wrapped an arm around her shoulders and held her to his chest. "Let's talk."

CHAPTER 8

Admittedly, Conner was nervous. He wasn't sure how to proceed, and he wanted to get them on the same page as painlessly as possible without sending his sweet sexy woman into a rage. She was quick with her temper when he expressed himself. Of course, there was always the possibility he was a bit poor at communicating. Shocking since he was a lit teacher and had never had any difficulty with the written word.

Truth be told, he'd never had trouble speaking or writing anything, until the sharp-witted Sabrina came on the scene and cut him down frequently and passionately.

She snuggled up to him, but her brow was furrowed when she lifted her face.

He smiled down at her and squeezed her closer. "You're very young, baby."

She rolled her eyes. "This again?"

He chuckled. "Just listen to me." He cleared his throat. "I'll admit you're older and wiser than your years would indicate, but nothing makes up for experience."

"I've been a submissive for eight years, Conner. How long have you been a Dom?"

"Almost twenty."

She visibly swallowed.

He took a deep breath. "I'm not saying this won't work. I sincerely hope it does. I'm just warning you I have firm expectations from my subs, and I've never had one as innocent as you."

She glared at him. Feisty as ever. "What makes you think I'm so innocent?"

"Baby, it's obvious. I don't care how long you've been dabbling in BDSM, your experiences are limited."

She pursed her lips and lowered her gaze. At least she wasn't arguing with him. Although, she still disagreed.

"I'm going to wager you've done little more than the most basic of submissive components. Kneeling. Spanking benches. Assuming a demure stance—albeit poorly." He chuckled.

She sucked in a breath, her face jerking up to meet his. She pressed on his chest to separate from him, but he held her tight.

"I don't mean any of that to sound insulting. I'm merely pointing out your lack of actual experience. I'm not that kind of Dom."

"I told you I was with a Dom full-time when I was eighteen."

He nodded. "And you told me he was forty. And I bet he helped you get your feet wet and then moved on."

Her mouth fell open.

Conner closed his eyes, trying to find the right words to keep from pissing her off. "Baby, you've never had a man in your ass."

She said nothing.

"Has anyone flogged you?"

She shook her head subtly.

"Have you ever worn a gag?"

"No," she mumbled.

"Butt plug? Nipple clamps? Spreader bar?"

She swallowed again, her eyes wider until she tipped her head out of view again.

"I'm not saying this to scare you. I'm trying to make a point. You're green, baby. You're twenty-six. You should be green. I'd be worried if some Dom you had at eighteen bound you in a dungeon and fucked your tight ass without letting you come."

She flinched.

He held on to her. And then he quickly flipped her onto her back, held her arms over her head, and hovered over her, giving her no space.

She held her breath, meeting his gaze, her mouth open, her eyes wide.

"Do I have your attention now?"

"Yes, Sir."

"Okay." He kissed her nose. "Now, I don't mean to insinuate that I'm going to overwhelm you all at once, but I'm an experienced Dom with insatiable appetites. I like my subs to do my bidding without question. I'll insist you obey me when we're in the role. And I'll punish you appropriately when you sass me."

She still didn't move a muscle.

"When we're playing, I expect you to follow my instructions. No lying. I expect you to be open and honest with me at all times, or this won't work.

"No cussing." He lowered his gaze pointedly. "You may think it's cute, but I don't like nasty language coming from your mouth."

She held his gaze, but remained mute.

"No jeans. No pants. I like your pussy available to me. If

we're at the club, keep your gaze down. Refer to me as Sir. Keep your hands at your sides or behind your back as instructed. Be respectful. I won't push you further than you can handle. And if I scare you, use a safe word—yellow to slow down, red to stop. Understood?"

She nodded. "How often do you expect me to submit to you? Full-time when we're together? Just at the club? What about in public?"

He set his forehead on hers. "I don't have all the answers yet. Having a submissive in my home will be new to me, so we'll have to wing it at first, figure out together how often we want to be in the role, establish boundaries for what works for us as we go along.

"What I know is that you're mine. I'll take things slow and keep your lack of experience forefront in my mind. But I won't go easy on you." He took her lips in a deep kiss with no warning, slipping his tongue into her mouth to dance with her own. *God, she's sweet.*

Her body relaxed slowly as he plundered her mouth. When a soft moan escaped her lips and she tugged on her hands to free them, he nibbled a path down her neck toward her breast. He'd been inside her twice. He had not had enough of her yet, however.

Switching both her wrists to one hand, he lowered the other to cup her breast while he flicked his tongue over the nipple.

Sabrina arched her chest, another longer, louder moan slipping out to fill the room.

"Stay still, baby." He pressed her back onto the mattress with his hand. "I need to taste you again. Either remain perfectly still so I can explore your body, or I'll restrain you and do it anyway. Understood?"

She nodded.

He lifted a brow.

"Yes, Sir." Her words were breathy. For once, he'd managed to knock the sass down. He had to battle to avoid smirking. She shivered.

Conner dipped his head again and sucked her nipple into his mouth.

She flinched, but didn't buck her chest.

Lord, her tit was the sweetest thing he'd ever suckled. He squeezed it with his palm, forcing the nipple up into his mouth. He could feel the vibrations of Sabrina's sounds through her chest as he fondled her rougher.

Before she completely lost it, he switched to her other breast, giving it the same attention. When he finished exploring her nipples, he eased down her body, releasing her hands. "Leave your arms over your head, baby. And spread your legs for me."

She did as he told her, biting her lower lip between her teeth and tipping her head back to expose her neck.

Conner crawled between her legs, spreading them wider until he held her thighs open as far as he imagined comfortable.

Sabrina whimpered. He knew she wasn't in pain. She had to be overstimulated.

Good.

He pulled her folds open with his thumbs. "So pink," he mumbled.

Moisture flooded the entrance to her pussy when he breathed against her opening. Her legs stiffened beneath his grip, pressing in an attempt to close.

He dug his fingers into her firmer. "Always open for me, baby." He blew against her clit, the nub sticking out from its hood and glistening with her moisture.

"Oh, God," she mumbled. "Conner... Sir..."

"I know, baby," he soothed. "I know." He stuck his tongue into her as far as he could reach and fucked her with it before pulling back out. "Such a tight cunt." He flattened his tongue on her folds and licked upward until he flicked the tip over her clit.

She nearly shot off the bed.

He was ready though, lifting his face to give her a stern look. "Still, Sabrina. You'll learn to stay still for me."

"Yes, Sir." He could barely hear her. Her head rolled from side to side. Her legs shook.

She was precious.

He was one lucky bastard. He returned his attention to her smooth mound. "I love the clean shave, baby. Do it every day." He set his cheek on her pussy and inhaled deeply, luxuriating in her scent and the smoothness of her skin. "Did you shave this evening before I came?" He knew she had. There was no stubble.

"Yes, Sir," she whispered, perhaps embarrassed to admit such a thing. Interesting, since that meant she intentionally put her jeans back on before he arrived.

"Good girl." Without warning he sucked her clit into his mouth and let his teeth graze the tip.

She was too close.

He could feel her entire body stiffening, so he released her. "Not yet, baby. You'll come when I say. Not before." If he wasn't mistaken, her clit actually throbbed. He smiled.

Finally he released her legs. "Leave yourself open. Don't move an inch. If you can do that, I'll let you come. If not, I'll stop and leave you hanging. Understood?"

"Yes, Sir."

Conner trailed a finger through her folds, gathering her wetness and stroking downward toward her tight forbidden hole.

She tensed, as he expected.

He repeated the action several times, spreading her moisture lower and circling her clenched ass. "Your entire body is mine, Sabrina. Not just parts of it. I'll expect you to surrender this tight hole to me gradually. I'm only going to use one finger tonight, but be prepared for more soon."

She moaned. Her legs clenched, but she didn't close them. Her butt cheeks squeezed tight.

"Open up to me, baby. I promise it will feel good." He tapped her rear hole with his finger. "One finger, Sabrina. That's nothing. Let go of the notion that it's wrong or dirty. It's just us here. Consenting adults." He circled the entrance again, spreading more of her arousal as it ran down from her pussy to coat his finger. That was how he knew she was ready. Her pussy didn't lie.

Finally her butt cheeks relaxed.

"Good girl." He slipped his finger inside her slowly, pushing through the barrier she created with her clenched muscles.

Sabrina moaned loudly. Her feet dug into the mattress as she obviously fought to keep from closing her legs.

"That's my girl. Just feel." He pressed deeper until he was up to the second knuckle. Meanwhile he licked through her folds again, spreading them open and dipping his tongue into her sheath.

"Oh God."

Gorgeous. Her sounds made his heart sing. Her noises filled the room. She was so aroused, she couldn't control them. And that was the point.

He was so screwed. He wouldn't admit it out loud, but this woman had him wrapped around her finger. She could blatantly defy him every step of the way, and he would still melt at her feet. It was going to be a challenge keeping her oblivious to the effect she had on him.

Pushing the rest of his finger into her, he circled her tight walls, letting his tongue and finger bump into each other through the thin barrier between them. He pulled his mouth away and traded his tongue for his thumb, spreading his palm open to fuck both holes with one hand.

Sabrina lifted her ass up.

He stopped his movement but didn't remove his fingers. "Uh uh."

She let herself relax back onto the bed. "Conner," she pleaded.

Her ass was so tight and her cunt so sweet. His cock ached thinking about taking her rear hole. Soon. Not today, but he wouldn't be able to wait long. He would need to prepare her, stretch her, sweet talk her into letting him in. For now, he lapped at her clit and then sucked it into his mouth again as he fucked both her holes with his hand.

Sabrina shot off immediately. He hadn't told her she could, but there was no way he could expect her to hold back under that amount of duress. Her body pulsed around his fingers and his tongue, her orgasm coming from everywhere at once.

Conner was humbled. The most delicious woman on Earth was his. And he intended to make sure she knew it every day of her life.

CHAPTER 9

On Saturday morning, Conner got to the gym late. Rafe and Zane were sparring in the cage. Rider and Gage were weight training. Conner joined Rider and Gage.

"Dmitry was looking for you," Rider said.

"Dmitry was here?" Conner hesitated. "Alone?"

"Yep. He said he knew you'd spoken to Yenin last week. He wanted to follow up on that."

Conner frowned. "That guy won't let it go. Shit. How many times do I have to tell him I'm not going to fight for the Russian mob?"

Gage chuckled. "I don't think Dmitry considers himself a member of the mob."

"I'm sure he doesn't. Most of the time I don't either. Except when he gets pulled into this shit with Yenin and hunts me down to do the asshole's dirty work." Conner picked up a set of weights and put them on the bar.

"What did Yenin say to you last week?" Rider asked.

"He practically threatened me. Said he needed me to fight for him this weekend. I said fuck no. And he insinuated he could make me." Conner froze. His entire body went stiff.

"What?" Gage asked. Several seconds went by. "Dude. You look like you've seen a ghost."

Conner spun to face Gage and Rider. Hell, if there was anyone he should talk to about this shit, it was them. Rider was a cop and Gage a K-9 trainer at the police academy. "Fuck." He set his hands on his hips as his mind ran through several possibilities. "I don't know why this didn't occur to me before now, but someone is anonymously trying to get me fired."

"From the university?" Rider asked.

"Yep. Somebody emailed the Dean, the head of my department, and the university president telling them I was involved with a student."

"Are you fucking kidding me?" Rider set his weights down and stepped closer. "Why would anyone do that? Do you really think Yenin would stoop that low?"

Conner shrugged. "No idea. But it's the first possibility I've come up with."

"Do you think anyone is making an assumption about Sabrina?" Gage asked.

Conner shook his head. "I've wracked my brain over this. I really don't think this has a damn thing to do with Sabrina."

"What makes you say that?" Rider asked.

"The timing. It makes no sense. I had only seen Sabrina on three occasions when the allegations were made. Someone emailed the university over the weekend after she showed up at my fight last Friday. I've thought hard about it, but I don't see how anyone could have seen us together. But fuck me. It is possible Yenin or one of his minions saw us at the fight." Conner slapped a hand on his forehead. He shook his head as he realized how illogical the scenario was. "No. This just doesn't add up. Even if Yenin did send someone to spy on me, how the hell would that person know Sabrina was or had ever been a student?"

"Wait," Rider interrupted, "this is pretty serious, Conner. Let's think this through. Why didn't you call me or mention this before now?"

Conner shrugged. "Hell, the allegations aren't valid, so I didn't think to give a fuck. No one can prove I ever dated a student because I have never fucking dated a student." His voice rose, and he glanced around to find several other members of the gym staring at him.

Rider spoke softer. "Okay. So, you saw Sabrina at the fight. You faced her outside the locker room and immediately left the arena. What happened next?"

"We went straight to my car where we exchanged words and then she stomped off, leaving me holding my dick." Conner chuckled. He couldn't help it. The situation may have been serious, but God he loved how the woman could spar. It was better than the cage.

Gage smirked. "You pissed her off that fast?"

Conner shook his head. "Trust me. It isn't difficult. Sabrina is hell on wheels when she puts her mind to it. And I might possibly have contributed to her ire on more than one occasion."

Rider spoke again. "Okay, so unless someone followed you from the arena to the car, that's rather unlikely. The time before that you saw her the previous Friday night, right? At the club?"

"Yes. She was with another Dom." He scrunched his face, remembering watching Doug spank her. "We argued that night too."

Gage slapped Conner on the shoulder. "Wow, dude. Smooth. It's a wonder the woman ever consented to do anything with you."

"Ha ha. Anyway, we didn't speak inside the club. No fucking way someone saw us there. I went outside. When she left we argued in the parking lot. The only person who saw that exchange was Frank."

"No way would Frank have any interest in getting you fired," Gage pointed out.

"Yeah. But at this point, that's about the best option I've come up with," Conner added. "See the problem? If Frank the door man is trying to get me fired from the university, what the hell is the world coming to? What motive would the guy have? I don't even know him. Unless he had been sleeping with Sabrina, I don't see why he would give a fuck that I was. And I know he never met Sabrina before that night. It was her first time at Extreme."

"Right. Let's rule out poor Frank." Rider pursed his lips and then continued. "Wait. You said you'd seen her three times. When was the other encounter?"

Conner winced. He had not intended to tell the guys about fucking his woman in the bathroom of King Pizza. Ever. It was their little secret.

"Yeah. Dude," Gage said, "if you managed to fight with her at the club and then the arena, you must have pissed her off royally at some previous encounter. I know she was in your class last semester, but you never mentioned seeing her after that ended."

"Yeah, I might have possibly run into her over the summer."

"Maybe?" Rider raised an eyebrow, and then a grin fell across his face. "Are you fucking kidding," he whispered. "Did you sleep with her?"

"Maybe."

"And you don't think that has anything to do with the allegations?"

"Not really. Super unlikely. Even more unlikely than Frank."

"Shit, Conner." Rider ran a hand through his hair. "At this point, it seems the most likely prospect is Sabrina herself."

"No fucking way." Conner shook his head. "Not a chance."

Rider didn't look convinced. "You fucked the woman over the summer. Then I'm going to assume you didn't see her again or contact her. When she saw you at the club she was pissed. Then she saw you at the arena and she was pissed. What makes you think she didn't email the school with some bogus story about you dating a student to get you in trouble for being such an asshole?"

Conner winced again. He shook his head again too. "Not buying it. Not a chance."

"Didn't she stalk you? Follow you from the university to the arena?" Gage asked. "And wasn't she fit to kill?"

"Yes, but come on. We've come so far since then. We're together now."

"So?" Rider lifted a brow. "That doesn't mean she didn't email the university between fighting with you and making up."

"No way. I'm telling you, Sabrina isn't a suspect in this. I don't believe it. She doesn't have it in her."

Rider still looked skeptical.

Hell, Gage did too. "Anyone else a possibility? Who else have you pissed off lately?"

Rider flinched. "Who haven't I pissed off lately? Seems the entire world is mad at me. May as well toss Missy in."

"Shit. Didn't think of that," Rider said. "Who else?"

"Oh, how about a faculty member? Tina Chang isn't pleased with me, either."

WANT

"Tina Chang? Isn't that the lady who stuck her tongue in your mouth at a company party?" Gage asked.

"Yep."

"Why is she mad?"

"She left me a voice message asking me—no *telling* me—she needed me to attend some family function with her last weekend."

"Why the hell would she do that?" Rider asked.

"Desperation I guess. But she also received the email alleging I am in violation of university policy. *And* she came to my office to speak to me about it."

"Doesn't mean she didn't send the emails. Shit, you have a lot of enemies." Gage chuckled sardonically. "Glad I'm not on your bad side."

"Hell, no one is on *my* bad side. It just seems I manage to get on other people's bad side with great frequency lately."

"What did the university say about the allegations?" Rider asked.

"Dean Sheffield called me into her office. She was very nice about it. As she should be. I've been on staff for fifteen years. My record is exemplary. She knows I would never date a student."

Rider nodded. "Nevertheless, she had no choice but to call you in and let you know what occurred."

"Right. And as far as I know, that's all that's happened so far. An anonymous tip that I was involved with an anonymous student. No names were mentioned. That's why I didn't lose too much sleep over it. Now, if this had happened over the summer, it would have been a different story. I'd have shit a brick."

"Why?" Gage asked.

"Because I never should have fucked Sabrina that day. It was a horrible judgment call on my part. I was thinking

127

purely with the little head. I swear I've never once done anything so fucking stupid in my life."

"You didn't know if she was still enrolled or not." Rider had pieced it together.

"Right."

"Geez, man. That has to have something to do with this. Are you sure Sabrina isn't a possibility?"

"Yes." Conner took a deep breath. "Look, if Sabrina were pissed at me for fucking her, she could have turned me in at any time. Why wait two months?"

"Oh, I don't know. Maybe because the next time she saw you, you were an ass, and before that she hadn't been nearly as pissed?" Rider leaned closer again.

Gage spoke on the tail end of that rhetorical question. "Just out of curiosity, why do you keep saying you fucked her? So harsh. When I hook up with a woman I've been lusting after for a while, I usually sleep with her, have sex with her, make love to her—something like that. Don't think I've ever said I fucked her first."

Conner curled up his face again. "Trust me. I fucked her. I'm not even sorry. She wanted it. I wanted it. It happened. After lusting after her for four months in my classroom, the next time I saw her in July, my cock got so hard it nearly jumped out of my pants. And the way she looked at me..." He ran a hand through his hair as he thought back on that excruciating meal. "She licked her lips and squirmed in her chair from across the room and..." How the hell could he describe that scene to the guys? "I'm just sayin'... She wanted me. I wanted her. It was obviously mutual. We didn't exchange words. We fucked. I left. That was it."

"Why the hell did you leave?" Gage asked. "If you wanted her that bad for that long..." His voice trailed off.

"I was stunned for one thing. And, ironically, I thought I had just fucked a student."

"But she wasn't a student," Rider clarified again.

"No. She only took that one class. Mine. She didn't enroll for the next semester. She's an editor. She wanted to explore some of the classics. I made her life rather miserable apparently."

The three of them stood there in silence for a while.

Finally Conner shook himself out of his reverie. "We better get back to work. We aren't going to solve this right now. And I'm not sure it requires solving. As long as no one sends any more emails to the dean, the allegations will fizzle out. There's no proof. There never will be. Either someone maliciously set me up, or someone thinks Sabrina is a student. Either way, I've done nothing wrong. Even if I at one point thought I had done something unethical, it turns out I didn't."

"Well," Rider lifted his weights, "if anything else happens, let me know. Maybe I can help."

"Thanks, man. Appreciate it." Conner sat on the bench to get started.

Rider turned back to face Conner again. "Have you told Sabrina all this?"

"No, and I don't intend to."

"Why the hell not?"

"Because it has nothing to do with her, and I don't want her to worry for no reason. If I paraded her into the dean's office as an alibi, her name would be as muddy as mine through no fault of her own. Even though she's innocent, no one would ever be sure. Trust me, I've put enough on her plate lately. She doesn't need any added issues."

"I'll bet you have." Gage chuckled. "Bet she had no idea what was coming when she fell for you. She's young enough she can't possibly be prepared for your brand of dominance. Does she know what she's getting herself into?"

Conner tried to send a glare toward Gage, but he was fighting a grin. "She's learning. I haven't been gentle. So far she's been up to the task."

Gage lifted both eyebrows. "Oh, how I wish I could be a fly on the wall while you tame that beast. It must be a wonder to behold. Imagine. Conner Bascott falling for a younger woman with marginal BDSM experience. A woman with claws and a mouth on her." He laughed as he walked away.

Conner grinned. Oh, yeah. And Sabrina Duluth was all his. She might be feisty, but that was half of the reason he was so smitten. A demure woman without a spine would never do it for him. It took thirty-eight years and one very outspoken woman for him to realize all the modest obedient submissives he'd been with in the past with their heads appropriately bowed and their hands crossed behind them would never have taken him down. Hell, he hadn't realized at any point in his almost four decades that he needed to be taken down a notch. If anyone would have suggested anything of the sort, he would have laughed his head off.

And then came Sabrina. Soft and sweet on the inside, hard and spicy on the outside. Yes. He was so going to enjoy every minute of training her to submit to him in the manner he preferred. And the best part of all? He got to watch the pure lust that spread across her face every time he punished her for deliberately disobeying him.

She walked a fine line, and she knew it.

Sabrina was his. If he admitted it to himself, he had known that from the moment he first entered that bathroom and realized she was everything he ever wanted in a woman. She didn't know it, but she brought him to his knees that day. That's why he couldn't stay or even speak. He was shook up. The look in her eyes as he stripped her and made her body hum... His cock got hard every time he thought about it. The visual was permanently etched in his mind.

He hadn't known at the time that she' dabbled in BDSM. Whether she knew it or not that day, she was a submissive. Conner knew it. And he took advantage of it.

And he would do it again in a heartbeat.

CHAPTER 10

Sabrina sat at her desk Saturday morning, struggling to pay attention to her manuscript. Her mind was swamped with thoughts of last night. Her concentration was shot. If she didn't pull her act together, she would get behind. Clients were waiting on her. Deadlines were looming. No one cared that she'd met a Dom and fallen under his spell, rendering her mind inoperable.

She closed her eyes, visions of Conner leaning over her body and commanding her every move making her heart rate soar. The look in his eyes as he kissed her good night at her front door sometime after one in the morning… The way he held her thighs spread open and gazed upon her… The feeling of his finger inside her back hole… The touch of his hands against her breasts…

She groaned and jumped up to shake the memories from her head. The man was completely under her skin. She struggled to concentrate with thoughts of his dominance shaking her to the core.

She had to work. Even though it was Saturday, she had too much work to take the day off. He said he'd be there that evening, and he was taking her out to dinner and then to the club. She wouldn't be able to enjoy herself fully if she didn't get enough done during the day.

How had the tables turned so abruptly? One minute they'd been at each other's throats and then next...they were fucking in her bedroom. She hadn't had a chance to ponder the arrangement. Truth be told, Conner hadn't given her the opportunity to deny him. He claimed her, and that was the end of it.

Not that she minded. Submitting to him wasn't optional in her mind either. Without speaking a word, he could command her with his expressions. Damn.

She forced herself to eat lunch and get back to work, finally managing to immerse herself in the novel she was editing. Before she knew it, there was a knock at the door, and she jumped in her seat.

She glanced around the room, startled. "Shit." It was later than she'd thought. The sun was already dipping in the sky.

She pushed back from her desk and hurried to the front door, not yet registering that she would find Conner on the other side. But there he stood, in the flesh, a smirk on his face as he glanced up and down her body.

She lowered her face to take in her appearance and groaned. "Oh damn." She held the door open farther to let him in. "I lost track of time. I haven't even showered."

"I see that." He chuckled. "Love the outfit, by the way."

She wore loose shorts and a tank top. No bra. Her hair was in a messy bun on top of her head. No makeup. She groaned again.

Conner took her hand, kicking the door shut behind him. He tugged her toward the bedroom, speaking over his shoulder. "I love that you're comfortable enough to let yourself be all natural with me."

She followed on his heels, struggling to keep up. She had no choice. After all, he nearly dragged her down the hall. What was the rush?

Conner didn't stop until he reached her bed, where he sat on the edge and pulled her to one side by the arm. He finally met her gaze. "I'm going to spank you now."

She opened her eyes wide. "Why?"

"Cussing, baby. Don't like it. I've told you enough times. You cuss, your ass will be pink."

"Shit." She moaned and jerked back a step. "I mean, I'm sorry, Sir. I'll try, but it's going to take me a while."

He smiled. "Take as long as you'd like. You'll try harder and learn faster if you like to sit comfortably." His hands were on her shorts, and a second later he had them and her panties around her ankles. "Step out."

She did as he said, grabbing his shoulders to steady herself. Her mind hadn't caught up enough to really consider what he was about to do. Before she could fully internalize his intention, he had her over his lap, her face on the mattress, her hands above her head.

He held her lower back firmly and spanked her, hard.

Sabrina winced at the unexpected pain. She'd been spanked many times over the years. Always for pleasure. Never for punishment. Or at least not seriously.

It smarted.

Again he swatted her ass, his hand landing in another spot at the juncture of her cheeks and her thighs. With no warmup, his slaps hurt worse than they would normally. The sensation was foreign.

He spanked her again, several times in fact, not letting up. She lost count. And just as quickly it was over, and he tugged her to her feet.

She heaved for oxygen, tears threatening to fall. She

didn't want to cry in front of him. She was mortified. "That hurt," she mumbled, squirming.

He held her arms to keep her in front of him. She felt decidedly naked. All she wore was her tank top. Her pussy pulsed with need and left her exposed. She squeezed her legs together, aggravated he'd caused that kind of arousal in her with a punishment spanking.

"Look at me, Sabrina."

She lifted her gaze, fighting the tears.

His face was firm. "No cussing."

"Yes, Sir."

"Spread your legs."

She hesitated.

"Now."

She stepped out.

"Good girl. When I punish you, you will not be allowed to come."

"Yes, Sir." Those words made her need worse. She thought she might faint from the pulsing between her legs. A deep ball of need squeezed inside her belly. *From a punishment.*

He turned her around and led her to the attached master bath. "Take a shower. The warm water will help. Then we'll go out."

Her ass hurt. Or maybe it just stung. It might have been her pride that hurt worse. Could she do this? Let Conner control her like this? He told her he would, but she hadn't been prepared for such a quick decisive introduction to his world. He wasn't kidding. He was an intense, firm Dom.

Conner flipped on the shower and held his hand under the spray while it warmed up. When he was satisfied, he turned around, pulled her tank top over her head and ushered her into the warm water.

Sabrina swallowed. The need to cry had subsided somewhat, but she still shook as she let the water cascade down her body. It felt good. She glanced through the glass door to see Conner leaning against the vanity, watching her.

Ugh. Was he always going to be this high-handed with her? Probably.

Making quick work, she washed her hair and put conditioner in it.

"Shave, baby."

She gulped at the thought of him watching her work the razor between her legs. If she didn't find a way to control her jittery hands, she would cut herself. Taking a deep breath, she started with her legs and worked her way up. By the time she reached her pussy, she had her nerves at least partially under control. She ignored Conner entirely to do so, pretending he wasn't staring at her.

After rinsing, she shut off the water and stepped out. Conner handed her a towel. "Do you like Mexican?"

She wrapped the terry cloth around her and lifted her gaze. "Yes, Sir."

"Excellent. There's a great restaurant I thought we'd go to and then the club." He stepped forward. "You okay, Sabrina?"

"Yes, Sir." She swallowed for the millionth time. She was sort of okay.

He scrutinized her face. "I'll be strict with you, especially at first. I don't have many rules. There are few things I won't tolerate. Cussing obviously. I want you to be respectful at all times. Even when we aren't in the role. Understood?"

"Yes, Sir." *When are we not in the role?* It seemed as though he expected her to obey him all the time.

"Good. Now, get dressed. Don't take too long. I'll wait in the living room." He released her chin and turned toward the door. "Oh, and Sabrina," he said over his shoulder.

"Yes?"

"A skirt or a dress. No pants."

She nodded. *Of course.*

When he left the room, she lowered her shoulders and took a deep breath. *Holy shit.*

She groaned at the thought, knowing she needed to curb her four-letter thoughts or risk a permanently pink ass.

Half of her wanted to scream and show him the door. The other half was titillated beyond belief. She wanted more. More of his sexy commanding self all up in her business. It was intense, but so fucking hot... *Fuck.* She enjoyed the spanking. And although it was frustrating how badly she needed to come, the edgy feeling was also titillating.

Making quick work, she removed the towel from her body and wrapped it around her head. She padded to the bedroom, shuffled through the hangers in her closet, and decided on a black dress that was decent enough for a restaurant but sexy enough for a night at Extreme also.

She'd only been to Extreme the one time, with Doug. But as far as she could tell, it was very similar to the other clubs she'd attended over the years.

The dress had an open back that didn't permit a bra. With her smallish chest, she didn't need a bra for support. She almost always wore one anyway for comfort and to keep her nipples covered, but the dress had built-in cups that afforded her that protection. She slid the soft material over her head and let it settle around her hips, wincing at the contact against her ass. She hesitated for a second before deciding against panties. The lace would be intolerable this evening.

Back in the bathroom, Sabrina removed the towel, worked her fingers through her hair, and started the blow dryer. In fifteen minutes, she had makeup on and her hair tamed to the point of barely damp.

She slipped on her favorite black heels and headed for the living room.

Conner stood from the couch as she entered. He held one of her romance books in his hands, his face impassive. "You read this all day?"

She nodded. "I do." He needed to curb his attitude about her job before she kicked him in the balls.

"But this is rubbish." He held it up higher. "How can you call it good literature?"

Her head nearly exploded. She set her hands on her hips and glared at him, choosing her words carefully. She wanted to tear him down effectively without cussing. "Dr. Bascott, you seem to be under the misinformed assumption that any literature that isn't part of your precious Brit lit isn't worth reading and therefore of no value."

"Exactly." He set the book back on the coffee table as though it were diseased.

"That's insane." She threw her hands in the air and stomped forward a few paces. "I make a good living editing romance novels, Conner Bascott. I love it. Contrary to your preconceived notions, there are hundreds of authors out there who need good editors, more than I can possibly handle. These days I turn down more authors than I take. With the age of self-pub, I can be selective. I'll have you know my job is serious, and I support myself just fine."

"Are you having a tantrum, Sabrina?"

Her eyes widened. On the tip of her tongue was a solid "fuck you," but she held it in, barely.

Suddenly, Conner stood tall and with a flourish broke

into a voice she'd never heard before. *"No sight so sad as that of a naughty child,'"* he began, *"especially a naughty little girl. Do you know where the wicked go after death?'"*

Sabrina was stunned. He thought he could quote Charlotte Brontë and take her down a notch? Hell no. *"They go to hell,'"* she replied, exceptionally proud of herself and her ability to come back at him with the next line in *Jane Eyre.*

In fact, she thought she would one-up him by tossing another quote back at him from the same book while his mouth hung open in surprise.

"I do not think, sir, you have any right to command me, merely because you are older than I, or because you have seen more of the world than I have; your claim to superiority depends on the use you have made of your time and experience.'" Sabrina stared at him hard while he recovered.

"Touché," he finally said, a grin spreading across his face. As if he hadn't seen her until that moment, his gaze roamed up and down her body, and his expression heated. "That dress is sexy. You look amazing."

"Thank you." She fought against a smirk that he'd just now noticed her. She sauntered to his side of the room and shuffled through the books on her coffee table, choosing one of her recent favorites, a BDSM that had made her panties wet and her toes curl when she edited it. She held it out to him. "Read this, oh wise one, and then tell me it has no value."

Conner stared at her outstretched hand for a moment before taking the book from her. "Challenge accepted."

"Shall we go?"

"Of course." His face settled into a more relaxed state, a smile curving his lips. If she wasn't mistaken, a soft chuckle escaped his mouth as he led her from the house.

He had parked behind her. As they headed for his car, he paused. "Jesus. What happened to your passenger door?"

Sabrina closed her eyes for a second. "I don't know. Someone obviously thought it would be funny to gouge it with their key."

"When did this happen?"

She shrugged. "Not sure. I noticed it on Friday. But I can't say when it happened."

He turned toward her, his brow furrowed. "Did you piss someone off?" His mouth quirked in a slight grin.

"Ha ha. I can't imagine how. I'm not exactly the piss-someone-off kind of girl."

He opened the door of his car to let her in. "Really?" He chuckled. "You?"

She glared at him, fighting a laugh. "Okay. I do manage to rumple your feathers. But our brand of disaccord is not something I've ever experienced with anyone else." She smiled sweetly as he shook his head and rounded the hood.

CHAPTER 11

It was eleven o'clock before Sabrina followed Conner into Extreme. After an enjoyable dinner, she was considerably more at ease than she had been at the house. Dinner had been like a normal date. He told her on the way that they weren't in the role and gave her permission to relax, as long as she didn't cuss or behave in a manner unbecoming. She wasn't sure what sort of things fell under that heading, but she didn't imagine she was the sort of person to violate any of his preconceived notions about propriety in public.

As it turned out, Conner Bascott could be an enjoyable date when he let his guard down and acted human. The three hours she spent with him since they left the house had been the best few hours in his presence to date. When he wasn't scowling, growling, or admonishing her about something, he could be almost normal.

His face lit up when he laughed. The wrinkles at the corners of his eyes were endearing when he smiled broadly. He shared details about his childhood and listened to her life story intently. By the time they were finished with dinner, she knew him better than most men she'd ever dated. He was an open book concerning his thirty-eight years.

The combination of his interests was fascinating. How many people taught British literature by day at a university, fought Mixed Martial Arts in the evenings, and practiced BDSM on the side? No one she'd ever met.

When they reached the entrance to the club, Conner turned toward her and took her shoulders, waiting until she lifted her gaze to meet his before he spoke. His face was serious again. "You'll sub for me inside."

"Of course." She nodded. They hadn't discussed the specific boundaries of when they would be in the role and when they wouldn't, but she knew he would dominate her inside Extreme.

"Good girl." He took her hand and nodded at Frank on their way past the doorman.

Sabrina lowered her gaze, taking a deep breath as they stepped inside. Her nipples grew stiff, and the feel of her dress swaying over her naked ass suddenly seemed exacerbated. She'd been aware of her sore butt when she first took her seat at dinner, but the feeling had subsided quickly. Now, the heated skin came to her full attention again.

Conner still had no idea she wore no panties.

With his fingers threaded through hers, he led her to a corner table in the bar area of the club. She realized when they arrived that the women she'd met at his fight last week were at the table.

They both smiled and greeted her. "Sabrina," Kayla said, "so nice to see you again. We were hoping you might show up here with Conner."

Sabrina smiled, wondering what Conner might permit as far as socialization at the club.

He nodded and held out a chair. "I'll get you a drink. What would you like?"

"Coke would be nice. Thank you."

He lifted a brow and leaned closer to her face.

"Sir."

"That's better. Be right back."

A flush stole across her face as she turned back to Kayla and Emily, both women giggling.

Emily spoke as soon as Conner walked away. "He's intense."

Sabrina glanced around. Rider and Gage were on the far side of the table engaged in a conversation with two other men. They weren't paying attention to the women.

"Is he always like this?" Sabrina asked.

A third woman, who Sabrina didn't know yet, chuckled. "Pretty much. When he has a submissive, that is. It's been a while since he's had a permanent submissive, though. He does scenes with lots of women, but none completely under his command." She leaned forward and held out her hand. "I'm Katy, by the way." She pointed toward a clean-cut man at the other end of the table. "That beast down there is my husband, Rafe." She smiled warmly.

The fourth woman also reached out a hand, which Sabrina shook next. "And I'm Jenna. The guy next to Rafe is mine. Mason."

"Mason. Got it. Hope there isn't a quiz later." Sabrina giggled. "Names take me a while. There're so many of you. Conner said there're six guys that hang out together?"

"Yep." Katy nodded. "The Fight Club." She rolled her eyes. "Jenna and I aren't super fond of watching men beat each other, so we don't go to too many of the fights. But I heard you met Emily and Kayla last weekend."

"I did." Sabrina grinned at both women.

Emily spoke next. "And she's one of us, so don't try to dissuade her. She loved the fight." She giggled.

"I did find it invigorating," Sabrina agreed as Conner returned to her side.

He handed her a soda and leaned down to whisper in her ear, brushing her hair back with his hand. Her neck tingled under his soft touch. "I'll give you fifteen minutes to get to know the girls better, and then you're mine." His lips landed on her neck as he finished, kissing her gently.

She shivered at the contact. When she lifted her gaze, his back was turned. He was already heading to the other end of the table. A glance at the four women with her told her everything. They were all smiling. Indeed, this was a Conner they weren't overly familiar with.

The fifteen minutes flew by as Sabrina tried to memorize everyone's name and get a handle on who went with whom. There was apparently one more guy who wasn't there that night. Zane. He was an EMT, and he was working.

The ladies were all kind, even exchanging phone numbers with Sabrina. They all said to call them any time. They would be happy to get together or go to a fight with her if she wanted.

Too soon, Conner stood from the other end of the table and headed her way. He was so damn tall, taller than the other guys. She knew they were in the same weight class, but as far as she could tell, Conner's height was not compensated by being skinnier. He was as buff as the other guys.

Conner took her hand, and she stood, her heart beating faster, wondering what he had in mind. This was their first foray at the club. She hadn't seen him in action in public, so she had nothing to go by. She should have thought to ask the other women what sort of scenes he liked to do while they'd spoken. Too late.

Before they took one step away from the table, a woman eased up on Conner's other side and wrapped herself around him until she was a second skin attached to his side, her hands reaching all the way into Sabrina's space. "Conner, honey, where have you been?" Her voice was sickly sweet, dripping with saccharine, and when Sabrina stepped forward, she found the woman pouting, her lip stuck out in a mock tease.

Conner stiffened. "Missy, how many times do I have to tell you it isn't happening between us?"

Missy, held on tighter. "Conner, darling, surely you don't mean it. We're so good together."

Sabrina saw flames. How dare this bitch get in her man's space? Granted, he'd only been her Dom for a short time, but nevertheless, he was hers. She had no intention of sharing, and from the look on Conner's face, he agreed.

"Missy, let go of me. Don't make this ugly."

The woman loosened her grip, but her face was full of shock, and she didn't release Conner. "Seriously, my love. Let's do a scene together. Yeah? You're so good with a whip." She had the nerve to look at Sabrina finally. Until that moment, the crazy woman hadn't seemed to notice Conner was with anyone. Or perhaps she had intentionally been snubbing Sabrina.

Her face held a deep disdain as she looked Sabrina up and down. "Surely you don't mean to Dom for this girl. She's a baby. I can't imagine her being able to submit to you at the level you enjoy." She had the audacity to lift a hand and trail it up Conner's chest until she cupped his face.

Sabrina wasn't sure whether she should be glad Conner didn't fling the woman across the room and injure her or be frustrated with him for not taking a firmer stance. In either case, there was no way for Sabrina to hold her own tongue another moment. "Listen, bitch." Sabrina straightened to her full height, a whopping five-five in her three-inch heels, and stepped closer. "I don't know what sort of history you have with Conner, but he's obviously no longer interested in whatever skanky proposition you have to offer. So back the fuck off. He might be too much of a gentleman to slap you, but I'm not."

Missy's mouth fell open again, her eyes wide. "You slut."

"I'm not the slut here, ho."

By then Sabrina was aware of several other people around. All the other women had stood, and their Doms had come from the other end of the table. Two of them pried Missy off Conner and tugged her off his side.

Rider spoke as they walked away. "Are you drunk, Missy? Or high?"

Conner took a deep breath and let it out slowly before he turned his gaze back to meet Sabrina's.

She had gathered enough of her wits to realize she'd just used a string of profanity. If he thought to punish her for the infraction, there was a good chance she would walk right out the door.

For a second, she was unsure. Conner's brow was furrowed. And then his eyes danced, his lips turned up in a smile, and he chuckled. "Well, I guess I don't have to worry about you holding your own against any of my exes."

Sabrina grinned back. "Nope. Though I do hope you don't have too many. It's exhausting." She leaned closer, lifting up on her tiptoes to reach his ear. "And don't even think about spanking me for cussing. It was necessary."

He nodded as he tugged her to face him. "I'll grant you that, under the circumstances, but don't make it a habit."

"Yes, Sir," she said, returning to the role. "Now, I believe

I've been challenged, so let's put one thing to rest right now."

"How's that?" He stared at her quizzically.

"You owe me a flogging." It took balls to say those words. It was true no one had ever hit her with anything but their hand. On the other hand, she trusted Conner implicitly, even after such a short time with him. She knew him to be a firm but fair Dom. She knew he'd been in the life a long time. And from the other women, she also knew he would never hurt her, at least not in any way that lasted more than the few hours of burning sting from a spanking or a flogging. He'd said so himself.

Extreme was a high-end club. Safe, sane, and consensual was their motto. She had no fear other than the obvious concern over the unknown.

A smile spread across Conner's face. He shook his head as he led her away. He didn't say a word, but brought her to the dance floor where he took her in his arms and swayed to the music. "Not going to flog you tonight, baby. It's too soon. You aren't ready. You don't know me that well."

"I trust you."

"I know you do. But that isn't the point. You don't have to prove anything to me. And you certainly don't have to prove anything to Missy. Besides, the guys led her out the door. She wouldn't even be able to see your victory." He grinned. "Another time."

She nodded, feeling somewhat deflated. Part of her wanted the experience. And part of her wanted to get it out of the way so she wouldn't have to keep worrying about how it might feel.

Conner's hands splayed across Sabrina's bare back as he moved to the music. "Love this dress, by the way." His palms pressed into her heated skin. "You're tits are free under it, aren't they?"

"Yes, Sir."

One hand eased down to cup her ass gently. "And you aren't wearing panties, either."

"You knew?"

He nodded. "Of course."

"How?"

"Well, there are no lines. I notice these things. And besides, I figured your ass was too sore to want anything rubbing against your skin."

"True."

His hand lowered. He had to bend his knees to reach the hem of her dress, but he managed, and then his palm landed flat on her bare ass, making her suck in a breath. She glanced around.

"Are you worried someone might see?"

She cleared her throat. "Sort of." She didn't want to admit she wasn't super fond of exposing herself in public. If it was important to him, she supposed she'd cross that bridge.

"Don't look so worried. I don't share pussy. I won't hesitate to expose your ass cheeks, and maybe breasts, but your pussy is mine to look at. I won't expose it to others."

She breathed out a sigh of relief. She could live with that.

His hand disappeared to ease back up to her spine. "Is the sting easing?" He lifted her chin with his other hand.

"Yes, Sir."

He narrowed his gaze. "Truth? Don't ever lie to me, especially not about something that important. I need to know my punishments are effective, but I don't want the result to be long-lasting."

Her pussy clenched as he said *punishments*. He had a way with words. "I'm fine, Sir."

"Good. Then you won't mind me looking to make sure." He took her hand and led her from the dance floor.

Her cheeks grew hot as a flush stole up her face. He intended to examine her ass? For what? Welts? Pinkness?

She followed at his back, unable to see where they were headed. Besides, she wasn't familiar enough with Extreme to know her way around yet. She had to force her gaze to remain lowered.

When he stopped and opened a door, she nearly ran into him. A second later, she found herself in a private room, the door closed, the lights on the dimmer turned all the way up until the room was bright. Conner led her to a couch in the small room, and he sat. "Lie across my lap, baby, so I can see your sweet ass."

Why did that idea make her so uncomfortable? The man had seen her ass already. He didn't even exude any sexual overtures. In fact, it was the pure clinical aspect of his command that made her shiver with unease.

Nevertheless, she did as he requested, stepping up to his side and lying across his knees.

His total dominance over her was palpable. He lifted her dress up her back and held it with one hand while he set his other hand on her ass and gently rubbed her skin.

Sabrina held her breath. How humiliating. How humbling. How submissive. She let out the air in her lungs and tried to relax. He was her Dom now. His intention was either to make sure she was indeed not injured or make sure she recognized his total domination over her body. Either way, she needed to suck it up and let him explore.

"Still pink, but it's only been a few hours. I expect you'll hardly know I spanked you in the morning." He squeezed first one cheek, and then the other, pulling them apart.

She heard his caring tone and felt his touch, letting both soak into her and ease her mind.

Suddenly his hand was between her thighs. "Spread your legs, baby."

She opened them, as far as she could perched precariously across his lap. Instantly her pussy flooded. The air in the room hit her bare skin and brought her attention to the need between her legs that had been there, not quite dormant, since he'd spanked her. She needed to come. In fact, she bit her lip to keep from begging. Her arousal shot sky high that fast.

"That's my girl." He worked his fingers between her thighs, nudging them wider and then stroking through her folds. "So wet for me."

She was. No denying it.

He gathered her moisture and circled her clit. When his finger landed directly on the swollen nub, she moaned. "Always so responsive. I like that." He pinched her clit and then left it to push two fingers into her pussy.

Sabrina feared she might come. "Sir, I need to come."

"Not yet, baby. I know you're needy. You've been such a good girl. You deserve the release. But hang on a bit longer." His words didn't help. Did he not realize that every time he spoke, her ardor rose higher?

Gentle fingers eased in and out of her languidly, as if they had all the time in the world.

They did not. Because Sabrina was about to explode. No matter how slow or fast he stroked her skin, the edge was right there.

"Control, baby. Wait for permission." His voice was low, soft. It vibrated through her. She gritted her teeth as he stroked through her folds and pushed his fingers back inside her deeper, as far as he could reach, his palm flat on her pussy, his pinky landing on her tight rear hole.

Finally, he moved again, fucking her with those fingers. Too slow.

"Oh God. Conner, I can't..." Her voice sounded like someone else's. Would he bring her to the edge like this often and command her to wait? And what if she came without permission? Was that an infraction she would be punished for? At the moment, it was almost completely out of her control and highly possible.

She hated to disobey him. But her brain was scrambled and her blood was all centered at her core, fighting for her release.

"Such a good girl. I'm proud of you." His thumb landed on her clit and pressed. "Come, baby."

Thank God. Her orgasm shattered her almost before he finished speaking. It would have happened either way. Did he know that?

Long drawn-out pulses jerked her body over his knees. His fingers slowed their motions as she came down from so high. When she was spent, he removed his hand and gripped her waist to reposition her sitting on his lap, her naked ass off the side. He held her against his chest and kissed the top of her head. "So proud of you," he repeated.

She melted. Those words were honey to a submissive. He'd proven he could be both harsh and extremely caring today. She was exhausted.

And she was falling for him. Hard.

CHAPTER 12

It was late when they left the club. Conner knew Sabrina was tired. She nearly dozed in his car.

He set his hand on her exposed knee and squeezed. "Come home with me." He carefully spoke so she might not be sure if he'd asked her a question or given her a command.

"Mmm." She rolled her head to face him as he glanced at her. "You think that's a good idea?"

"Why wouldn't it be? I know we've only been seeing each other a short while, most of that time rocky, but I've made my intentions clear. I want you in my life. I want you in my bed."

Her eyes were wider when he glanced at her again, her bottom lip between her teeth as she mulled over his proposition. She was no longer lounging in a doze. "Would you be mad if I said *no*?"

He took several deep breaths before he spoke. "I think confused would be a better description. Not angry. Frustrated perhaps."

"It's all happening so fast, Conner. A week ago we were at each other's throats."

He smiled. "No. No. You were at *my* throat. I was completely focused on getting in your pants." He tried to make light of the conversation, while inside he fought the urge to demand she see reason. She was his. He didn't see any reason to put off the inevitable. He wanted her in his home. He wanted to be with her every chance he could.

"See? That's just it. We had a great evening tonight. Not going to deny it. Dinner was lovely. But it was essentially our first date—the first time we've ever sat down and had a normal discussion without fucking or fighting. I'll admit, it worries me."

"The fucking or the fighting?" he asked jokingly.

"Neither. The serious parts. When we're fighting, my heart races and my blood boils, and frankly the more red I see, the more I want to fuck. And when we're fucking, I lose all sense of reason. It scares the shit out of me."

He jerked his gaze toward her. "Did you just cuss at me?"

She groaned. "Conner. God. Let up on that."

"Not going to happen, sweetheart."

She blew out a breath.

He thought it prudent to address what she'd said instead of her deliberate defiance. "What do you mean you 'lose all sense of reason'?"

"I'm not sure I make good choices. You scramble my brain, easily. One look from you, and I melt."

"And this is a bad thing?" He stopped at a light and turned to face her.

She shook her head. "Never seems like it at the time, but later…"

"Later what?"

"Later I feel…weak."

"Weak? You? We *are* discussing Sabrina Duluth, right?" The light changed. Conner pulled forward into the intersection and then made a decision he hoped he wouldn't regret. He headed for his house. He needed to straighten out her misconceptions, and he didn't intend to put it off another day.

"Yes." She didn't find his words funny. She faced the front and didn't comment as he drove, even though she had to know he wasn't aiming for her house.

Five minutes later Conner pulled into his driveway, pressed the button on his garage door opener, and slid into the garage. When he shut the car off and turned again toward her, she looked livid.

"So that's it? You asked me if I would come home with you. I said I wasn't comfortable with it. And you did it anyway?" She crossed her arms over her chest and shut herself off from him.

He hated that nonverbal act, but he needed to ignore it for now. "No, that's not *it*. I'm not trying to be an ass, but I do want to talk to you. I don't want to drive you home and drop you off in the middle of this discussion. It's important." He opened the door and got out of the car.

Sabrina didn't move while he rounded to her side and tugged her door open next.

"Really?" She glared at him.

"Yes, really. Please. Come inside."

She humphed as she unfolded herself and stepped out.

Conner led her to the door and pushed the button to close the garage while he let her inside. For a second he wondered how she would perceive his home. He'd been a bachelor for twenty years. He wasn't one of those disastrous messy guys, but he did realize he also wasn't Mr.

Tidy. Luckily, he had a cleaning woman who came every other week and kept his house presentable. And she'd been there yesterday.

Sabrina said nothing. In fact, her arms were once again crossed under her chest, exactly how he detested, and then she spewed more cuss words to seal the deal on her defiance. "This is fucked up, Conner. You're bullying me."

He grinned behind her. He couldn't help himself. His cock literally stiffened when she disobeyed him. Suddenly he knew beyond a shadow of a doubt he wanted to spend the rest of his life with her. And he never wanted her to change. Her defiant nature was half the reason he'd fallen for her so hard and so fast.

While she'd been in his class in the spring, he'd lusted after her. When he'd fucked her in the bathroom at King Pizza, he'd lusted after her. But throughout all that, his drive to have her had been mostly physical.

As soon as she'd confronted him at the club and then at the arena, his attitude had changed from lust to something much deeper. She wasn't a pushover. And he didn't want a pushover for a life mate. He wanted someone with a spine that could stand up to him when he was a tyrant, call him on his overbearing tendencies, spar with him. Make him work for it.

Not that he frequently intended to let her win or have her way, but he enjoyed the battle.

He felt more alive than he'd ever felt in all his years.

Who would have thought one tiny woman twelve years younger than him could wreak such havoc on his entire system?

He turned her and pressed her back into the kitchen counter, his hands on her shoulders. He hadn't turned on the lights. The dim illumination from the small light above the stove allowed him to see her expression. Closed. Pissed. Insolent.

He knew it was a bold move, but he chose his next words anyway. "You do realize your ass is going to be very sore tomorrow, right?"

She rolled her eyes, but said nothing.

"Drop your arms, Sabrina. And may I recommend you not speak again unless you can control your tongue. Because I assure you I can control how hard I strike your ass and how many times."

Her arms fell to her sides slowly. Her gaze was on his chest. She didn't lift her face.

"Good. Now we're getting somewhere." He stepped closer, pinning her, his hands easing down her biceps until he set them on the counter on either side of her. "Now, I want to talk. I want you to hear me out. I also want you to engage in the conversation. Respectfully and without cussing. Clear?"

She didn't answer.

"Sabrina. Are we clear?"

"Yes, Sir." Her words were a mere whisper. She shifted her feet. Her chest rose and fell a few times as she took several deep breaths.

"You're aroused," he blurted before he could stop himself. *Holy shit*. He knew she was. *God is good*.

Sabrina said nothing, but she squirmed some more and balled her hands into fists at her sides.

"Sabrina, look at me."

She hesitated and then lifted her gaze. Her face was impassive.

"I know you're mad, and we're going to hash that out, but I want you to be honest with me. Is your pussy wet?"

She stiffened.

"I'm trying to be a gentleman here. I'll give you about

five seconds to answer my question, and then I'm going to check for myself."

She chuckled. Not in a good way. "A gentleman? You're a total bastard." She pressed on his chest, shocking him, and ducked quickly under his arm to escape. She stomped through his kitchen and into his living room, slapping her hand on the wall and dragging it across until she found a light switch and flipped it on.

Conner followed her, fighting a grin. He ignored her blatant defiance. "Answer the question."

She spun around and put her hands on her hips. "No. I'd rather not. You said you wanted to talk. Talk. And then take me home."

Conner opted to challenge her. "Five...four...three..." He stepped forward as he spoke, closing the distance between them.

Sabrina stepped back. "You wouldn't." Her eyes widened. She rounded the couch and stood behind it, gripping the back.

"Two...one..." He reached out with one long arm and grabbed her, wrapping his arm around her waist. He was so much larger than her. Did she think she could take him on in a battle? In the blink of an eye, he had her pressed over the back of the couch.

Her arms flung forward to break her fall, landing on the couch cushions, but her feet came off the ground.

Conner stepped between her legs fast, nudged her thighs wider with his knee, and leaned over her body to set his cheek against her ear while he used his free hand to push her short skirt over her ass and then cup her pussy. He paused a moment and closed his eyes as he stroked his two middle fingers through her folds and gathered her immense wetness. "Oh, baby."

Sabrina moaned.

Conner removed his hand and stood her upright on wobbly legs.

"Bastard," she muttered.

"You could have just answered the question," he whispered into her ear, well aware of the shiver that shook her body from head to toe as his lips landed on her neck. Reluctantly, he stepped back and grabbed her hand, leading her around to the front of the couch and then tugging her down next to him. He turned to face her.

Sabrina's skirt flipped up as she sat. She kicked off her heels. He knew her naked ass was in direct contact with the cool leather of his enormous black couch. She didn't react, however.

"I thought it was clear we were together, baby." He took her hand and lifted it to his cheek. She wasn't being super receptive to him and wouldn't meet his gaze, but she let him manhandle her a bit. "Look at me."

Gradually, she tipped her head. "We *are* together, Conner. That doesn't mean I want to move in. Normal people date, you know, like on weekends."

"We aren't normal people, and you know it."

She closed her eyes and then opened them again. "You know what I mean."

Conner released her hand and cupped her face with both palms. "You're mine, baby. You've admitted as much yourself."

She bit her lip.

"What? Did you lie?"

"No. It's not that I lied. It's that when I'm naked and exposed with you, I'm totally yours. There's no way to deny the magnetic pull you have on me."

"And it's not there when you have your clothes on?" He furrowed his brow. What the hell was that supposed to mean?

"I didn't say that." She blew out a breath. "Conner, you're intense."

He chuckled. "I know this."

"You suck the oxygen out of a room."

"Are you saying you can't breathe?"

"I'm saying I can't even *think*. When I submit to you, it's like I'm under hypnosis. I'm not myself."

"Who the hell are you then?" Could she be more confusing?

She squirmed free of his hands and turned her entire body to face him, scooting back to lean against the arm of the couch.

He lowered his hands to her thighs and leaned closer, not willing to give her as much space as she thought she wanted. "Sorry. Go on."

"I don't suppose you have a bottle of wine?"

Jesus. The woman was all over the place. Conner shook his head to keep up.

Her face fell.

"Oh. I didn't mean to imply I don't have any wine. I was just trying to get the cobwebs out. You have me spinning." He stood. "I'll get you some wine." He headed for the kitchen. Maybe alcohol would loosen her up and get her to make more sense. "Red or white?" He called over his shoulder.

"Red. If you have it."

He grabbed a bottle of Merlot, quickly extracted the cork, and returned to her side with two glasses in one hand and the bottle in the other. He poured both glasses, set the bottle on the coffee table, and handed her the liquid fortification.

Sabrina took a long drink. "Mmm, that's good."

"Glad you like it. It's one of my favorites."

"I didn't figure you for a wine drinker."

"What did you figure me for?" He smiled, thankful she was relaxing.

"Beer? Or Red Bull." She giggled.

"I love it when you laugh. You should do it more often." He leaned back, sitting much closer to her this time and reaching over to play with a lock of her hair.

She dipped her head into his hand. And then she took another sip.

Thank you, wine.

Sabrina grew serious once again, tracing the top edge of her glass with one finger.

He wanted to suck that finger into his mouth. "So, I'm suffocating you?"

She rolled her shoulders and sat up straighter. "No. It's not that. I enjoy being with you. Tonight was awesome. Well, except for the part where that other woman wrapped her arms around you like she owned you." She grinned.

"Were you jealous?" He tried not to smirk. Score one for himself if she was jealous.

She furrowed her brow. "Maybe. I'm not sure jealous was the right word, but I did see red."

"I'm not with Missy. I'm with you." He shrugged. Surely that much was obvious. "Trust me, you're not in competition with Missy."

"That's good."

"What else is eating at you?"

"It's weird. I need to get used to your domination. It's confusing me. I've never been with anyone who practiced outside of the club. It's always been more of a hobby than a life choice."

"I see. Well, I've also told you it's been a very long time since I've had a submissive outside the club myself. So we'll figure this out together."

She nibbled on her lower lip.

"You said you felt weak. You realize that's jacked up, right?"

She furrowed her brow. "Now you're gonna tell me how to feel?"

He shook his head. "Not at all. I just want you to understand who holds the power in this relationship."

She chuckled and took a sip of her wine.

He let her hair cascade through his fingers and danced them down her arm, watching as goose bumps arose in their path. "Sabrina, you're misinformed. The submissive always holds the power. I'm at your mercy. It may seem as if the opposite were true since I make the rules and I dole out the punishments when you break them. But you're the one in complete control."

"How do you figure that?"

"The power is all in one little word: *no*. Or *red*."

"That makes sense," she mumbled.

"I know I'm a harsh Dom. I really like control, and I'll expect you to turn it over to me. But the firmer the Dom, the stronger the submissive. You see?"

She nodded.

"I don't expect you to submit to me twenty-four seven, but can you trust me to recognize when it's appropriate and when it's not while we forge this path together?"

She nodded again.

"Try to relax. Turn the reins over to me. That's a huge ask. I'm requesting that you trust me enough to know when's a good time to dominate you and when it would be better to give you space."

Sabrina licked her lips.

He wanted to lick them also, but thought better of it for the time being. Instead he reached for her free hand and held it in his, tracing his thumb over her knuckles. "Stay." It took herculean effort to put himself out there like that. If she said *no* again, he would take her home, but Lord how he wanted her in his bed.

She took another drink of the wine. "Do you always strong-arm your submissives like this?"

"No. I've never met one I wanted as badly as I do you." Now his heart was lying out between them for her to trample or accept.

She sucked in a sharp breath. "How many women have you brought home from the club like this? No. Fuck. Don't answer that." She jerked her hand back.

"None."

"What?" Her gaze darted to meet his. "Seriously?"

He nodded. "I've had a few relationships that lasted longer than ours over the years. Of course. You have to know that. But it's been years since I've had anything serious enough to want her to sleep in my bed. I bought this house five years ago. No woman has slept here." *Please change that tonight.*

She continued to stare at him, shock written on her face. Finally she swallowed. "Will you negotiate about the cussing?"

He smiled broadly. Really? That was her main concern? "No."

She rolled her eyes.

"In fact, I'm not going to go easy on you at all. You've ruined my plans for the night with your mouth. I want you to stay. And I want you to do it knowing I'm going to spank you hard and leave you needy."

She gasped and then drew her legs closer to her body.

"The idea makes you wet."

"You can't know that by looking."

He cocked his head to one side. "Are we going to have

this discussion again?" He grabbed her wrist to feel her pulse and then dropped it. "Oh yeah, very wet."

She didn't move.

"Admit it, or I'll check again. And you know I will."

She took another drink of wine. The glass was almost empty now.

"I'm not a fan of hesitation, Sabrina."

"Fine. Yes. I'm aroused. Every time you mention spanking me, I get hornier. Happy?"

"Immensely."

"So, the plan is, you want me to stay so you can spank my ass and leave me wanting? Who would agree to those terms, knowing the outcome was not in their favor?"

"*You* would. That's why I'm so smitten by you. That's why you're mine." He set his own glass on the coffee table and took hers from her hand to do the same. And then he leaned into her space, forcing her to recline against the plush arm of the couch, and took her lips in a gentle kiss.

She melted under his touch, softening to him, a low moan melding with his in her mouth.

He set his hand on her thigh and eased it up her body, pushing the silky black material of her dress up as he went until he cupped her breast.

Sabrina arched into his touch. Her head fell back as she broke the kiss. "Conner…"

"Stay," he mumbled against her neck.

"Mmm." Her noise was noncommittal.

"Stay," he repeated as he nibbled down to her cleavage. He wasn't playing fair, and he knew it.

Her hands landed on his shoulders. "Fine. You win."

He lifted his head. "It wasn't a contest. It was more of a plea. I want you in my bed. I may never let you leave."

She chewed on her lower lip and then released it. "I

can't stay forever. I need to get some work done tomorrow. You've thrown me completely off schedule."

He grinned. "Me? What did I do?"

"Muddled my brain so I can't edit."

He widened his smile. "Perfect. My work here is done." Conner flicked his thumb over her nipple and watched her face as she sucked in a sharp breath. Just as quickly, he released her and stood, tugging her with him.

She wobbled on her bare feet, holding on to his forearm.

Before she could protest, he lifted her into his arms and carried her through the room, stopping to flip off the lights as he made his way down the hall. When he reached his bedroom, he set her on her feet next to the bed and tugged her dress over her head, leaving her naked to his view.

He sat on the edge of the bed and held her at arm's length. "You're exquisite, baby." His gaze wandered down her small frame, taking in her pert breasts, the nipples puckered. Next he lowered his head to her pussy. She fidgeted. He wanted to fuck her so bad. And it wasn't going to happen. That didn't mean his cock was on board, however. "Kneel, baby."

She did as he instructed, setting her hands on his thighs. Without asking permission, she palmed his cock with one hand and worked the button on his jeans with the other.

Conner held his breath, wondering what her motivation was while fighting the urge to come before she got him out of his pants. Finally, he grabbed both her wrists. "Don't move." He set her hands at her sides and left her kneeling in front of the bed in order to stand and remove his clothes. As soon as he was naked, he stroked his stiff length from base to tip.

Sabrina remained where he left her.

"Good girl." He eased back onto the bed, positioning himself in front of her again. "Sucking me isn't a requirement. And it won't change my mind about your own disobedience." He gripped his cock again, pumping it several times.

"Yes, Sir." She licked her lips and leaned forward, demure for the first time in many hours. "May I, Sir?"

CHAPTER 13

Sabrina stared at the bobbing cock in front of her. Nothing mattered except taking it into her mouth. She was well aware of the pulsing in her pussy and the way her nipples puckered, but those factors only drove her need to taste him higher. Even if he kept his word, which she had little doubt of at that point, she still wanted to suck him off.

At least she'd have the satisfaction of knowing she could take Conner Bascott down to his knees with her mouth. Weakening him was a sight to behold.

"Look at me, Sabrina."

She lifted her gaze.

"You are clear that I will not fuck you tonight, right?"

"Yes, Sir." Why did he have to say it so many times? Every time he reiterated his position, the knot in her belly tightened. Wetness leaked between her legs and ran down her thighs. It unnerved her. She leaned forward and reached with her hands to cup his balls.

"Keep your hands at your sides."

She paused for a second and then dropped her hands and leaned forward to lick his cock. Conner held it for her, angling it toward her mouth. Precome dripped from the tip, and she lapped at it, smiling as he moaned.

"You undo me, baby."

She sucked him into her mouth and drew him deep, forcing his hand to inch down the shaft. Working together, she thrust again and again while he held his dick at the level of her mouth. It was so sexy bumping into his fingers with each pass.

Without the use of her hands, she struggled to keep her balance.

Conner went rigid when she sucked harder. Suddenly, he set his free hand on her head and forced her to release him. His other palm still gripped his cock, thrusting up and down the length rapidly.

Sabrina couldn't move. He held her in place with a firm grip on the top of her head. She watched with rapt attention as he masturbated, not understanding why he hadn't let her complete the task.

With a long groan, he reached his peak, angling his cock at her chest while his come spurted out to land on her breasts.

Sabrina gasped, her eyes wide with both shock and arousal. No man had ever so boldly shot off on her body before. It was hot. Her nipples puckered harder as his come dripped down the tips. She fisted her hands to keep from reaching for him. He obviously intended for her to remain still. Her pussy gripped at nothing. She would give anything to rub her clit and finish herself off, but that wasn't in the cards.

Conner Bascott was the master of this scene. His rules. His game.

And she knew without a doubt she would enjoy every minute of whatever he dished out. Whatever had possessed her earlier, making her think she should go home, vanished. She was right where she belonged. On her knees at Conner's feet, his come dripping down her chest like a piece of art. Her pussy longing for action. Her heart seeming to lean forward in her chest as this man claimed her as his own.

When he was spent, Conner released his cock and reached forward to drag the side of his finger up one of her breasts until he flicked over the tip. He brought the finger —covered in his release—to her lips. "Suck, baby."

Sabrina opened her mouth and let his finger in. His flavor coated her taste buds, reminding her she was his to control.

He pulled his finger out with a pop and repeated the action on her other nipple.

She sucked again, cleaning his pointer of the come gathered up to the second knuckle.

"Good girl." He sat back and released her head finally. "Don't move."

She dipped her face to the floor in subservience as he stepped away and padded across the room. She listened to the water running in the bathroom. Moments later, he returned with a damp cloth. His come still coated her chest and belly. She actually hated for him to remove the evidence of what she'd done to him.

A short yelp escaped her lips when the washcloth landed on one breast. It was cold. Her nipple puckered.

Conner chuckled. He'd done it on purpose. "I believe you enjoyed that a little too much for such a naughty girl."

She winced. He wouldn't forget her earlier infractions. And he wouldn't take it easy on her.

When she was cleaned of his come, he set the cloth aside. "Stand."

Her knees wobbled as she rose to her feet.

Conner stood. "Lean over the side of the bed, baby. Hands over your head."

She shook as she did so. She knew he would spank her now. He'd made that clear. She wanted him to. It would absolve her of the infraction so they could wipe the slate clean and start fresh. Not that she didn't intend to cuss in his presence again, but she would think twice about when and where next time, knowing her pussy would be left empty and longing afterward.

She braced herself, slightly worried. He'd spanked her before, but this time was different. He wouldn't be gentle.

"Scoot back a few inches so your tits hang off the mattress."

Oh God. Did he have any idea how aroused she was? What if she came without permission while he spanked her, or after?

"Why are you being punished, Sabrina?"

Oh shit. He wanted her to speak? She gulped. "For cussing, Sir."

"Do you deserve to be spanked?"

"Yes, Sir."

"Have I not made myself clear on many occasions that I won't tolerate that foul mouth of yours?"

"You have, Sir."

"I'm not going to go easy on you, baby. It will hurt. Especially since your ass is still pink from earlier. I want you to remember this punishment for a while. Perhaps it will help you curb your language if you have to wince to sit tomorrow."

"Yes, Sir."

"Don't move." He set his hand on her lower back and braced her. "Spread your legs apart farther."

She stepped out with both feet.

"Ten swats. You may not come at any time."

"Yes, Sir." Her voice wobbled.

"If you find yourself close, say the word *yellow*. If you come without permission, your punishment will be much worse."

She couldn't imagine what might be entailed in "much worse," but she didn't intend to find out.

"We can take it slow if you can't control the need to come, but don't let yourself go over the edge. It's clear to me the idea of being spanked makes you very horny."

Damn him.

The first swat landed on the juncture of both cheeks, taking her by surprise with its intensity. Holy fuck. He wasn't kidding. It hurt.

And son of a bitch her pussy pulsed with renewed need.

No one had ever hit her that hard. Her whole body came alive.

A second slap landed lower, almost at her thighs, causing her to sway forward with the impact.

She moaned. Her clit vibrated as though it had received the brunt of the attention instead of her ass.

When the third strike landed on her right cheek, she yelped. "Yellow, Sir." She struggled to breathe. The sharp pain stung, but it seemed the harder he spanked, the more she needed release. Her face heated with embarrassment, and she was glad it was somewhat hidden by the mattress.

"Good girl." He soothed her burning ass with his palm. "Let me know when I can continue."

Never.

She wasn't at all sure she would ever be able to endure seven more similar swats against her burning, needy ass. Even her tight rear hole wanted attention. She gripped her cheeks together.

"Ready for more, baby?"

"Yes, Sir." Might as well get it over with. To prolong the experience would do her no good.

Two rapid swats in succession landed on her left cheek, one high and one low. "Stop wiggling, Sabrina." His hand firmed on her lower back. "I'm not fond of a moving target."

She hadn't known she was moving. She curled her toes to grip the carpet beneath her feet.

Two more spanks, lower, at the juncture of her thighs again.

"Yellow," she yelled. "Sir." She held her breath and then released it. "Oh God. I can't. I'm going to come."

"No." Conner squeezed her thigh hard, his thumb reaching between her legs to land dangerously close to her pussy. "You won't come. Control, Sabrina. This isn't for your pleasure."

There was no way in hell for him to dictate what she found pleasurable, but he knew that. She gasped for air, gritting her teeth and then holding her breath. All her concentration centered on her pussy. She was so wet. One light touch and she would shoot off.

"Three left, baby." He eased his grip and massaged her cheeks again. "Ready?"

"No, Sir." She was not. If he spanked her, she would come. And the thought completely unnerved her.

"I know it's hard, baby. It's supposed to be hard. Get a grip. I'll give you about five seconds and then I'm going to continue." He lifted his hand.

She held her breath. *Please, God. Don't let me come.*

The last three spanks landed fast and hard between her cheeks.

She rocked forward on the last one but managed to keep from coming.

"Good girl." He stepped behind her and stood between

her spread legs. "I'm proud of you. I misjudged you when I said you were too young. I apologize." He set both palms on her sore ass and rubbed gently.

Sabrina couldn't believe his words. So sincere. Maybe the age difference jokes were over now. Her chest swelled at the thought of pleasing him. Her face was hot and undoubtedly beet red. Tears threatened to fall from the sharp slaps and the emotional overload.

Her legs turned to jelly, shaking uncontrollably.

Conner released her. "Don't move. Stay right there. I'm going to grab a few things."

A few things? What few things?

He was back behind her in moments. Before she caught her breath, his hands were on her ass again. This time they were covered in something wet. "It's a special oil, baby. It will ease the sting." He massaged it into her ass and thighs roughly while she fought the continued need to come. "You did so well. I'm so pleased."

"Thank you, Sir."

"Your legs are still shaking."

They were.

"I need you to stay in this position a little longer." He released her finally. A ripping noise filled her ears. Condom? No, too loud for that. "I'm going to put a small plug in your tight hole, baby."

What? Oh God. Was she ready for that? Why now?

"Don't stiffen up." He set one hand on her ass again, pulling that cheek away from the other. The overwhelming exposure was enough to make her knees buckle. His other hand was around her in an instant. "Stay with me. Just another minute."

She locked her knees.

Conner stroked a finger between her cheeks as he righted himself again. "Open up for me. If you clench, it will only make it harder. The sooner I get the plug in, the sooner you can relax."

Relax? With a plug in my ass? I don't see how this is possible.

Deep breaths. This was unavoidable. Most of her truly wanted him to fuck her in that tight forbidden hole. She was curious. Women said they enjoyed it. She wasn't opposed to the idea at all. But was all this embarrassing fanfare necessary? Conner was staring at her asshole. How horrifying.

He held her cheeks spread wide. When he tapped the little hole, she winced.

"I haven't done anything yet, Sabrina. And this isn't going to hurt. It's so small you'll hardly notice it. Relax your muscles. Any discomfort is all in your head."

He was right. But that didn't make it easier.

She smashed her face into the mattress and willed her rear to accept this plug.

"Good girl." A blunt object pressed at her entrance and swirled. "I'm going to insert it now. Hold still."

She did as he instructed, expecting more of a stretch than what actually occurred. The plug must have been quite small. It only took him a second to pop it into her. She felt the unusual stretch of her rectum around the foreign item, but it didn't hurt. It also wasn't nearly as large as Conner's cock.

"That's my girl." He twisted the external section of the plug, making every nerve ending in and around her ass come to life. Even her pussy contracted. And then he was gone.

She didn't move a muscle while he padded to the adjoining bathroom again and then returned.

He pulled the comforter and sheet back from the head of the bed. "Climb up, baby."

Her ass stung, and she winced again as she crawled

onto the bed and then collapsed on her belly. The plug felt like it had a ten-inch ball extending from between her cheeks. Irrational, but since she hadn't seen it, she didn't know what it looked like.

Conner chuckled as he climbed up beside her and eased the sheet over her back. He brushed her hair from her face and kissed her cheek. "You're an amazing woman, Sabrina. Thank you."

"For what, Sir?"

"For staying, and for allowing me to so totally control you." His hand landed on her lower back, and he snuggled in beside her. "You warm enough?"

"Yes." She was warm. Too warm. Her pussy still throbbed. She squirmed against the sheet beneath her and moaned as her sensitive clit rubbed the material.

Conner's hand firmed on her back. "Stop wiggling. I know you need to come. You will not. I'm not a lenient Dom. You should know that by now. I mean what I say. When you cuss, you will find your ass sore and your pussy needy. But I won't back down on my word. Tonight you will sleep with that need welling up inside you. Tomorrow you will not cuss at me."

She swallowed. He might be right about that. The way she felt right now was enough to cause her to watch her language. He said she would learn. She hadn't believed him.

Apparently she should have listened. She'd never wanted to fuck so badly in her life. The thought of shutting her mind down and sleeping was inconceivable. All her blood had congregated at her pussy. Her clit was smashed against the bed and pulsing. It wasn't enough. Her arousal was so palpable she could smell it in the room.

Conner kissed her shoulder and held her close. "Sleep, Sabrina."

For a long time, she lay there concentrating on breathing. She was aware when Conner drifted off, leaving her wanting. It took at least another half an hour before she calmed down enough to let sleep claim her.

∾

"Yes. Oh God, yes," Angelica screamed as Leo jerked her head back by her hair and fucked her harder. She was on her hands and knees, her legs spread. And he was the best fuck she'd ever had. Sure, he was rough, but she liked it rough. And he was older. But she liked her men older too. Like Dr. Bascott. The older ones were the only ones who were capable of being rough enough to really get her blood boiling.

And Leo was one hot fuck.

She had always imagined Dr. Bascott would be a similarly hot fuck. One day she intended to find out.

She closed her eyes as Leo slammed into her over and over. If he would just rub her clit…

Finally, Leo leaned over her and nibbled her earlobe. "That feel good, sweetheart?" His accent sent a shiver down her spine, as usual. Whatever it was, it was sexy as hell.

"Yes," she hissed. "Harder. Please." She squirmed.

He chuckled and released her hair to grab both her hips. Holding her steady, he fucked her faster. His fingers dug into her skin. She didn't care if he left bruises as long as he didn't stop.

Her belly quivered with need.

Just as she was about to beg him to stroke her clit, his hand snaked around her body and pinched the little nub hard. "Come, baby. Show me how much you like it," he growled.

Angelica let go, pulsing around Leo's cock as her orgasm swept through her.

God yes. It was that good. The best she'd ever had. If she didn't have a serious hard-on for another man, she would consider keeping this guy.

Leo came right behind her, grunting his orgasm into her pussy. When he finally stopped humping her and relaxed his hands, she collapsed onto the bed, her hair falling across her face in complete disarray.

She breathed heavily as she glanced around without moving more than her eyes.

She had no idea where she was. She'd met him at a club, same as always. This time she'd really laid it on thick— short skirt, tight shirt, plenty of cleavage, perfect makeup.

They'd never exchanged numbers, but she'd seen him the last four Saturday nights at that particular club.

This time she'd hit the jackpot. He'd taken her home.

Or so she thought. This place didn't seem like anyone's home, but she didn't care. She had a good buzz, and since she had not managed to make any headway with Dr. Bascott no matter how hard she tried, Leo would do. He was at least as sexy as the professor.

He was ripped. His cock was huge. Tattoos covered his back. She couldn't make out any of them in the darkened room, and she hadn't seen him without his shirt on before now. But she longed to run her fingers over every line on his body.

Leo left her on the disheveled bed and made his way to the adjoining bathroom. When he returned, he sat beside her and slapped her ass. "Time to go, sweetheart. I've got an early day tomorrow. I need my beauty rest."

What? She shifted her body enough to look up at him. He was kicking her out? Already?

She had hoped to spend the night and repeat that performance a few times. She stuck out her lower lip and pouted, lifting her chest off the bed enough to tempt him with her ample tits. "Ahh, Leo. I was hoping we could do that again." She lifted one hand and cupped his face as she rose up onto her knees and climbed onto his lap, straddling him.

Her pussy was primed. She was ready for more.

He didn't wrap her in his arms as she would have liked. Instead he lifted her off him and set her on the bed, standing as he did so. "Sorry, babe. You can't stay any longer." He grabbed his jeans and pulled them on.

Leaving the fly open, he tossed her the shirt she'd worn and then located the other pieces of her clothing and gathered them off the floor to set next to her also.

Seeing no other option, and somewhat annoyed with his behavior after fucking her, she jerked her clothing on and stooped to find her heels. She picked them up, but held them in her hand instead of putting them on. Her purse sat on the bedside table. She grabbed it last.

"Ready?" Leo opened the door and led her out of the room.

She was steaming mad by then. She wasn't used to being tossed out quite so unceremoniously. The gall.

She followed him silently on bare feet, noticing more about this strange house on the way back through. She hadn't bothered to pay attention to much of anything on the way in. She'd had one thing in mind. Getting laid.

They rounded a corner and stepped into an enormous living room. The room was bright, even though it was the middle of the night. And even more shocking, a man sat on one of the many couches, reading glasses on his nose, his head buried in a magazine as if it were midday.

He lifted his gaze as she followed Leo into his line of

sight. The man was older. Perhaps fifty. He stared at her, as if assessing her and finding her lacking.

Angelica shivered. For the first time since she'd entered the compound, she had a sense of dread.

The gray-haired man didn't smile. He didn't seem capable. His brow was permanently furrowed. "Leo, my boy. Who do we have here?" he asked, not taking his gaze off Angelica. His accent was similar to Leo's and unrecognizable to her, but English wasn't his first language.

"Just a girl I picked up at the bar."

She flinched. She didn't want to make a big deal out of their evening either, but that didn't mean she liked the men she fucked to so flippantly refer to their tryst.

"Sit." The man patted the seat next to him. Too close to his side.

For a second, Angelica thought he was talking to Leo, and then Leo pointed to the couch and stepped out of the way.

She almost swallowed her tongue. *Sit? What the fuck for?* Any residual buzz she'd had from drinking at the bar earlier disappeared in an instant. "I need to get going," she muttered, pointing over her shoulder. She didn't have the foggiest notion where the exit was, nor did she have a car. Leo had brought her in his sports car. Hers was still at the bar.

"I'm sure you have a few minutes to spare. Sit." His voice was firmer this time, his accent sending a chill down her spine. He turned his gaze to Leo. "Leo, be a good boy and get me a brandy, would you?" He didn't finish the sentence as though it were a question. It was far closer to a command.

Leo shuffled across the room toward a long bar she hadn't noticed until then.

"Sit, my dear." The man lowered his face to stare at her over the top of his glasses. His face was unreadable. Hard. He wasn't a man she wanted to cross. That much she knew.

Tentatively, she took a seat on the couch, not quite as close as he probably intended, but close enough to temporarily appease him until she could figure a way out of the mess. She set her shoes and purse on the floor at her feet.

"So, tell me about yourself. What's your name?"

"Angelica." Why was he asking her this?

"Relax, Angelica. I'm just making conversation. What do you do?"

"I'm a student at the university."

He lifted a brow. "How old are you?"

"Nineteen." She sat up straighter. She was old enough to make the choices she made. Who was he to judge?

"And you met Leo at a bar? How did you get in?"

"Fake ID," she muttered. Hell, everyone had a fake ID. So?

The gray-haired man ignored her infraction. "The university, huh. An intellect. How precious. What're you studying?"

"Literature."

"Oh." His brows rose. "A lit major. Then you must know Dr. Bascott."

She flinched. Could this night get any weirder? "I do. I have a class with him this semester."

The man grinned for the first time. "Ah. Excellent. He's an amazing professor. Is he not?"

"He is. How to you know him, sir?" She tried for polite, relaxing marginally. If this man knew Bascott, how bad could the guy be?

"We go way back." He waved a hand through the air,

dismissing her question. "I haven't spoken to him in a while. I should really give him a call. Is he still fighting?"

"Sir?" What did he mean by fighting?

The man narrowed his gaze at her as though assessing her reaction. "Perhaps he doesn't reveal that side of himself to his students." Gray-haired guy twisted his neck to look at Leo. "Leo, when was the last time you saw our friend Conner?"

"It's been a few weeks. We sparred for practice together, oh, I don't know, maybe three weeks ago?" Leo glanced up at the ceiling as if pulling the answer out of his memory.

"*You* know Professor Bascott too?" She whipped her head fully around to face Leo.

"Only in the MMA circles." Leo returned and handed Gray a tumbler, notably not offering Angelica anything. Leo plopped down in a chair across from them, nursing a drink of his own. Something dark and on the rocks.

"MMA?"

"Mixed Martial Arts," Gray responded.

She had no idea the professor was a fighter. But holy shit that was hot. Just thinking of the buff professor battling it out in the ring made her pussy clench. No wonder he was so smoking hot.

Was his fighting a secret? Maybe no one at the university knew what Dr. Bascott did in his spare time. If it had anything to do with these guys, it was probably illegal. Something about this older man seemed illicit.

The older guy tipped his head back and chuckled. "I wonder what he's up to these days? Leo, is he still with that girl he was dating a while back?"

"Not that I know of."

"Huh. Too bad. She was cute." The man seemed to be commenting to nobody in particular.

What girl? Angelica's curiosity was piqued. Surely he wasn't referring to that bitch Sabrina. Was he?

"Yeah, she was hot," Leo added. "Tiny though. She didn't have anything on Angelica." He winked at her as he spoke.

Holy fuck.

"Sabrina?" she asked.

The older guy snapped his fingers. "Sabrina. That was it. Long brown hair. About this tall?" He held one hand up in the air.

Yep, that had to be her. How had that bitch managed to ruin Angelica's night without even being present? Fuck her. And how the hell long had she been seeing Conner?

Angelica almost smiled. She'd suspected, but if Conner really had been fucking Sabrina all last semester, he truly would be in a heap of trouble.

Perhaps the reason he'd been so curt with the woman was simply to throw the rest of the class off of his dalliance.

Oh, Professor Bascott. Shame on you…

"What was her last name, Leo?" The older guy seemed to be ignoring Angelica.

"Duluth," she responded.

"Yes. That was it. Huh. Small world. How do you know her?" Gray asked.

"We were in the same class last semester."

"She's a student? Dating the professor? Isn't that against policy?"

Angelica nodded. If what this guy was saying was true, then it would seem Dr. Bascott had been a very naughty boy. She should have thought of that sooner. If the two of them fucked in a restaurant in July, it would stand to reason they had screwed around before that also.

"Huh, well ain't that a crazy coincidence?" The guy

stood and slammed the rest of his drink down. "I really need to hit the sack. Leo, are you taking this lovely lady home?"

"No. Her car's at the bar where we met. I'll get her a taxi." He lifted his drink as though after consuming it he wouldn't dare get behind a wheel, even though he'd driven her to the strange compound in the first place after drinking.

Bastard.

CHAPTER 14

It was bright. Too bright. Sabrina opened one eye to get her bearings.

Then she moaned.

Shit. Conner's house.

Soft music reached her ears from somewhere in the house. Classical. Soothing. In contrast with her confused mental state.

She was afraid to move. How bad would her ass hurt?

Shit.

She'd slept in Conner's bed, in Conner's house. She'd let him spank her. Hard. And he hadn't permitted her to come.

Had she lost her mind?

She shifted a few inches, still on her belly, but testing the rub of the sheet against her ass. Not bad.

Deep breaths. She needed to get up, take a shower, go home. She had work to do. Taking entire days off wasn't her style.

Sabrina eased from the bed until she stood naked in the room. She didn't make a sound.

She was okay.

She spotted Conner's black T-shirt from the night before and snagged it to pull over her head. She needed to face him at some point. Better to get it over with.

She had no idea why she felt shy about seeing him.

Because you let him spank you hard.

Yep. That was a little embarrassing.

First she silently made her way to the adjoined bathroom, realizing with every step she still wore his plug. What would he say if she took it out? Better to leave it for now. She used the toilet and washed her hands.

When she padded into the living room, she paused to take in her surroundings. She hadn't paid very close attention to anything the night before. She'd been too worried about what Conner's intentions were, and then she'd been too horny to see straight.

His couch was an enormous black leather piece that was currently occupied by its owner. Whatever he was doing must have been very interesting because he hadn't noticed her enter. She was behind the back of the couch, so from her angle, she couldn't see what he was engrossed in. His head was dipped low. Reading?

She took a moment to soak in the rest of his great room. Everything was warm and inviting. Not nearly what she would expect from a bachelor pad. All browns and blacks. Throw pillows graced the matching black leather arm chair and were tossed on the floor in front of it.

She inched forward until she was feet away from Conner.

Finally, he lifted his gaze. A huge smile spread across his face, and he raised one arm over the back of the couch toward her. "Hey, sleepy."

She closed the gap between them until he could grab her and tug her up against the back of the couch. That's when she realized what he was reading. And his chest was bare. Delicious.

He lifted up the book. "Gotta apologize to you again. This isn't half bad."

She smiled. "Told you."

"I admit, I expected only smut. But there's a story under it."

"Of course there's a story, doofus." She swatted at his shoulder, wondering if doofus was an acceptable word. He didn't comment, so she assumed her sore ass was safe.

"Come." He nodded in front of him and released her.

She rounded the couch, realizing his intention when she reached him. He nodded at the floor, intending for her to kneel.

She eased onto her knees, relieved to find he wouldn't require her to sit. She was still leery about what her ass might feel like.

He cupped her face. "Did you sleep well?"

"Surprisingly yes, Sir." She let her gaze roam down his face to stare at his chest. The tattoo over his right shoulder was so intricate and amazing it made her lick her lips. And his pecs... Jesus. There had to be a law against such divine exposure.

He grinned. Good. And then he kissed her nose and leaned back to tuck a lock of hair behind her ear.

"I'm a mess. I need makeup remover and a shower. I really should get home."

He frowned. "Is there a rush?"

She shrugged. "I need to do some work today."

"Do you work every day?"

"Most days. Yes."

He sat back and picked up the book again. "You edited this?"

"I did."

"You did well, Sabrina."

She narrowed her gaze. "I continue to amaze you with my less-than-stellar profession."

He chuckled. "True. Do you write also?"

"Mmm. A little."

"Published anything?"

"No."

"Why? You're a fantastic writer. And so knowledgeable about the genre."

She laughed. "That's the second time you've told me you found my writing acceptable. It still sounds odd coming from the man I thought detested my work for so many months."

"I told you already that wasn't true."

"Yes, but it will take a while for it to sink in. To answer your question, if I were independently wealthy, I would probably take the time to write a book. But since I'm not, and there are bills to pay, I edit. Writing is a risk. A risk only those who can afford to take may assume."

"Really? How long does it take to write a book like this?"

She shrugged. "Depends on the muse, I suppose. Some authors can do it in weeks. Others need years. I like to pay my bills *every* month." She grinned widely.

"Shame."

"Perhaps. There's no guarantee I would even be any good."

"But you have some writing already? Something stashed under your mattress, so to speak?"

"A bit." She chewed on her lower lip. *Don't go there, Conner.*

"So, you're also scared."

He went there.

"Of course. Everyone is."

He frowned. "Don't hold yourself back out of fear. Your life will slip by while you watch."

"Thanks, Freud."

Conner leaned in and cupped her face again. "I'm not trying to psychoanalyze you. I just think you should think about it."

"Noted."

"Stay. I'll get you something to eat."

Sabrina didn't move. She wondered about his version of dominance while he was gone. This was the first time they were truly alone together for an extended period of time. He'd made it clear he was very dominant. Would he expect her to submit every time they were alone? And what about the exchange of dialogue they'd just engaged in? He let her speak freely, look at him, and even drop the title of Sir.

Suddenly he was back. He took the same spot on the couch and held out a glass. "Juice?"

"Thank you, Sir." She took it from him after a slight hesitation where she hedged, wondering if he intended to feed her himself or let her take control.

It seemed he would allow her to drink at her own pace.

He also held a plate of food that smelled delicious. Bacon. Eggs. Toast. Her stomach growled.

"I wasn't sure what you liked to eat in the morning. I'm a pretty big breakfast eater, so I made you some too and kept it warm."

"Thanks. I don't always eat so much, but I'm actually starving."

He handed her the plate and took the glass of orange juice from her to set it on the coffee table, freeing up her hands so she could hold the plate with one and eat with the other. She did so while he watched. It was unnerving. But she was hungry.

A phone rang, jarring her to glance toward the kitchen. Conner didn't move.

"Feel free to get that, Conner."

"The machine will pick it up. I'm sure it isn't important." His gaze never left her.

Sabrina continued to eat, the ringing piercing the otherwise silent room several times before the machine loudly announced in Conner's deep voice that the caller should leave a message.

"Conner... Darling... It's Tina."

Sabrina's back arched. She widened her eyes. Her chest pounded.

Get a grip. Could be his sister.

Conner rolled his head back against the couch and gripped his jean-clad thighs with both hands, clearly annoyed, but he didn't jump up.

"...You owe me one. That was so embarrassing last weekend. My parents don't believe I actually have a boyfriend."

At that line, Sabrina dropped her plate. Luckily there wasn't anything left on it, but it slipped from her hands to land on the carpet.

Conner grunted and lifted his head to meet her gaze, a scowl on his face.

She stared at him, not lowering her face as they listened to the rest of the conversation. Why was he allowing this to go on? If he had another woman... Fuck. She couldn't even ponder the idea. This made no sense. If he had someone else, or recently...why the charade? And why didn't he turn off the volume?

Instead he remained still, holding her gaze, his lips pursed, his eyes dancing with frustration.

"...So, I told my mother you'd be with me next weekend

for our usual family dinner. Don't let me down. Please, Conner." Finally, the line went dead.

Sabrina flinched when the machine clicked off. She held her breath. Waited.

"Sorry about that."

That's all he was going to say? "Conner?"

"Co-worker. She has some notion she owns me. She does *not*."

"Good to know, under the circumstances, but what on earth makes her think she's your girlfriend. Is she?"

"Of course not. If she were, I wouldn't have sat here letting you listen to her."

"I thought of that." She nibbled her lower lip. "Was she? At one time?"

"Never. Unfortunately she likes to believe otherwise. We had one brief incident about a year ago at a company function. I had a bit too much to drink, and she cornered me in a hallway and stuck her tongue down my throat. It wasn't pleasant." He winced. "I've tried to be polite toward her. I have to work with her. But she won't take no for an answer. It's getting out of hand. I'll have to talk to her again."

"Clearly. That borders on sexual harassment."

"It does." He leaned back again and ran both hands through his hair. "I'm not really in a position at work right now to charge someone with sexual harassment, so I'd rather handle it on my own or ignore the woman entirely."

"What situation at work?"

"It's nothing. Don't worry about it." He didn't elaborate. After a few seconds, he leaned down to pick up her plate and set it on the coffee table. "Come. Let's shower so I can get you home, and you can get some editing done."

Sabrina's heart raced as she rose from the floor and

followed him. His amazing back kept her occupied all the way to the bedroom, the gladiator shield mesmerizing.

Conner flipped on the shower when they reached the bathroom. He turned toward her while it heated and grabbed the hem of her shirt.

She was aware of her sensitive ass as the cotton eased up, but it didn't hurt.

He dropped the shirt on the floor and turned her around. "Lean over the edge of the vanity, baby."

She took several deep breaths, still rather uncomfortable with the way he handled her nudity. She wasn't used to such intimate scrutiny.

"Spread your legs farther."

She stepped out, wetness leaking between her legs. Her pussy pulsed with sudden need. It threw her off balance the way his demands made her so horny. His brand of dominance was nothing like anything she'd ever experienced.

Until now, she'd gone to the club, played with different Doms, and even dated a few. But nothing in her past had ever come close to this intense relationship. She'd done scenes. At specified times. Usually at clubs. Never at her home. And rarely at a Dom's home.

This was so much more. What Conner expected of her was several notches up from anything she knew.

His hands landed on her ass and squeezed. "Still pink, baby. Does it hurt?"

She winced, but then panted as she realized her flesh was fine, just a slight sting when he initially grabbed her.

"Sabrina?"

"Not much, Sir."

"It looks how I would expect this morning. But I want to be sure it feels similarly. My intention isn't to leave you in pain for days on end. A spanking should hurt enough to encourage you not to repeat a behavior. That's all. Anything more is too much."

"I think it's okay, Sir." She did. But she also didn't want him to do it often.

His fingers landed on the plug and twisted. "I'm going to remove this now. I'm proud of you for leaving it in. Legs wider, baby. Relax." His free hand gripped her waist.

She stepped wider.

"Good girl." The plug popped out far easier than it went in.

She released a breath. She'd lived.

Conner stepped to her side and used the sink to wash the plug. When he was finished, he put it in a drawer, opening and closing it so fast she barely had the chance to see the contents.

What she did see made her eyes widen, however. There were other toys in that drawer. Most of them in the original packaging.

Oh God. Was all that for her? Had he purchased it in the last few days?

"Don't nose around in there, baby. I can see the curiosity on your face. Leave the contents a mystery." He took her shoulder and urged her to stand upright. His serious expression made her lick her lips.

"Yes, Sir."

He took her hand then and led her to the shower.

The warm water felt amazing, and she stepped under the spray to let it run down her face and body.

Conner didn't say a word while he grabbed the shampoo from the shelf and poured it in his hand. Before she knew it, he had his hands buried in her hair, massaging her scalp.

She moaned. It felt so good. Her body relaxed, and she closed her eyes as he took care of her. She took mental notes. *He doesn't demand feeding you himself, but he likes to wash you.*

"Keep your eyes closed, baby." His voice was husky. She had no intention of opening them anyway with soap running down her face.

Every sound was louder with her eyes shut. A pop, and then his hands were on her shoulders, smoothing soap down her arms and then over her breasts. He lingered on her nipples, rubbing them until they stiffened.

She leaned toward him, her mouth opening. She didn't care that soap ran into her mouth. Her arousal shot up a notch with every touch.

"Good girl. Just feel. Eyes stay closed. You've done so well. You deserve a reward."

A reward. Thank God. Her body hummed with need.

He pinched her nipples and then let his hands smooth down to her belly and then her thighs. He made his way down her legs, kneeling in front of her, before he eased back up. "Spread your legs, baby." His breath hit her pussy as he spoke, the cooler air in contrast to the warm water.

She opened her stance as his fingers found her center. She grabbed his shoulders to keep from falling. Steadying herself, she concentrated on his every touch. He stroked through her folds several times and then his fingers danced around her clit. "May I shave you?"

Her eyes shot open. What? He didn't notice her infraction, however, since his gaze was focused on her pussy. And she was forced to close her eyes just as quickly when soap ran down her forehead.

"Please? I'll be careful. Promise," he continued when she didn't respond.

"Um." She couldn't imagine herself consenting to that. No one had ever suggested something that intimate. *Shave my pussy?*

She'd never even gone to a waxing center to get a Brazilian. The idea made her cringe.

But this was Conner. He had wormed his way into every single aspect of her life so quickly and thoroughly she really shouldn't be shocked at his suggestion. "Okay," she muttered.

He stood and kissed her gently on the lips and then eased her under the spray of water. Shampoo ran down her, rinsing the soap from her face.

When he helped her out of the direct spray, she blinked her eyes open.

Conner stared down at her. He hadn't given her permission to look at him yet, but he didn't mention it. He stroked his thumb over her lower lip as he backed her up to sit her on the built-in bench seat. "Scoot back. Put your heels on the tile. Spread wide."

She shivered as she followed his instructions. In this position, her lower lips parted and her clit throbbed. So erotic.

Conner grabbed a bottle of shaving cream and tipped it up to squirt a mound of it into his palm.

Sabrina winced. He was really going to do this. She hoped he was quick about it because she didn't think she would breathe the entire time.

He kneeled between her legs and flattened his palm on her pussy, smearing the cream everywhere.

Holy mother of God. She almost came.

And then his hand was gone, and he used it to hold her wide and steady while he stroked over her tender flesh with the razor in his other hand.

The scraping noise unnerved her more. She didn't dare move a single muscle. Instead she watched closely as he worked his way down toward her ass, holding her folds in every direction as he made sure he didn't miss a spot.

When he was satisfied, he set the razor aside. "Don't move yet, baby." He grabbed the nozzle from the wall and removed it. She hadn't realized it was detachable, and she didn't have time to think before the spray landed directly on her open pussy, rinsing away the shaving cream.

Sabrina screamed out when the water hit her clit.

Conner grinned. "You like that."

She panted. "Conner… Stop… I'm going to come…"

He dropped the spray head, and it swayed along the wall, the water hitting them both haphazardly as he leaned into her. He gripped her thighs with both hands, held them wider, and sucked her clit into his mouth with no warning.

Sabrina came so hard and fast, her breath left her. All the blood ran from her head to her core, leaving her dizzy. Her legs shook as pulse after pulse of her orgasm pressed against his relentless mouth.

He didn't stop.

She never had a chance to ease down from her high before it built again.

Still he licked and nibbled her sensitive clit. And then he released one thigh and thrust several fingers into her pussy.

She screamed again. Her head rocked back until it hit the tile wall. Her eyes rolled back. Her vision blurred. Her arousal rose higher. She gripped involuntarily at his fingers with her pussy.

It was too much and not enough.

She curled her fingers around the edge of the bench seat, unable to get a grip on the slippery tile.

So close.

And then he was gone.

Her head yanked forward. She tried to concentrate on his face through the fog. "No. Oh God. Conner. You can't stop." She gulped.

"Need to be inside you, baby." He flipped off the water and lifted her into his arms so fast, her head was spinning.

Suddenly, the shower door was open and the cool air of the house hit her wet skin. She shivered, squirming in his embrace. Still so needy. Her mouth hung open, but she couldn't speak.

Conner strode quickly through the room and out the door, not stopping for towels. Thank God.

He tossed her unceremoniously onto the bed. "On your hands and knees, Sabrina."

Her limbs didn't work. She was shocked. She remained on her ass, watching him while he grabbed a condom from the bedside table, ripped it open, and rolled it down his cock. Water dripped down his body from his hair. He didn't seem to notice or care.

"Knees, baby. Now. Flip over." He stepped toward her.

She blinked, trying to assimilate the meaning of his words.

He didn't wait. He grabbed her waist and flipped her over. "Can you hold yourself up?"

She nodded, completely unsure. Her sopping wet hair matted to her cheek, soaking the bed in front of her.

"Lean forward on your forearms, baby. You can rest your head on the mattress."

That suggestion was easy. She nearly collapsed. The only reason her knees didn't buckle was because he grabbed her thighs with his hands and spread them wider, almost too wide. And before she knew what was happening, he gripped her waist and thrust into her.

"Yes…" A loud groan left her lips on the end of that word. "Oh God, yes."

His cock seemed larger than ever. Every movement drove her higher as he fucked her hard.

She dug her forehead into the mattress between her

hands to steady herself, gasping for air. She blinked as drips of water ran into her eyes. The sheet was soaked now. It stuck to her face.

While he fucked her hard and fast, one hand disappeared. A finger landed seconds later on her forbidden hole, tapping it and then rubbing the sensitive flesh of her ass before pressing into her without warning.

Sabrina moaned so loud she shocked herself. That's how good it felt. So aroused she lost all sense of reason and didn't care what he did. And that finger rubbing against his cock inside her was heavenly. "Yes…" she muttered again. "God, Conner. Please… More." More what? She had no idea.

And then he added a second finger.

Ohh… So full. So fantastically delicious. She'd never felt like this before.

Too soon, she was on the edge.

Conner reached under her and pinched her clit with his free hand.

She shattered, her orgasm seeming to rip her into a million pieces. Nothing would be left of her.

Still he thrust. "That's it, baby." He rubbed her clit then, harder, faster, pushing her orgasm into another one before it subsided.

No thoughts would gather in her head. She wanted to beg him to stop. It was too much. Too sensitive.

She wanted to beg him to keep doing what he was doing. And how the hell was he managing so many assaults at once?

His cock thrust faster, his fingers in tandem, and his other hand pressed hard against her clit. "Come again for me, baby. Take me with you."

Could she? Her breathing was erratic.

"Do it, Sabrina," he commanded. "Come. One more time."

As if her body obeyed him even when her mind wasn't capable, she followed his demand. The deep pulsing grip she had on his cock as a third orgasm shook her entire body seemed to cause her to float away from herself as if she'd died.

The intensity was overwhelming. She gulped for air. None seemed to come into her lungs.

And then Conner groaned loudly, his voice piercing the fog. He removed his fingers from her ass and her clit and gripped her hips to hold her steady, his cock deep inside her, pulsing into her depths forever.

When he was done, he didn't move.

She could hear him breathing at least as heavily as her.

He leaned forward and kissed her lower back as he eased out. "Don't move." He walked away.

Don't move? She collapsed seconds later, her body falling onto the soaked bed, sprawled out on her belly while she continued to take deep breaths. Her wet hair covered her face. She couldn't see through the curtain of it. She didn't care. She couldn't move. Perhaps she'd never be able to move again.

He was back, chuckling. A towel landed on her back and he dried her still-wet skin before he climbed up to one side of her and gathered her back against his front. He brushed her hair from her face. "Are you alive?"

"No." It was the only word she could manage. And it was appropriate. She was certain she had actually died, and this was heaven.

He pulled the comforter over them awkwardly, considering they were lying sideways across the bed. "Are you cold?"

She didn't know.

He chuckled again. "Maybe I *have* killed you. That would be horrible to explain to the police." He kissed her shoulder, nibbled a path to her ear.

She concentrated on breathing. If she remembered correctly, that was the most important part of staying alive.

There was silence for several minutes while her body came back to Earth. Conner stroked her skin everywhere with his free hand, up and down her side, across her breast. Her damn nipple stood at attention every time he grazed over it. "You okay?"

"I think."

"Did I push you too far?"

"No." She swallowed. "God, no."

His laugher was silent, but she could feel the vibration of it shaking her body. "So you would do that again?"

"I'm thinking about when it might be too early to toss out a string of cuss words."

He laughed harder, his hand trailing down to stroke her still-heated ass. "Not today, baby. You need a break."

"If that's how you plan to fuck me after you spank me every time, it might be worth it."

He rolled her to her back and met her gaze. His face was filled with mirth, the wrinkles around his eyes spreading wide to go with his smile. "I might have to get more creative."

"Mmm. I might not mind." She shivered. Even with the comforter, she was cooling down against the wet sheets.

"Tell me you're mine."

"I've already told you that."

"Do it again."

"I'm yours."

He kissed her, deep and thoroughly. And then he set his forehead against hers. "How about we shower again, separately this time, and then perhaps we can actually face each other without fucking for a few minutes."

"We can try." She shrugged, not at all sure it was possible and not at all sure she cared. His dominance was intense at times. The last twelve hours had been amazing, though. If she could endure a spanking like last night, being left needy to sleep, having him shave her pussy, and then letting him fuck her hard with his fingers in her ass... she could not only endure anything he dished out, but probably enjoy it.

CHAPTER 15

Conner took Sabrina to his favorite burger joint for lunch. It was a gorgeous day, and the place had outdoor picnic tables that were perfect. It didn't seem like they could do any talking as long as they were in the privacy of the house. Every time he looked her in the eye, they started kissing.

She wanted to go home and work for the afternoon. Conner needed to grade papers anyway, and there was no way he would get anything done with her in his house. As loath as he was to admit it.

"I can't believe you eat this stuff," she teased, holding up a thick burger loaded with cheese, bacon, and all the regular toppings. She could barely get her mouth around it.

"What? Are you saying my favorite indulgence isn't delicious?" He covered his heart in mock hurt.

"No." She pointed at his chest with a general wave of her hand. "I'm saying how the hell does someone as fit as you eat this and stay so buff?"

He laughed. "I work out. A lot. Hard. I can eat whatever I want in between."

"Even at your advanced age?"

He wadded up his napkin and threw it at her across the table. And then he stood, leaned over the red-and-white checkered table cloth, and grabbed her face to lean over and whisper in her ear. "I didn't hear anyone complaining about my *advanced age* this morning while I had my cock in her sweet wet pussy and my fingers in her tight virgin ass."

She giggled, a shiver shaking her as he let her go. Her eyes danced with mirth when he sat back down.

What he wanted to do was take her over his knee, perhaps to make her come screaming his name rather than spank her.

Suddenly a shadow fell over him as someone stepped in between him and the sun. When he turned to look up, he was shocked to find Dmitry Volikov straddling the bench seat of the picnic table.

He plopped himself down too close for comfort and grabbed one of Conner's fries. "Hey."

Conner narrowed his gaze at Dmitry, stiffening. "What are you doing here, Volikov?"

"You're a difficult man to track down."

"I heard you were looking for me at the gym. If this is about fighting for Yenin, forget it. Tell him I said *fuck no* for the millionth time."

Sabrina flinched, a soft gasp escaping her lips.

The last thing Conner wanted to do was mix Sabrina up with the Russians. It left a bad taste in his mouth. Dmitry was a good enough guy most of the time, but Conner wasn't sure he trusted him.

"Dude, you think I haven't already conveyed that message?" Dmitry turned toward Sabrina and smiled as though he'd just realized Conner wasn't dining alone. His gaze ran up and down her torso, taking her in.

Conner's blood boiled. "You still haven't answered my question. What are you doing here, Dmitry?"

Slowly, Dmitry let his gaze slide from Sabrina to Conner. "Anton is in a state. I wanted to warn you."

"I got that the last time I saw him." *When he threatened me.*

"He talks about you a lot." Dmitry leaned closer. "A *lot*." He glanced at Sabrina again. At least he had the sense not to blab everything he knew to her.

Conner had to appreciate that much. He sat back, wiping his fingers on his napkin. At least he'd finished his burger before Dmitry ruined his appetite. "What do you want me to do?"

Dmitry shrugged. "Watch your back."

Conner sucked in a sharp breath. "You think it's that bad?" So much for keeping Sabrina out of the loop. She would have questions now. Rightfully so.

"I do."

Conner hesitated. "Why the hell do you fight for that asshole?"

Dmitry chuckled sardonically as he stood. "If you think it's that simple, you're dumber than I thought."

Conner swallowed. He knew the Russian fighters had a plateful of issues, but weren't they working for Yenin voluntarily? "If you need the money, go pro. You're good enough."

Dmitry shook his head as though Conner were dense. At that point, Conner was inclined to agree. "I wish I had your lily-white life with the picket fence, dude, but not all of us live that way. Stay clean. Don't let him bully you."

"Trust me, man. I wouldn't fight for him for all the money in China."

Dmitry tapped the table with his fingers. "What if it were for all the money in Asia, and you didn't have any other income?" He lifted one eyebrow and then turned and walked away.

Sabrina gasped. "What the fuck?" she mumbled when Dmitry was out of earshot.

Conner jerked his head back to face her.

She winced when he met her gaze.

"For once, I'm going to have to agree with you. *What the fuck* is right. Dammit." He stood. "Let's get out of here." He took her hand as he led her to his Mustang, glancing over his shoulder as they went. It wasn't logical to think they were being followed. Or hell, maybe it was. As fucked up as his life was, he wouldn't put anything past anyone lately.

As soon as he had Sabrina safely in the car and had entered his own side and shut the door, she spoke again. "You gonna tell me what that was all about?"

"Yeah." He didn't say more as he pulled away from the curb. He wanted to get out of Dodge first. He'd tell her about Yenin after they got to her house.

They drove in silence. He gripped the steering wheel, paranoia setting in. What the hell did Dmitry mean when he said fighting for Yenin would pay a fortune? What bothered him more was that he suggested Conner could be out of a job. Was it possible Yenin was behind the ridiculous accusations at work? It made sense. After all, the allegations were false and anonymous.

Conner followed Sabrina into her house and shut the door behind him.

She dropped her purse on the kitchen table and turned to face him. "Talk."

He plopped onto the couch and glanced around again at the number of books in her living room. He didn't think any normal person could read that many books in a lifetime. And he would bet money she'd already read most of them.

He leaned his elbows on his knees as Sabrina sat next to him and curled her legs under her.

"Dmitry's a good enough guy. I don't think he meant any harm."

She startled. "If that guy was one of your friends, I'd hate to meet any of your enemies."

Conner smiled briefly and then leaned back against the couch to give her some details. "There's this Russian mob guy named Anton Yenin. He thinks he owns Vegas. And in a way he does. He has hounded me to fight for him for years, but for some reason he's gotten demanding about it lately, and even threatened me if I didn't."

"Shit. Are you serious?"

"That's two." He narrowed his gaze at her. "Stop cussing."

Sabrina jumped up and put her hands on her hips. "Conner, don't change the subject. This is *fucking* important." She emphasized the word *fucking* and stiffened as though challenging him.

Conner blew out a breath. "I agree. It's important. And I'm trying to tell you the saga. If you would just listen. You don't need to sully yourself with foul language. I got the picture."

"Sully myself? Listen to you." Her voice rose. "There's some fucking asshole mob guy fucking threatening you, and he sent his fucking minion to find you and add to that fucking threat, and you want me to fucking watch my fucking language?"

Conner pursed his lips. "Sometimes you suck at submission." He wiped his palms on his jeans, itching to take her over his knee and knowing now was not the time.

He'd made himself very clear on the issue of cussing—and she had failed at it miserably since he'd started dominating her. What the hell kind of submissive would she be long term?

He stared at her, wondering how they'd gotten so far off track since that morning when it had seemed the world was a perfect place for the two of them.

"I think I should go." His patience was waning. He had a shit ton of problems on his plate, and he didn't want to fight with Sabrina on top of everything. He was afraid he might say something he couldn't take back if he didn't leave. He stood.

"You have *got* to be kidding."

He shook his head. "Sabrina, you're pissed. And frankly I'm pissed also. And I have a very full plate. I don't need you topping me right now in addition everything else. I'm going to leave. I'll call you later." He headed for the door, knowing it was the right thing to do.

Ordinarily he wasn't as short tempered as he had been for the past week. However, ordinarily he didn't have some crazy person trying to get him fired, a Russian asshole threatening to make him fight underground, some insane professor pretending he was her boyfriend, and a submissive from the club trying to claim him as her own when it was totally over between them before it had ever started.

Sabrina was a woman he wanted a future with. At least he thought he did. If she had a submissive bone hiding inside her somewhere. But right now, he needed space. He needed to go to the gym and work out his frustration. There was no way he could reason with her this afternoon.

"Fine. Go."

He walked out the door without looking back, madder

than ever. At himself more than anything. Was he doing the right thing?

If it meant the difference between saying things he couldn't take back and holding his tongue, then yes, he needed to walk away.

He nearly jogged to his car and pulled away from her house before he could talk himself into going back inside to reason with her. Neither of them was in the right frame of mind to be rational. Later. If she was still speaking to him...

～

Sabrina winced when the door slammed shut.

What the hell had just happened?

She flopped down on the couch and groaned. That had not gone well. And she accepted the majority of the blame. Why on earth had she thought goading him would be a good idea?

Obviously the man had a lot going on. Maybe she didn't know him as well as she thought.

Hell...that was an understatement. She didn't know him well at all. She knew he was the sexiest man she'd ever seen. He worked out hard and fought amateur MMA. He was a firm Dom. What else did she really know?

That he made her panties wet every time he entered a room.

That her heart raced just thinking about him.

That he could make her come harder than anyone she'd ever been with.

Fuck.

Oh, and he didn't tolerate cussing for some reason.

Some Russian mafia guy was after him.

Some other professor wanted in his pants.

Some gorgeous submissive at the club thought she deserved to put her claws in him.

Hell, there might even be a student or two who would fight over him given the chance, like that Angelina girl, or whatever her name was, from last semester. If he had to deal with very many coeds like her, she didn't envy his job.

Sabrina closed her eyes and groaned again. She needed to apologize for her insolence. Later.

She ran a hand over her face and stood. They both needed a time out. And she had work to do. Perhaps if she buried herself in her editing, the day would fly by. Later tonight she would text him and apologize.

Sabrina hauled herself off the couch and headed for her office. She booted up her computer and tucked herself into her seat. Over a dozen emails had accumulated since she'd last gone through them yesterday. She opened the first one and worked her way through them, intending to address only what was most urgent on a Sunday afternoon.

The third one made her blood run cold.

What the...?

Dear Ms. Duluth,

If you value your dignity, I suggest you find someone else to play house with. Your current dalliance is not in your best interest. The professor is about to learn a hard lesson. I suggest you make yourself scarce fast before you find yourself in a heap of trouble. These sorts of things can follow you for a lifetime.

Sincerely,

A Concerned Citizen

Sabrina held her breath and read the short message over and over. What the hell? Suddenly, she noticed there was an attachment. A zip file.

Fuck.

With shaking fingers, she clicked on the download button. After a few tense seconds, a stream of pictures popped onto the screen. Sabrina sucked in a sharp breath and jumped to her feet, releasing the mouse as though it were poisonous.

Fuck. Fuck fuck fuck. How the hell did someone get these photos?

She shivered as she stared at each shot as it flipped by, each one remaining for only a few seconds before another showed up like a slide show. A pornographic slide show.

The first few were innocuous enough. A picture of her leaning toward Conner outside Extreme. It had to have been that first night. Though how anyone managed to catch a shot that demonstrated anything but aggravation was beyond her.

The next shot was of her in his car outside the arena the next Friday night. It was blurry.

The third was of the two of them at King Pizza at lunch. She looked very submissive in that shot. It stunned her to think she'd appeared so vulnerable in public.

And then her gut clenched. She grabbed her belly to avoid vomiting on her keyboard as her eyes widened. There she was, completely naked, lying over Conner's lap as he spanked her on her own couch. It was a bit blurry also, obviously taken from outside the front window through a gap in the blinds. She knew for a fact the blinds hadn't been open when she stripped in the living room.

The next one made her grab the back of the chair and hold on to avoid collapsing. She was bent over the side of Conner's bed as he pushed a plug into her. Her face conveyed extreme rapture.

All the blood ran from her head, leaving her faint.

Why?

She sank to the floor finally and leaned against the wall,

lowering her head between her knees before she hyperventilated. She needed to catch her breath before her mind would work again. She squeezed her eyes shut and inhaled long and slow. Oxygen. And then action.

But what was she going to do?

She stiffened. Even before she'd opened the email she'd been pissed with Conner. Now she was livid.

It's not his fault someone is stalking us and taking pictures. Her rational self made a plea for Conner.

Her heart told her to run.

She glanced around the room, feeling violated. Someone had fucking followed her, or Conner, and taken pictures at nearly every juncture. How many more were there? There could be hundreds for all she knew.

Shit.

Should she call the police?

Wait. What about Rider, Emily's boyfriend? He was a cop. Maybe she should call him.

Ugh. The last thing she wanted was for anyone to actually see these degrading pictures.

How humiliating. She shivered again and wrapped her arms around her middle as though cold.

She stayed like that for a long time, unable to move. Unable to make any decisions.

Holy shit.

Maybe she should heed the advice of the email and stay away from Conner. Clearly he had a closet full of ghosts if someone was following him all over creation and taking pictures of him.

Why? What was the objective?

Or perhaps the stalker's goal was simply to get rid of Sabrina.

Hmmm. That was a possibility. There seemed to be a plethora of women who wanted in Conner's pants badly.

Maybe one of them sent the message. Whoever it was, they were articulate.

That professor who wanted him to go out with her? Or what about the girl at the club, Missy? She didn't seem like the type to use such proper English, but who knew?

Would a professor at the university be threatening Sabrina so she could sleep with Conner? Not likely. Because even without Sabrina in the picture, that didn't mean Conner would go out with the woman.

What about the Russian guy? Jesus. She knew the Russian mob wanted Conner to fight for them. That was abundantly clear. But what did that have to do with Sabrina?

Fuck.

She pulled herself off the floor and made her way out of the office without glancing back at the computer screen. She would vomit if she saw those images again.

She padded to the kitchen, unease creeping up her spine.

Was someone outside even now, watching her? She glanced at the front window. The blinds were closed, just as they had been the other night. One slat was askew.

She inched closer. Yep. One slat was definitely lying on its side, having gotten caught in the strings. That was for sure where the picture had been taken.

Sabrina reached out and righted the slat before turning toward the kitchen.

No way in hell could she edit as she'd planned for the afternoon.

She needed to talk to someone.

Rider seemed like the best option. She wasn't calm enough to call Conner. And she wasn't sane enough to make good choices under the circumstances.

She grabbed her cell phone from her back pocket and

scrolled down to find Emily's number. Thank God the woman had exchanged numbers with her.

Sabrina lowered herself onto a kitchen chair as the phone rang.

Emily picked up on the fourth ring just when Sabrina was starting to worry.

"Sabrina. Hi. How are you?" Her voice was full of excitement.

"Not so great actually. I don't suppose Rider is with you. I could use some advice. It's kind of personal."

"Oh. Okay. Sorry. He's at the gym. I think Conner is with him in fact."

"Shoot. Right. That makes sense."

"I could text Rider and ask him to contact you when he's done. I can't guarantee he would keep it from Conner, though. The guys are pretty close."

"Yeah. Of course. It was a bad idea." Sabrina nibbled on her lower lip, thinking about Plan B. She couldn't just sit there and wait. The stress was killing her.

"You could call the gym. Joe, the owner, might pick up, and he could track the guys down if it's urgent. I'm sure they left their cell phones in their lockers. It's tough to get ahold of them when they're working out."

"I'm sure." She glanced out the window. She didn't think she could stay inside the house one more minute alone anyway. Even if she had spoken to Rider over the phone, her skin was crawling. "I think I'll just drive to the gym. That'll be faster. Can you text me the address?"

"Absolutely. Sorry I couldn't be of more help. I hope everything's okay." She didn't add the lilt to the end of that sentence that would have turned it into a question. Bless her.

Sabrina didn't want to discuss it with Emily right then.

It wouldn't do any good. "I'm sure it'll be fine. I'll get back with you later this week, okay?"

"Sure. Be careful. Talk to you soon." Emily hung up. Thank God she was so polite and easy.

Sabrina wasted no time grabbing her purse, slipping on her shoes, locking all the doors, and heading for her car.

CHAPTER 16

Conner was in the cage sparring with Zane when he caught Sabrina out of the corner of his eye. He held up a hand to keep Zane from knocking him flat and turned to face her.

She stood just inside the door talking to Joe, but glanced at him and gave a half grin.

What was she doing there?

They'd fought. Did she want to apologize? He hoped not because he owed *her* the apology, not the other way around. He'd worked out with weights before sparring with Zane and realized he was being an ass.

Actually, she looked a little distressed and glanced around the room as Joe walked away from her. He didn't head toward Conner, however, or even glance at him. He scurried to the other side of the gym and set his hand on Rider's arm.

Rider lifted his gaze toward the front door and nodded. As he set his weights down, he glanced at Conner with a furrowed brow.

"Is that Sabrina?" Zane asked.

"It is." Conner tugged off his gloves as he made his way to the gate.

"She looks kind of pale."

"I see that." Conner grabbed a towel and wiped his brow as he walked.

Joe led Sabrina into his office. Rider followed ahead of Conner. What the hell?

Conner caught up with Rider at a jog. "What's going on?"

"No idea. Joe said she asked to speak to me." Rider paused and turned toward Conner. "Maybe…"

"No fucking way. Don't even suggest it. I'm going in too."

"Of course you are." Rider kept going. He pulled the door open to the office and stepped inside with Conner on his heels.

Joe stood just inside. "I'll give you all some privacy." He shut the door with a soft snick as he left.

"Sabrina? Are you okay?" Conner kneeled in front of where she sat in a folding chair.

She looked like she was holding on by a thread, and the moment he met her gaze a tear slipped down her face. She shook her head.

Rider shut the blinds on the large window that normally allowed everyone in the gym to see into the office.

Conner took her hands in his. "Baby. What is it?"

He was aware of Rider leaning against the desk next to him. The office was small.

She lifted her face to Rider. "I'm sorry to bother you. I didn't know where else to go. And I thought you could help."

Rider grabbed a chair and pulled it up next to Conner. "Of course."

"What happened, baby?"

She glanced at Conner and then ducked her face. "I got an email."

"Okay."

"A threatening email. Warning me to stay away from you."

Conner flinched. "Seriously?"

"Yes." She lifted her face and bit her lower lip.

"Did it say who it was from?" Rider asked.

"No." She shook her head. Tears fell faster.

"God, baby. I'm so sorry." He ran one hand through his hair and held one of hers with the other. "This is so messed up."

He glanced up at Rider. "What the hell?"

"Dude, you have so many enemies right now, I can't even begin to sort this out." He looked at Sabrina. "Can you show us the email?" He rounded the desk to sit in Joe's chair and power up his computer.

"Yes. But there's more." Her voice was lower, almost too low.

Conner dipped his head, trying to catch her gaze. "What?"

"There's a zip file attached." She jerked her gaze to Rider, ignoring Conner. She spoke quickly. "I'll show you the email. I know you need to see it. But is there any way we could keep the attachment closed?"

"Why?" Conner gripped her hand tighter. "Sabrina. Look at me."

She took a deep breath, but her eyes were closed and she didn't meet his gaze. "Someone's been following us."

"Who? You and me?"

"Yes."

"And they took pictures. Is that what you mean?"

"Yes." She opened her eyes finally, more tears falling. "Do not open them in front of anyone. Please."

"It's just me and Rider, baby."

She shook her head vehemently. "Conner. No."

He stiffened. "Wait. Are you saying there are nude pictures of us?"

She nodded, biting her lip.

Rider jumped up and handed her a tissue from a box on the desk, leaning over to reach her. "Okay. Listen. No matter what, we're going to have to call this in, Sabrina. That's serious."

She nodded, sobbing now. "I know. That's why I came to you. I couldn't think straight, but Rider, I'm not kidding. I don't want anyone to see those pictures." She shivered. "Not even you."

Conner's blood boiled. What the hell? It seemed like ten thousand people were after him from several angles. And he had no idea why. He'd never done anything to anyone in his life. He needed to stay calm for Sabrina. She was hysterical, or at least had been. Her face was red from crying more than just the last few minutes. He pulled her head against his shoulder. "Sorry, baby. I'm a sweaty mess."

"Don't care," she mumbled, grabbing his biceps and holding on tight.

Finally, he released her. "I'll trade places with Rider and see for myself first. Okay?"

"Not really. But what choice do I have?"

Rider stood and swapped with Conner, circling the desk so the screen was out of his line of sight.

Conner handed Sabrina a post-it. "Write your email info on here so I can pull it up."

Her hand shook as she took the pen from him and jotted the information down on a sticky note.

A few minutes later he had her email open and clicked

on the anonymous message. It reminded him so much of the email threats he'd gotten at work, he had trouble remaining steady.

Sabrina ducked her head.

He could hear her breathing heavily. She didn't glance up at the screen while Conner read the email to Rider.

"Jesus," Rider said as Conner finished. "Have you told anyone else yet?"

"No. I called Emily to get your number, and she said you were here." She shrugged. "Maybe it was stupid and I should have called the police, but I didn't know what to do."

"It's okay." Rider set a hand on her shoulder. "You're here now." He kneeled beside her. "But we need to take this to the station. Especially if there are photos."

"I'm going to open them now," Conner announced.

"I'd rather you didn't," Sabrina mumbled. She rubbed both temples with her fingers.

It took a moment for the pictures to pop up, and then the screen was filled with a slide show of the two of them together. He breathed heavily, thinking about some asshole following him around taking pictures of them at Extreme and then the arena. And then his breath caught in his throat. "Fuck." His heart raced. He wanted to punch a hole in the nearest wall. "Son of a bitch."

"I guess we'll definitely be taking this in to the station," Rider concluded. "I'm going to jump in the shower. I'll give you two a few minutes alone." He slipped from the room without waiting for a response, shutting the door behind him.

Conner quickly shut down the email, making sure the pictures weren't saved to the hard drive. He deleted the download file and checked everywhere to make sure Joe or anyone else who sat at the desk couldn't find them. He even checked the trashcan to make sure they weren't there either.

When he was satisfied, he scooted back and rounded the desk to take Sabrina in his arms. "I'm so sorry, baby." His actions and his words didn't match the rage he felt inside. But she didn't need him to wig out right then. She needed him to hold her.

She cried some more and finally wiped her eyes with the back of her hand. "Go shower," she muttered. "I'll wait here." She lifted her gaze. "You don't think the owner will mind, do you?"

"Joe? Of course not. I'll speak to him on the way by. He's the nicest man you'll ever meet. Like a father figure. He has taken all us on like we're family. And he'll feel the same about you once he gets to know you."

She blinked at him.

"Don't give me that look." He kissed her lips gently. "I know we fought earlier. I was an ass. I'm sorry. We'll talk about it later, but this?" He pointed back toward the computer. "This is not going to break us."

She nodded, clearly not sure she agreed.

And that was fine. Conner would make her see reason. It would just take time.

CHAPTER 17

Sabrina sat in a private room at the police station with Conner by her side, holding her hand, and Rider across the desk with another man she'd just met.

His name was Jacobson, and he was a sergeant. "So, we tried to track the email, Ms. Duluth, but we've been unsuccessful so far. Whoever sent this covered their bases. It's someone who either knows a lot about computers or knows someone else who does. We'll have someone in the department work on it. See if we can crack it. I can't promise anything. It's hard to keep up with technology these days."

Sabrina nodded. She was numb. Everything was a blur. Someone had printed out the email. To her knowledge, no one had opened the attachment. "Can you keep the attachment unopened?" she pleaded.

"I'm sorry, but a limited number of people are going to need to see the pictures in order to investigate this."

She nodded, fighting fresh tears. She couldn't do this. She couldn't.

Conner put an arm around her and held her closer. It didn't help. She was holding on by a thread.

Jacobson spoke again. "I'll have Maria come in. Perhaps having a woman will help. She's very understanding and a great asset in these situations."

Conner responded to him. "Sounds good. Thanks."

Jacobson left the room while Rider handed her another tissue. "Sorry, Sabrina. I wish there was another way."

She lifted her gaze to Conner. "Maria? She's a stranger. I just can't do this. It would almost be better for Rider to see them."

Rider cleared his throat. "Unfortunately that wouldn't do any good. I'm not assigned to this case, Sabrina. I'm a street cop. I don't investigate this type of crime. This needs to be handled by the organized crime bureau."

She jerked her gaze to Conner as Rider slipped from the room, leaving the two of them alone. "What's he talking about? Why on earth would this require an investigation from the organized crime department? Isn't that like mafia guys and stuff?"

Conner nodded. "Yeah." He blew out a breath. "Since Anton Yenin has been hounding me, we have to treat any threat as possibly originating from him and his men."

"Shit." She fiddled with the tissue in her lap. "This is a disaster." She stood, separating herself from Conner to pace the tiny room.

"I'm so sorry."

She didn't respond. Half of her wondered if she shouldn't just take the email at face value and walk away. Too bad if Conner was the hottest man she'd ever met and could make her body sing like nobody would ever be able to compete with. Perhaps that wasn't enough. Not if mafia guys were going to start hanging around threatening her. Or hell, jealous ex-girlfriends.

She didn't meet his gaze.

When the door opened, she flinched and spun around to face the newcomer.

A tall woman in uniform with thick brown hair pulled back in a low ponytail smiled and held out a hand. "Hi. I'm Maria Contreras. Sorry to have to meet you under such circumstances."

Sabrina shook her hand. "Me too."

Conner introduced himself and shook her hand also.

"We can do this whatever way is most comfortable for you." Maria addressed Sabrina directly. "Just the two of us or with your boyfriend." She rounded the table and sat on the far side, tugging a laptop out of her shoulder bag to set it on the table.

Sabrina winced. Did she want Conner in the room?

"I'm in the pictures too," he said. "They are of both of us."

"I understand that, sir. But my job is to handle this in whatever way will make Ms. Duluth most comfortable. If it's easier for her to work alone, then that's what we'll do."

Oh, shit. Now she had to make a decision. She chewed her lower lip while she stared at Conner.

He swallowed finally and stood. "I'll step out, baby. If it makes you more comfortable." He wrapped his arms around her and held her tight for a brief moment.

She shook her head. "No. Stay. We need to face this together."

Conner smiled wanly and pulled out the chair Sabrina had vacated.

She resumed her seat as he sat next to her once again.

Maria grabbed a pad and pencil from the corner of the desk. "Is there anything you'd like to tell me before we open the pictures? Anything that will make it easier?"

Sabrina cleared her throat. "We uh…"

Conner squeezed her hand. "We practice BDSM," he offered. "We're consenting adults. Nothing happens between us we don't agree on. However, someone managed to get several photos we'd rather didn't exist."

"I understand." She set a hand on the table, reaching across but not touching. "Trust me. I've seen all sorts of things working here. A few pictures of consenting adults having sex is not going to ruffle my feathers."

Sabrina didn't think these photos would be described as "consenting adults having sex," but she didn't say anything. She nodded. "Let's just get this over with."

"Okay." Maria turned the computer around to face Sabrina. "I'll let you pull up the email."

Sabrina's hands quivered as she clicked on the keys, opening the nasty email for the third time today. She'd be glad when she no longer had to look at those pictures.

Maria stood and pulled her chair around so they could all see. She flanked Sabrina on one side while Conner sat on her other side.

When the pictures popped up, Sabrina relinquished the mouse to Maria, who hit pause on the first one and asked for details.

Maria took a lot of notes while Sabrina and Conner described where they'd been for each photo. She tried to determine the angle of the photographer to discern where he or she might have been standing.

Sabrina braced herself as the screen switched to the one of her over Conner's lap.

Conner set a hand on her back. "Breathe, baby. It's going to be okay."

She jerked her gaze from the photo to him. "How? How the hell is this going to be okay?"

He winced.

"Conner, some asshole took nude pictures of me

letting you do lewd things in your home and mine. For all we know, he has two thousand pictures. I'm mortified beyond belief. How am I supposed to explain this to my family if it gets out? My parents?" She ran her hand over her eyes again. "Mom, Dad, yeah, this is my new boyfriend, the one you already know because his face is plastered all over the Internet spanking and plugging my *ass!*"

Lucky for Conner, he didn't placate her. If he had said one word in contradiction, she might have slapped him.

"I know this is hard," Maria said softly. "Let's get through the details, and then you won't have to look again."

"Yeah, well, it doesn't really matter now because I'll never be able to get the vision of those pictures out of my mind. I can't imagine being able to sleep again in this lifetime, either."

Maria took her hand and squeezed briefly. "I'm so sorry, hon."

Sabrina stared back at the screen and described how she knew where that picture had been taken between the slats of her blinds.

By the time they flipped to the next photo, she spoke hastily through renewed tears as they fell down her face. The look of actual arousal in her eyes while Conner pushed that plug into her made her want to scream.

Conner took over, explaining where his bedroom window was located and that apparently the curtains hadn't been completely closed at his home, either. That shot in his bedroom was taken from the back of the house inside the fenced backyard. He was livid as he explained where the photographer had to have been standing.

Sabrina stared at her expression the entire time. She remembered how aroused she'd been at that moment.

Would she ever be able to relax again enough to reach that level of arousal?

How many years would have to go by before she would be willing to have sex with any man in any location? It seemed like she would never feel safe again.

She'd never been raped, and she wondered how much deeper that level of violation must feel. Because right now, she wanted to fall into a crack in the floor and die.

Maria finished her notes, shut down the computer, and turned to face Sabrina, taking her hand again. "Sabrina, I'm so sorry this happened to you. I know you must feel very vulnerable. And that's totally understandable. I recommend you see your physician and get a prescription to help you sleep. You might have trouble shutting down your mind for a few days. If it persists, you'll need to seek counseling."

Sabrina nodded. She was so tired. She wanted to go home.

No. She didn't want to go home. She didn't know where she wanted to go, but not to her house where some fucktard had taken advantage of her privacy. And certainly not to Conner's house. She would call a friend. Dana. They'd been friends for a long time. Dana would let her stay at her house.

Except shit. She didn't want to explain this situation to a living soul.

Dammit.

Conner stood and shook Maria's hand. "Thank you for your kindness."

The door closed with a snick, leaving Conner and Sabrina alone again.

She didn't have the energy to face him. "Can you take me back to my car? I want to be alone."

"No." He leaned against the door and waited for her to face him from the chair.

"What? Conner, don't mess around. I'm tired."

"Your car's at my house. That's where I had some of the guys take it when we left the gym."

Right. She'd given him her keys and rode to the police station in his car.

"Fine. Take me there. I need to get my car."

"You aren't going to take off on me and go off by yourself, Sabrina."

"Yes, actually, I am." She stood, wiping her hands on her jeans and facing him head on.

He shook his head. "I know you're mad. You have every right to be angry. Hell, you had every right to be pissed off before the email came. I'll grant you that. But you're my submissive, and there's no way in hell I'm going to let you traipse off alone right now. It's not safe. And besides, I want to be near you."

She planted her hands on her hips. "Conner, you don't own me. I'm telling you *no*."

"Stay at my place."

"Not a chance in hell."

"Okay. Good point. Then let's go to a hotel."

"How is that going to help? Do you think I'll feel safe at a hotel?"

Conner pulled out his phone and tapped a few buttons, never taking his gaze off her. After a few seconds, he spoke. "Rafe. Hey... Yeah, I guess you heard we had a bit of a problem... No, she's fine. She's standing right in front of me... Yes... No... Listen, do you think you could spare a few rooms in your basement for the night? Or maybe a few days... Yes. I'd appreciate it... Okay... Right. Thanks. We'll be there in a bit."

She planted her hands on her hips. The audacity of this

man. "Seriously, Conner. You're steam rolling right over me."

"Do you have a better idea?"

She glared daggers at him.

"I didn't think so. Neither of us would feel comfortable in our own homes tonight. You aren't interested in a hotel. I'm betting you don't want to explain this situation to any of your friends. So, that leaves Rafe. I chose him because he and Katy have an enormous home with a finished basement. No windows. You can sleep knowing no one can possibly take your picture. And they have more than one room down there, so you can have one all to yourself if you're too pissed at me to share my bed."

Damn. Why did he have to make so much sense?

Finally, exasperated and with no better option, she consented. "Okay."

"Excellent. We'll stop by your place and grab some clothes and then mine." He opened the door to the room and stepped into the hall.

It was late afternoon as she followed him to the car. She hadn't eaten since lunch, but she knew if she even considered swallowing, her stomach would revolt.

They rode in silence to her place where she hastily gathered several things and put them in an overnight bag. She also grabbed her computer. If she didn't find a way to work tomorrow, she was going to fall too far behind. Though at the moment, the concept of editing a novel seemed entirely foreign to her.

At Conner's place, she waited impatiently by the door to the garage, refusing to step farther into the house. He was quick. And he insisted she leave her car and ride with him.

She was too tired to argue.

CHAPTER 18

"Do you want to stop and get something to eat first?"

Sabrina stared at him from her spot squished against the passenger door. "No."

"I'm sure you haven't eaten since lunch, baby."

She flinched when he called her *baby*. She wasn't in the mood for him to be nice. She was nursing a full-fledged tantrum. And she deserved it.

"Stop if you want. I'm not hungry."

He pulled through a drive thru and ordered chicken strips and fries, the largest order. And then he stopped in a parking place in front of the fast-food restaurant.

Thank God. She didn't want to face people. She sure as shit didn't want to go into an establishment and try to eat.

The chicken smelled good though, and her stomach rumbled loudly when he opened the bag.

He smiled at her when she glanced up. "I ordered plenty. Please. Try to eat something."

She took a chicken strip and managed to bite into it, awakening her taste buds as she chewed. It was fresh, and it was good. She managed to eat the entire strip and a few of his fries.

He didn't pressure her to talk, and as soon as they were done, he pulled back out onto the road.

She noticed he frequently glanced in the rearview mirror, undoubtedly making sure no one was following them.

It took only ten minutes for them to arrive at Rafe and Katy's house. It was a gorgeous two-story that sat nestled in a quaint neighborhood.

Katy met them at the door, smiling. "Come in." She gave Sabrina a brief hug and nodded behind her. "I'll show you around the basement. You can make yourselves at home. There's plenty of space."

Sabrina followed her down the steps with Conner at her heels, grateful that Katy seemed to have been briefed at least enough to not ask any questions. Sabrina couldn't remember if Rafe had been at the gym that afternoon or not, but in any case, among this obviously tight-knit fight club, word would have gotten around.

Katy flipped on lights as she went down a short hall. "Bedroom. Bathroom. Another bedroom. Living room." She held out her arms to encompass the enormous comfortable space that contained a large-screen television, huge comfy couches, and a wet bar. "If you need anything at all, holler." She squeezed Sabrina's hand on the way by and left them alone without another word.

Sabrina turned toward Conner, feeling slightly chagrined at the way she was treating him. But she was too exhausted to get into it with him. She needed to be alone. "I'll take the smaller bedroom." She passed him on her way by, grateful he didn't try to stop her.

After quickly changing into an oversized T-shirt, she

slipped between the covers of the queen-sized bed and curled up in a ball.

Her mind raced. Someone was following them. Hopefully they hadn't managed to track them to Rafe and Katy's home. Sabrina would feel awful if anything happened while they were guests in someone else's house.

It was a fact she felt better in a room with no windows. It was pitch dark with the door shut and the lights turned out. She listened as water ran in the bathroom next to her and then heard another door open and close.

Tears fell again. She couldn't stop them. This wasn't her life. She was an editor, for crying out loud. The most excitement she'd ever had in twenty-six years had been the time she got a speeding ticket in a school zone. That was as close as she'd come to any interaction with the police. Filing a stalker report wasn't on her bucket list.

She buried her face in her pillow for a few minutes, fighting the urge to scream.

Fighting the loneliness.

Fighting the need to snuggle up next to Conner and let him hold her.

Losing every battle.

She was supposed to be mad at him. He stomped out of her house that afternoon, unwilling to take a threat from the Russian mafia seriously. Or maybe that was just how she perceived his reaction. Surely he wasn't blasé about that Dmitry guy warning him about some Russian mob guy.

She flipped onto her back and closed her eyes, inhaling slowly several times. If she could just control her breathing.

In.

Out.

In.

Out.

Was Conner asleep? Did he have the same level of anxiety she suffered from? Was he even concerned? She couldn't be sure. He'd treated her with kid gloves all afternoon. But was the threat as serious to him as it was to her? After the way he seemed to blow off their encounter with Dmitry at lunch, she couldn't know for sure what he might be feeling.

Time ticked by in silence while she stared at nothing in the darkness, unable to close her eyes.

Finally, her bladder protested, and she eased out of bed, tiptoed across the room, and slipped into the hall as quietly as possible. A small night light in the bathroom led her way. She used the toilet, splashed water on her face, and took a drink from the spout.

When she stepped back into the hall, Conner was leaning against the opposite wall. He wore low hung sleep pants and nothing else. He took her breath away. "You okay, baby?" His voice was deep, concerned.

She nodded. They stood in silence for a long time. Finally, he reached out a hand.

She stared at it for a moment. If she went to him, she would be opening herself up to incredible vulnerability. If she didn't, she would never know if he was capable of handling her the way she deserved.

She took a breath and stepped into his embrace. He wrapped his arms around her and hauled her against his front. His chest smelled fantastic, and she took a moment to simply inhale his scent while he nuzzled his face in her hair. "I'm so sorry, baby. Please forgive me."

"For what exactly?" she asked his chest.

"For walking out on you earlier instead of talking it out. For not being there when you opened that damn email." He smoothed his hands up her back, over her shoulders, and across her cheeks until he nudged her away from his chest and held her face back to look into her eyes. "For falling so hard for you I can't find it in myself to let you go, even though I know this situation is ugly and could get uglier before it's over."

She sucked in a breath. *Wow.*

"If I were a better man, I'd tell you to stay away from me, but I'm not. I'm in so deep I can't do it. I want you near me any way you'll allow. If it means sleeping in separate bedrooms in Rafe's basement for the foreseeable future, I'm okay with that. Whatever it takes to ensure you're safe while keeping you close."

When he eased the grip he had on her cheeks, she leaned her forehead against his chest. "Would you mind if I slept in your bed? I can't relax alone."

He squeezed her tighter and then led her to his bedroom. He didn't shut the door to the hall, so the faint light from the bathroom was enough for her to make out the furniture.

Conner held the covers back and helped her climb in. And then he slipped alongside her and hauled her back against his front, wrapping his top arm around her and setting his lips on the sensitive skin behind her ear. "Thank you, baby."

She closed her eyes, trying to relax her racing heart.

She could feel his erection against her ass. There was no way to hide it.

And contrary to what she would have chosen, her nipples hardened as they grazed against the cotton of her T-shirt where his forearm stretched across her chest.

Conner kissed her neck gently. "Rest. We're safe here."

He was a genius, coming up with this plan to hide out where there were no windows and she could sleep without worry of some photographer snapping a shot of her in bed.

"Thank you," she mumbled as she let sleep drag her under.

～

It was dark when Sabrina opened her eyes. For a moment, she was disoriented. And then the memory of what had happened slammed into her.

How long had she been asleep?

"You okay?" Her gaze shifted to the man hovering over her. Conner. He brushed a lock of hair from her face and cupped her cheek.

"What time is it?"

"About two."

"In the morning?"

He grinned. "Yes."

She groaned. "I didn't sleep long."

"No. You must have been having a bad dream. You startled me as you gasped awake."

She didn't remember any dream. Probably a good thing.

She closed her eyes and leaned into Conner, setting her cheek on his chest. "This situation is a disaster."

He threaded his fingers in her hair and let the strands fall between each finger. It felt good. Soothing. "I know."

"Have you slept?"

"No."

She figured as much. "What time do you have to be at work?"

"Nine. I have office hours and then two classes. Will you stay here while I'm gone?"

She hadn't thought that far. She sat up and faced him, taking in his expression from the dim light. "I can't stay here forever, Conner. I have a life."

"I know." He continued playing with a lock of her hair. "Stay today at least. Let me think. I need to figure this out."

"Okay."

"Thank you." He let out a breath and pulled her on top of him. "I know we haven't been together that long, and we've had a rocky start, but I'd feel better if you would let me keep you safe. I have no idea who's behind this shit, but I intend to find out. If I had to worry about your safety on top of everything else, I don't think I could function."

"Okay," she repeated. She could work from here today. After she got more sleep.

Conner hugged her tighter and seemed to loosen up. Had he been lying there worrying about her safety all this time?

She felt bad about that. He didn't need her being defiant and contrary on top of everything else. For once, she vowed to play the obedient submissive for a day. She almost chuckled internally at the thought of not arguing with him or cussing in his presence.

This should be interesting...

～

The next time Sabrina woke up, it was to the hum of a cell phone nearby.

She glanced around. She was alone. The shower was running next door.

A phone buzzed again.

She reached for the bedside table and nabbed the phone before she realized it wasn't hers. It was Conner's. He had texts messages coming in rapidly. She tried not to look at them.

The clock on the nightstand said seven thirty this time. At least she'd slept a few hours.

Pulling herself out of bed as the water shut off in the bathroom, she took the phone with her and padded toward the bathroom.

"Hey, baby." Conner smiled as she rounded the corner.

"Do you always leave the bathroom door open?"

"I wanted you to feel like you could come in if you needed."

She held out the phone, warmed by the idea he'd been thinking of her. "Your phone's been beeping. You have a lot of action this morning."

He leaned toward her and kissed her forehead as he took it. Shocking her, he grabbed her waist with both hands, even the one holding the phone, and lifted her onto the counter.

"Conner... What are you doing?"

"I have to leave soon. Sit with me while I get ready."

She squeezed her legs together. He smelled so good and he looked like a god standing there in nothing but a towel, his hair dripping onto his shoulders and running off the shield tattoo and across his chest. She licked her lips at the vision. It was too early to be turned on by this man. She wasn't a morning person. But she wasn't a dead person, either. He was hot.

Conner scanned through the messages. "Jesus," he muttered.

"You're popular before eight. No one texts me this early." She grinned at him.

"Yeah, well, no one wants to be this kind of popular. Three of them are from Tina Chang, that professor I told you wants in my pants." He picked up his razor as he spoke. "The others are from the dean. I need to leave early and meet with her before my office hours." He cringed as he spoke but didn't glance at Sabrina.

"Does the dean want a piece of you also?" she teased. At least she thought she did.

He glanced her way for a second. "Yeah, for totally different reasons, however. I'm pretty sure she's gay. I don't think she wants to fuck me." He smiled, but it didn't quite reach far enough to be believable, and then he changed the subject. "Can you work from here today?"

"Of course. All I do is read smut, you know. It's not important." She narrowed her gaze at him, hoping to get him at least a little fired up. She preferred him a little edgy over this new cool, fake nothing. Their morning banter was simulated.

"Ha ha." He set the razor down, rinsed his face, and then turned to step in front of her. "Spread your legs, baby."

His words made her arousal shoot sky high as he nudged her knees and slipped between them, tugging her closer until his cock pressed against her pussy from behind the towel.

He took her face in his hands and tipped it up to meet her gaze. "I give in. You win. I'm sure your job is legit."

"You better say that. It's possible I make more money than you. So don't knock it. Plus, as an added bonus, I love what I do. Now, you need to get out of here so I can do it. I'm behind. I have clients waiting on me."

He brushed her hair from her face. "Do you think you can work comfortably here today without stressing?" His face was scrunched with concern.

"We'll see. Sometimes, even under the worst of circumstances, I can bury myself in a manuscript and block out the world." She licked her lips. "Although, I will say, I've never been stalked before by a crazy person who took lewd pictures of me and then threatened to pass them around if I didn't stop dating some guy."

One side of his mouth quirked up in a half grin. "Some guy?" He yanked her closer until her ass barely rested on the edge of the counter. His hands wandered down her body, grabbed the hem of her T-shirt, and yanked it over her head before she knew what he was up to.

His lips landed on a nipple the next second, knocking the wind out of her, and she arched into his mouth.

"Some guy?" he muttered against her chest, slinking down her body, leaving a trail of kisses along her belly until he reached her panties. He clamped his mouth over her pussy and sucked through the thin lace.

Sabrina moaned as her need grew fast. How did he have this power over her? She was supposed to be ticked with him still. But it was impossible to be very angry when he reached under her panties and finger fucked her hard.

"You mean the guy who has you on the counter with your legs spread open and your pussy dripping wet with need? That guy?"

"Yes," she uttered breathily. She gripped his shoulders to keep from falling backward and banging her head on the mirror.

"Mmm." He hooked his fingers in the sides of her panties then and tugged them down, forcing her legs together to get them off.

And then she was naked…on the counter…in the basement…of some friends of his she barely knew.

And Conner dipped his face between her legs once again, grabbing her thighs and pressing them wide. His tongue plunged into her pussy, his nose bumping her clit.

She didn't have any purchase to thrust upward with her legs hanging down the sides of the counter. Completely at his mercy, she gasped as his fingers teased her clit and then pinched it. And then he traded his mouth for the fingers, sucking her swollen nub between his lips and fucking her pussy with three fingers.

"Oh, God. Conner..." She stiffened as her arousal climbed fast. She needed him inside her. "Please..."

He didn't stop. In fact, he increased his efforts and thrust his hand harder. His breath landed across her wetness as he mumbled against her. "Come for me, baby. I need to taste you."

That was all it took. Her clit pulsed as he covered it with his mouth again. She dug her nails into his shoulders, unable to keep from marking him.

If he noticed, he didn't care.

When she finally relaxed against him, he pulled back and smiled up at her. "Good morning." He licked his lips.

Sabrina nearly collapsed. Thank God she was holding on to him still, or she would have. She felt like Jell-O.

Conner steadied her with both hands at her waist and lifted her off the counter. "You okay?" he asked as he set his forehead against hers.

"No."

His smile widened. "Good. Then I've done my job." He eased back. "I have to go. I'll call you between classes. Text me if you need me."

She nodded. He was going to leave her there... Naked... Legs wobbly... Nowhere close to sated...

She could hear him chuckling as he walked away.

Sabrina took a deep breath and stepped over to the shower. The room was still filled with steam. She flipped the water back on and then shut the bathroom door.

Might as well get some work done as long as I'm up anyway.

CHAPTER 19

Conner took his seat in the dean's office at eight thirty. She was alone this time.

Dean Sheffield cleared her throat. "We got another round of emails this weekend."

"I bet you did." Conner stiffened.

"What makes you say that?" she asked.

"I've had a pile of problems myself this weekend. It appears someone is stalking me. I had to go to the police yesterday."

"Oh, God. I'm so sorry."

"Yeah, you and me both. And my girlfriend." He pursed his lips. "Please tell me you didn't receive pictures of us."

Dean Sheffield gritted her teeth in a wince. She opened a folder, pulled out the top paper, and laid it in front of Conner.

Conner slumped back in his chair in relief. It was the shot of the two of them in his car at the arena. "Is this the only one you got?"

"Yes." She cocked her head to one side and narrowed her gaze. "Are there others?"

"There are. This one is harmless, but some are not. I would appreciate it if you didn't open any attachments in the future. Trust me. You would regret it if some of the pictures I've seen are sent to you."

"Conner? Who's the woman? The email claims she's a student. There's no way for us to determine that from this picture. It's too blurry and taken from too far away through a car window."

"You're going to have to take my word for it. She's not a student." There was no reason to admit she had been. He wasn't currently breaking any rules, so the point was moot.

"Is she your girlfriend then?"

"Yes. And I have no idea why someone's trying to convince you I'm breaking any moral codes here. I am *not*. I never have been. Believe me, these people have plenty of other pictures that would give you a much better view of her face. They've chosen this one on purpose for some reason, probably because they either know she isn't a student or aren't positive."

"It would help if you told me who she is. That way we could at least eliminate the possibility." Dean Sheffield leaned forward.

Conner stared at her, making a decision. "I'd rather not."

"Why?"

"Because she's been through enough dealing with this. I don't want her dragged into another interrogation. I'd rather leave her out of this."

Dean Sheffield blew out a breath. "That's not very forthcoming, Dr. Bascott."

"I realize that. But my decision stands. She isn't a student at this university. I don't want her name being dragged through the dirt."

A few seconds of silence passed before Dean Sheffield spoke again. "What's going on, Conner?"

Ah, so now she wanted to get friendly and switch to his first name. "I don't know. And I'm being honest when I say that."

"Someone wants to get you fired."

"That seems pretty obvious."

"You have the police involved now, so that should help."

"I hope. But until someone manages to trace where these emails are coming from, I don't have much to go on."

"Maybe the police will crack that." Dean Sheffield stood. "I'll let you get back to work. I know you have classes to teach today. Please, keep me informed, will you?" She held out a hand, and Conner shook it as he stood.

"I will. If I find out anything, I'll let you know." Conner left the office and made his way back to his building at a quick pace. His office hours started in five minutes.

As soon as he rounded the corner in his building, pulling out his keys, he found Angelica Hudson already waiting with a huge smile on her face.

Shit. He'd forgotten she intended to return this morning. She was the last person he felt like dealing with. The girl rubbed him wrong. It seemed lately she came to him for no apparent reason. All he needed on top of everything else was a student with a crush on him.

"Good morning, Dr. Bascott. I've got the first draft of my paper worked out." She followed him into his office and took a seat across from him as he set his briefcase down next to his desk and plopped onto his chair.

"Good. Let's see what you've got." He needed to focus. This was his job. But dammit, this girl was not quite right. Her shirt was too tight, and her cleavage was hanging out for anyone to ogle. Conner had less than no interest in her chest. Again.

When she leaned forward and set her forearms on the corner of his desk, he was sure she was putting him on. Really? Who did that?

He ignored her and took the pages from her hand.

She had done the work. Maybe she just didn't have good fashion sense.

"Do you have the outline with you?"

She pulled it out. "Sure."

He needed to look it over. He hadn't paid much attention to it the first time. "Need a refresher." He tried to smile as he took the page and glanced down the front.

She wasn't a brilliant student by any stretch of the imagination, but she did have a good premise. And the rough draft at least followed the guidelines.

"This is a good start. Make sure you're backing up all your facts and you have enough to support your theory."

"Okay. Thanks." She didn't move from the chair as he handed her both sets of papers back. "Are you okay, Dr. Bascott? You seem distracted."

"I'm fine." He smiled. "I'll see you in class this afternoon?"

"Of course." She grinned as she stood. Was it his imagination, or did she make an effort to adjust her breasts as she prepared to leave?

She stared at him for several seconds, her mouth opening as if she intended to say something else. But then she closed her mouth and pursed her lips as she turned around and left.

He exhaled as the door shut behind her. Jesus. He ran a hand through his hair. He needed to get a grip.

To distract himself before class, he opened his computer and worked on lesson plans for the next few weeks. When he finished, he opened his email.

Fuck.

He recognized the sender immediately. The same anonymous address as he'd seen on the dean's email and also Sabrina's. He hesitated a moment before clicking the button to open it.

Dr. Bascott,

You are treading on thin ice. You might want to reconsider some of the choices you are making, or you will find yourself losing everything you hold dear.

Sincerely,

A friend

"A friend, my ass," he muttered. "Dammit." What the hell was this all about? Who was trying to frame him and get him fired? And why?

His mind was preoccupied all afternoon as he taught two classes and then trudged to his car. He'd forwarded the email to Sargent Jacobson to add to the file from yesterday.

As he folded himself behind the wheel, he caught the glimpse of someone coming toward him out of the corner of his eye. "Fuck," he muttered.

Professor Chang approached at a near jog, waving her hands in the air. Just what he didn't need today on top of everything else. She was out of breath when she reached his side and leaned both hands on the frame of his car to gaze at him where he sat.

"Tina, I'm kinda in a hurry. Can this wait?" *Forever.*

She shook her head. "I just heard the news. I'm so sorry."

"What news?" Okay, so she piqued his curiosity. However, he for sure didn't need any more news.

She shook her head. "Someone's trying to get you fired."

He gripped the steering wheel with both hands. Great.

How many people knew about this? "You already knew this. You received the emails yourself. What's new?"

"The rumors are growing by the minute. Conner. Be honest with me. Did you sleep with a student?"

Shit. "Of course not, Tina."

"Listen, Conner." She leaned into the car farther, her breasts at his eye level.

What is it with women and their damn breasts today?

"If you need anything… I mean maybe I can help." She grabbed his tie and gave it a sharp tug. "An alibi or something."

Shock didn't begin to describe his reaction. Tina Chang was offering to say she had slept with him? His ears started ringing with anger. For all he knew, Tina set the entire thing up herself so she could rescue him and get in his pants.

He shook his head and grabbed his tie higher up to yank it from her hand. "I really have to go, Tina." He actually had to shove her a bit forcefully to get her out of the way so he could shut the car door. And without looking back, he sped away.

His heart pounded as he made his way through the streets of Vegas toward the gym. He couldn't possibly go back to Rafe's yet. He was fuming with aggravation. If he didn't burn some of it off, it would ruin the tentative hold he had on his relationship with Sabrina.

"Fuck." *Sabrina.* He pounded a fist on the steering wheel. Maybe he should let her go? His world was insane. Somebody wanted him fired. And that same somebody obviously didn't want her in his life.

A punching bag would do him wonders.

He whipped his car around every corner until he zipped into a parking spot at the gym and climbed out of the Mustang. Slamming the door, he rounded the hood and stomped toward the back entrance.

Joe glanced up as Conner entered. He paid the man no attention. Not even a nod. It wasn't like him to ignore the gym owner, who was not only his trainer but his friend. But Conner didn't have it in him to face anyone.

Not until he punched the fuck out of something intangible. And perhaps not even then.

In minutes, he had changed clothes and made his way to the back corner of the main room to tackle one of the enormous punching bags hanging from the ceiling.

No one bothered him. Thank God. There weren't very many people in the gym at this hour. Most arrived later in the evening. It was only four thirty.

He didn't know how long he fought against the bag before a hand landed on his shoulder. "Dude. Why didn't you at least put gloves on?"

Conner jerked his gaze to find Zane staring at his hands. "Fuck." Conner's knuckles were a bloody mess, and he hadn't even noticed. He was also breathing heavily. Sweat poured down his face.

Zane gripped his shoulder and nudged him backward. "Let me look at that." He didn't ask a question. The man was an EMT. When he used that tone with anyone, they didn't balk. Including Conner. Besides, he was completely spent.

He staggered backward and dropped into a folding chair along the wall. "Did Joe call you?"

"Yep." Zane kneeled in front of Conner and lifted his left hand. He had a bag of supplies next to him. He was prepared. How long had he been watching? "Hold this." He lifted a shallow bowl up and nudged Conner's other hand with it.

Conner winced as he took the edge and held it under his left hand.

Zane poured something clear over his knuckles. It wasn't fucking water, either. It stung like a mother fucker. Zane chuckled. "He lives."

"What's that supposed to mean?"

"I thought maybe you were a robot the way you were going after the punching bag. I was wondering how long you might continue the battle before you realized you were bleeding." He dabbed at the wounds with a piece of gauze, not lifting his gaze and not asking any questions.

When he was satisfied with that hand, he switched to the other. "The shower is going to sting like a bitch, dude."

Conner winced again as Zane poured more of the evil liquid over his right hand. The pain was actually welcome. It temporarily distracted him from reality.

When Zane was finished, he set the bowl on the floor and took a seat in the chair next to Conner. "Wanna talk about it?"

"Not really. You can get the gist of the story from Rider and Gage. I'm in no mood."

"Yeah. I figured they knew what was going on with you, but I didn't want to pry into it without your permission."

Conner lifted his gaze. "We're a team here. The Fight Club." He gave a wry half smile. "Pry away." He stood then and walked to the locker room. The shower called to him. And he needed to face Sabrina soon. Though what he was going to say to her was a mystery.

CHAPTER 20

"What happened to your hands?"

Conner tried to smile at Sabrina as he stepped into Rafe's kitchen. He shrugged. "No big deal. I forgot to wear gloves."

"You forgot? How is that possible, Conner?" She had a knife in her hand and a cutting board under her wrists. The huge wooden board was covered with vegetables. She immediately set the knife aside and turned around to wash and dry her hands.

Rafe sat at the other side of the island nursing a beer, apparently watching Katy and Sabrina cook.

Conner strode directly to his friends' refrigerator and grabbed a beer. He downed half of it before he faced Sabrina again. She stared at him with a narrowed gaze. "We should talk," she mumbled.

"Yes." He took a deep breath. He wasn't stable enough to face her yet. "But can it wait? I've had a long day. I need to catch my breath."

Sabrina took his arm in her hand and squeezed. "No it

can't fucking wait," she gritted out, tugging him toward the stairs.

Oh goody.

He followed her reluctantly down the steps, shutting the door behind him. He didn't figure there was any way in hell they would be keeping their voices down, but at least the barrier would possibly keep Rafe and Katy from having to listen to their exact words.

When Sabrina spun around on him in the huge downstairs living room, she set her hands on her hips and nailed him with her gaze. Yep. She was livid. "You never even called the entire day."

Shit. She was right about that. He had said he would call. He opened his mouth, but she cut him off with a shake of her head.

"Do you have any idea what I've been through today?"

He flinched. He hoped nothing. He hoped she'd been here in Rafe's home editing quietly.

"I didn't think so." She glanced at his hands. "While you were off punching the fuck out of something—at least I hope it was something and not someone—I was at the police station half the day dealing with the next round of emails."

He startled. *Fuck.* He stepped forward.

She held up a hand, palm out. "Don't even think about it. I'm exhausted. Way too tired to fight with you, and I don't want any part of you to touch me right now."

He cleared his throat. "I know you're pissed. You have every right to be."

"Pissed? That doesn't come close to how I feel."

"Sabrina…" He backed up a few paces and fell into a giant cozy arm chair, downing the rest of his beer as he did so.

She didn't say anything else.

"You do realize this is exactly what the person wants, right?" he asked.

"What person? What are you talking about?"

"Whoever is sending these emails. Hell, whoever is fucking with me at work. Jesus, even your keyed car might have something to do with this. Someone doesn't want us together." And that wasn't the half of it. Someone wanted him fired. He just hadn't yet put it all together to see how it was connected.

"Well, whoever it is can have their way. I'm done." She threw up her hands and stomped into the bedroom she'd used last night before coming to him.

He gripped the empty beer can so hard it crumpled, cutting his fingers in a few new places. Finally, he pulled himself to standing and strode over to the doorway where she was stuffing her belongings into her overnight bag. She didn't pay any attention to him.

"You're right. You should go." It took every ounce of courage he had to say that. It wasn't that he didn't want her. He would give anything to storm across the room, throw her on the bed, spank her ass for doubting him, and then fuck her senseless.

But for now, he needed to let her go. And he needed her to think it was over. It was the only way he could deal with this shitstorm of a world he'd fallen into without taking her down as a casualty.

He knew if he let her go home and didn't follow her or contact her in any way, whoever was stalking her would leave her alone. It wasn't about her. It was about him.

He had no idea why, but somehow he needed her to think this was over so she would be safe. "This isn't going to work between us. All we do is fight. It's how we started out."

She inhaled sharply, her fingers hesitating as she

jammed her clothes into her bag. A sniffle made him stiffen. If she started to cry...

She held it together, sort of. Though he hated the thought of her driving. He would get Rafe to take her to his house to get her car. His chest literally hurt. Is this what it felt like to have a broken heart?

No, he realized. Whatever Sabrina was feeling was a broken heart. Not him. He knew he was totally head over heels for her. Falling so hard that those three little words he'd never said to a woman in his life hovered on the tip of his tongue.

But this was for the best. For now. All he could do was hope when the storm settled, he could crawl back to her and beg for forgiveness. If the damage wasn't too extensive. If he came out on the other side unscathed.

Sabrina grabbed her bag, hefted it over her shoulder, and stomped by him as he jumped out of the way. If he touched her, he wouldn't be able to go through with this farce.

She headed for the stairs.

"I'll have Rafe drive you."

"I'll talk to him myself. Don't bother."

"I want to help."

She spun around to face him, meeting his gaze. "Fuck you, Conner Bascott. Fuck you and your spinelessness. Rafe can take me to my fucking car, and I'll drive myself to my own fucking house and live happily ever after without your help, thank you very much."

And with that she was gone.

CHAPTER 21

Sabrina buried herself in her work. For the rest of the week, she stayed inside her house, hovered over her computer, wearing sweatpants and only showering occasionally.

She allowed herself to glance at her email two times a day. Sure enough, as she'd expected, nothing else arrived to threaten her.

She still hated that so many pictures of her naked body in compromising positions were out in the ether floating around. But she couldn't do anything about it. The police were investigating. All she could do was wait and hope they caught whoever had been stalking her.

They got what they wanted, so she prayed they held up their end of the bargain too and didn't let her face leak out all over the Internet.

One good thing was her work. She could stick her head in a manuscript and escape into the fictitious world of the characters, blocking out the ache constantly tightening her chest every time she came up for air, to eat or sleep or bathe.

She didn't hear from Conner. And by Friday she was pretty certain she never would. Obviously he didn't have the balls to face whatever this threat was at her side. Which pissed her off and fueled her anger.

She missed him. She missed sparring with him verbally. She missed his mouth on her body, his hands on her ass, his cock in her pussy...

The need to see him grew by the day. She knew he was fighting at the same arena she'd followed him to a few weeks ago. Had it only been two weeks? It seemed like a lifetime.

In a split-second decision, she jumped in the shower, put on clean jeans and a T-shirt, and left the house. The arena was big. She could watch him from some corner. At least she would get to see him, even if he didn't see her.

The thought of staring at his delicious chest covered with the gladiator tattoo over one shoulder made her mouth water.

One last indulgence. That's what she told herself. She just wanted to see his face, even from afar, soak in his sexiness, and then she would know he'd moved on. It would kill her to do this, but she needed the closure.

At eight thirty, she slipped into the arena and made her way to a far corner, nowhere near where she'd watched him the first time. She could see Emily and Kayla standing near the spot where she'd met them. She smiled. They were both on their tiptoes. Rider was in the ring. The tattoos on his shoulders were as impressive as Conner's—wings. He looked like he could fly. The announcer referred to him as "The Enforcer."

She smiled again, thinking about the play on words. The man certainly enforced the law, both inside and outside the cage.

She knew Conner was next. His fight was all she

251

wanted to see, and then she would slip back out. Rider won in the middle of the third round when the other man tapped out.

Sabrina held her breath as she waited for a glimpse of Conner's fine body.

It didn't take long. In a few minutes the announcer was at it again. "...And in the red corner we have Conner 'The Gladiator' Bascott. Weighing in at one eight-four, this middleweight champion of the arena has never lost a fight..."

She tuned out the rest of the speech, focusing on Conner's fine frame as he stepped into the ring. Her breath caught in her throat. His brows were furrowed in concentration—or aggravation. She couldn't be sure.

He glanced around the crowd for a moment before returning his focus to his opponent and stretching his neck from side to side.

Was he looking for her? An ache formed in the pit of her stomach. She shook the thought from her mind. *Of course not, silly.*

The bell rang, and Sabrina flinched as the match began.

If she wasn't mistaken, she thought she could actually hear him give a war cry from her spot so far away. It was ridiculous, considering the size of the crowd and the volume in the arena. The fans loved this man. And she'd been able to call him her own for a few brief days. A time better forgotten if she knew what was best.

Obviously, she was a glutton for punishment.

Conner was in rare form. He looked fit to kill. She'd never seen him so aggressive. Granted, she'd only watched him fight the one time, but the look in his eyes was feral. She could tell even from a distance. He swung out several times, landing more punches in less than a minute than the average fighter. Especially his opponent.

Sabrina actually felt sorry for the other guy. The dude had no idea he was fighting someone with so much pent up anger this week.

Not that she blamed Conner. He'd been through a lot. She assumed she didn't know the half of it.

Conner made an impressive leg kick that caused the other guy to stumble backward, slamming into the fence. While the guy put up his hands to block the barrage of punches coming at him on the heels of the kick, Conner pressed forward. Finally, he grabbed the man around the neck and held him in a choke hold.

Sabrina held her breath. She didn't blink as she watched the situation unfold. The crowed grew wild, screaming so loud their words were indiscernible. She fisted her hands at her sides as she watched.

Suddenly, Conner gave a jerk, and the two of them went to the floor. Conner grappled for position, scrambling to get on top of his opponent until he had the upper hand, his forearm lying across the other man's neck, cutting off his airway and leaving him completely immobile.

The seconds ticked by slowly while Sabrina gritted her teeth. "Come on, Conner," she mumbled under her breath.

Finally, the guy tapped out, and Sabrina let out a long breath.

Conner jumped to his feet as the announcer declared him the winner. He waved at the crowd briefly before ducking his head and exiting the cage.

Sabrina glanced at Emily and Kayla. They hadn't moved. Gage hadn't fought yet.

Good. Sabrina could slip out of the arena undetected.

She wormed her way through the throng of people and back out to the lobby. In her haste to escape, as she came around the corner, she ran into someone. She reached out to steady the woman with both hands before the lady could fall on her ass. "I'm so sorry. I—"

The woman staring daggers at her was the same fake blonde who had hit on Conner at Extreme. "Missy?"

"Watch where you're going, sister." She looked perturbed as she shook Sabrina off and smoothed her hands down her short skirt. "Hey, you're that girl who was with Conner at the club."

"Yeah." Shit. She hoped Missy didn't tell Conner they'd run into each other. "What are you doing here?"

Missy's face split wide with a grin. "I'm with Conner." She lifted her chin and set her hands on her hips.

Sabrina's eyes widened. She couldn't breathe. All the air fled her lungs as time stood still. *No. It can't be true.*

"Excuse me. I need to go meet him. He'll be waiting." Missy pushed past Sabrina, leaving her head spinning as she watched the bitch's ass sway back and forth. Missy's heels were so high Sabrina wondered how she didn't fall.

She finally shook herself and blinked. In record time, she pushed her way through the crowd and out the front door. She could barely hold herself together as she jogged to her car. As soon as she was safely inside, she started the engine and fled the parking lot before letting the tears fall down her face.

Holding on by a thread, Sabrina made her way back home and inside before totally losing it. She flounced onto the couch and curled up on her side, not bothering to turn the lights on.

For the first time in five days, she really let herself cry. Hard.

How had her life gotten so off track?

She sobbed forever it seemed before she ran out of tears and lay there staring at nothing, pulling the throw blanket over her body and closing her eyes.

Welcome sleep sucked her under in seconds.

∾

It was bright out when Sabrina blinked awake. The living room itself was dim because she hadn't opened any blinds or curtains in the last week, but she could see the bright sun peeking around the edges of the windows.

She struggled to sit, wincing at how stiff her body was from lying in the same curled-up position all night. Taking several deep breaths, she ran her hands through her hair and stared at the ceiling. *Oh God*. What the hell was she going to do next?

Like a freight train derailed from the tracks, she felt frozen in her place, unsure if the damage could ever be repaired.

She thought back on the previous evening. Could Conner really have been there with that skanky bitch? Realistically she doubted it. The woman could have been lying. Sabrina wouldn't put it past her. But what the hell was Missy doing at the arena?

Conner hadn't seemed to be interested in the woman the last time Sabrina had seen him with her. But things could have changed. Or perhaps he went crawling back to anyone he could find to blow off steam. He might have needed to dominate someone, and Missy was an easy choice.

The idea made Sabrina shiver. Had Missy been behind all the emailing, car keying, and threats? Was she smart enough to orchestrate such a thing just to win a Dom?

It was illogical. So far from unlikely that Sabrina couldn't fathom the possibility.

Missy didn't seem to have enough brain cells to rub two of them together, and she certainly didn't seem capable of hiring a stalker to follow Sabrina and Conner around town. Could she have done the job herself?

Fuck.

Sabrina stood and made her way to the kitchen. She needed coffee first and then a shower.

By the time she was caffeinated and clean, she resolved to face the man who had her in knots. If he thought he could blow her off and ignore her, he was sadly mistaken.

Sabrina may have spent the week licking her wounds, but she wasn't a woman to take rejection sitting down. He owed her an explanation. Or at the very least some words that would give her closure. Otherwise, she would sit and pine away for his ass for months.

With this renewed sense of action, Sabrina dressed in jeans and a cute blouse. Conner hated when she wore jeans. Too bad. He was going to have to get used to her defying him on occasion. She pulled on her black boots, the ones with heels high enough to be dressy, but not so high as to be presumptuous. They could go either way. Today they were just boots with jeans.

She headed for her car and then sat there for several moments wondering where to start. She didn't want to call him and give him a heads up. She wanted to hunt him down.

The gym.

It was the most likely choice for a Saturday morning.

Sabrina didn't see his car as she pulled into the parking lot, but she decided to get out and go inside. One of the guys would be there. They might be able to direct her in the right direction. The last thing she wanted to do was head straight for his house if Missy was by any chance there in his bed. That would be the height of mortification.

She stepped from her car, tucked the keys in her pocket, and turned toward the entrance to the gym.

A man spoke, startling her. She hadn't noticed him. "Well well, if it isn't Sabrina Duluth."

She froze, a few yards from the older guy she didn't recognize. He had a strong accent. Russian maybe? *Shit*.

"I must say, I'm surprised to see you here this morning."

"Who are you?"

He chuckled sardonically. "A friend of The Fight Club." He waved a hand through the air as though his identity wasn't all that important. "Too bad about your man. You must feel awful."

"Pardon?" Her blood ran cold. "What are you talking about?"

He flinched and set his hand over his chest, feigning shock. "Oh, pardon *me*. I didn't realize you didn't know." He shook his head. "Strange man, Conner. I'm surprised he didn't just man up and use you as an alibi. At the very least you could have lied."

"Lied about what?"

"Don't play stupid with me, Sabrina. I know all about your affair with the esteemed professor. Tsk tsk." He lifted a finger and shook it back and forth in the air, reaching too close to her face for comfort. "You know it's against school policy for a teacher to fuck his students. For shame."

She stood rigid, trying to make sense of the man's words. He seemed dangerous. Every cell in her body screamed at her to get the hell away from him, and fast. But first she needed answers. As luck would have it, she didn't have to ask for them.

The gray-haired man glanced at his watch and spoke again before her tongue could form more words. "I'm sure his career is completely in the dumpster by now. His meeting with the ethics committee started about an hour ago. Such a shame too. I heard he was a beloved professor."

She couldn't believe what she was hearing. Ethics

committee? Meeting? Why? Surely he wouldn't get fired for dating a former student. They'd done nothing wrong.

And why did this asshole know so much about it?

Slowly, the pieces came together. She knew with clarity she was staring at the Russian mobster who wanted Conner to fight for him. What the hell was he doing in the parking lot of the gym, hanging out next to his car?

Waiting for Conner…

Fuck.

And he didn't realize Sabrina wasn't privy to anything he was telling her.

Why the hell had Conner allowed himself to get into this situation when all he had to do was bring Sabrina forward? Before she could ponder it another moment, she turned and ran back to her car.

"Where are you going, Ms. Duluth? Don't you want to wait with me? I'm sure he'll come straight here as soon as his career is in the shitter." His voice rose, but she didn't hear anything else because she was inside her car, speeding away in seconds.

As she drove to the university, she tried to concentrate on everything she'd heard. It didn't make sense. None of it. If somebody set Conner up to lose his job, why on earth wouldn't Conner just tell her? Especially if she could have exonerated him with a simple meeting?

She stayed well over the speed limit all the way to campus, praying she didn't get pulled over. She didn't have time for that. "Come on. Come on…" Tapping the steering wheel with her fingers as she waited at a red light didn't help her nerves.

It was a Saturday morning. Why were they meeting on a Saturday? She sped directly to the administration building, having no idea where else to start. The lot had several cars in it already, and Sabrina added hers to the mix, crooked and straddling two spots. She didn't care. She was out of the Honda and running toward the entrance without a glance back.

Luckily, someone was working at the information desk. Out of breath, Sabrina addressed her. "There's a meeting going on somewhere. Do you know where it might be?"

"What meeting?" The student looked confused.

"With the dean maybe? The ethics committee?"

"Oh." Her eyes went wide. "I saw the dean heading for the conference room upstairs earlier." She pointed to the top of the staircase. "Maybe she's still there." She tucked a lock of red curls behind her ear.

"Where is it?" Sabrina nearly yelled.

The girl flinched. "Probably the one the right."

Sabrina took the stairs two at a time, nearly sprinting. When she reached the second floor, she flung open the first door on the right she came too. No one was inside. Leaving that room, she headed for the next. She didn't even think. She just tore forward, her only thought that Conner was an absolute idiot if he let himself get fired without bring Sabrina in.

As she jerked the next door open, she sucked in a sharp breath.

Several men turned around to face the door and stare at her.

A woman stood at the head of the room. "This is a closed meeting. You can't be here."

Sabrina scanned the occupants until she found Conner sitting at the front.

He jumped to his feet when he spotted her. "Sabrina?" He wore a suit, and he looked pale. Stress lines marred his features. "What are you doing here?"

She stepped inside.

The woman spoke again. "Ma'am, you can't be here," she repeated.

Sabrina ignored her and padded farther into the room. "What's going on?"

"Sabrina, can we talk about this later?" Conner implored.

"No, we can't talk about this later. Later would be too late, wouldn't it?" She made it to the front of the room.

"How did you know where I was?"

"Long story." She stepped right in front of him, ignoring the mumbling coming from the other men in the room. She glanced around and noticed there were also two other women. Everyone was dressed in their best suits.

"Sabrina…" Conner's shoulders slumped. "I have it under control," he whispered, taking her arm and tugging her back in the direction she'd just come.

"It doesn't seem that you do," she admonished, jerking her biceps free of his grip. "Not if you let things go this far without telling me. Why would you do that?"

"Conner?" the woman standing questioned. "Is this the woman?"

"It is," he muttered. He turned around and faced the group, motioning toward Sabrina. "Sabrina Duluth. You can look her up if you want. She was indeed a student here last semester, but only for the one semester. We didn't begin seeing each other until several months later."

"Why, Conner?" What the hell possessed him to let things go this far when all he'd needed to do was ask her to come in?

He stared at her for a second. "I didn't want you mixed up in this. It wasn't your problem. And neither of us did anything wrong."

"So? If someone accused us of something we didn't do,

don't you think it would have helped to allow me to corroborate?"

He blew out a breath. "Yes. It would have helped me. But it would have put a flag on your name."

"What?"

The woman at the front of the room stepped forward. She reached out a hand. "Dean Sheffield. Nice to meet you."

Sabrina shook her hand while Dr. Sheffield smiled and then turned to Conner. "How noble of you, Dr. Bascott." She smirked. "Stupid, but noble."

"Someone clue me in here," Sabrina demanded. "I'm at a loss."

Dean Sheffield continued, scrambling around on the podium for a paper. "Would you be willing to sign an affidavit stating that you were not involved with Dr. Bascott in any manner that was inappropriate during your semester at the university?"

"Of course."

"That will do it." Dean Sheffield lifted her gaze. "The rest of you are excused. I think we're done here."

There was a noisy shuffling of briefcases and shoes as everyone gathered their belongings and left the room.

Sabrina lowered herself into a chair two down from Conner. She fought to catch her breath still. "Conner. You're going to have to explain this to me."

Dean Sheffield stepped forward with a form in her hand. She took the chair next to Sabrina, farther from Conner. "I see what he did. It wasn't the smartest choice, but I get it."

"What?"

"I didn't want your name dragged through the dirt while I fought this ridiculous allegation. Nothing anyone accused me of was true. And I knew I could eventually prove it without hauling you into it." He plopped down in his seat and leaned his elbows on his knees.

Sabrina took the paper from the dean and absently signed it. "It would seem things got out of hand. Just how far were you willing to go without bringing me into it?"

Conner frowned. "I don't think it was out of hand. Do you, Dean Sheffield?"

"Not yet." The woman raised her eyebrows as she shook her head. "I was getting a little worried."

"Weren't they about to fire you?"

Conner froze, his hand lifted in the air. "Who told you that?"

The dean sucked in a breath. "And how did you find out we were here?"

Sabrina licked her lips. "Some Russian guy. I went to the gym to look for you, and he cornered me in the parking lot. Interesting conversation."

"What did he look like?"

"Stout. Gray hair. Maybe fifty. Receding hairline. Heavy accent."

Conner jumped to his feet. "Let me get this straight. You spoke with Anton Yenin at the gym just this morning?"

She nodded. "I don't know his name, but I spoke with some old Russian asshole, yes."

"And he told you I was getting fired right now?"

"Yes."

"Well, there you have it." Dean Sheffield stood. "You want me to call the police, Conner?"

Conner shook his head. "No. I'll handle it." He didn't take his gaze off Sabrina. His face turned red. He looked livid. With her? Finally, he grunted and stomped back and forth. "Jesus, Sabrina. He could have kidnapped you or killed you or worse."

Worse? What the hell was worse than kidnapped or

killed? She shivered, pondering the options. And then she furrowed her brow at him. "Why are you yelling at me? All I did was drive to the gym to look for you. I didn't do anything wrong."

Conner stopped moving and turned to face her. Several heartbeats went by while the dean excused herself quietly and left the room. The door shut with a resounding snick.

They were alone.

Conner's glare softened slowly. Suddenly, he took two strides and hauled her off the seat to her feet, pressing his lips to hers. He kissed her hard, slanting his head to one side and gripping her biceps. His kiss was desperate. Needy.

And her entire body responded in kind. Instant heat rushed to her center and tightened her pussy, making her moan into his mouth.

When he finally broke the kiss and leaned his forehead against hers, holding her tight, he muttered, "God, I missed you. Do you know the hell I've been living with since you walked out that door Monday?"

"Yes." She knew. She'd lived with the same hell. "Wait. You haven't been with Missy?"

"What?" He reared back a step, not releasing her biceps. His brow was drawn tight.

Sabrina cleared her throat and shook her head. "Of course. How stupid."

"What made you think I was with that crazy woman?"

"I saw her last night."

"Where?"

Sabrina bit her lip. "At the arena," she whispered.

"You were at my fight?"

"Yes."

He grinned. "Why didn't you say anything?"

"I just wanted to see you. Needed to. I didn't want you to know."

"Missy was there?"

She nodded. "I ran into her, literally, on my way out. She told me she was there with you."

"She was *not*."

"I gather."

Conner pulled her into his embrace again, wrapping his arms around her.

It felt amazing having him so close. She breathed in his scent, wishing her heart would stop racing. She still had a thousand questions.

"We need to go to the police station."

"Yeah," she muttered into his chest. What she really wanted to do was go back to his place and strip him of his clothes so she could trace his tattoo with her tongue.

Later.

He let her go long enough to grab his things and then took her hand and led her to the parking lot and straight to his car.

"I have my car here."

"Leave it. We'll get it later. I'm not letting you out of my sight."

She smiled as she relaxed into his Mustang. Somehow it was all going to work out.

CHAPTER 22

Four hours later, Sabrina sat in the back of the squad car with Conner beside her still holding her hand. She chewed on her lower lip and then took a deep breath. "I hate this idea."

"I know, baby." He turned to face her and lifted her chin with a finger. "It won't take long, and then we can go back to my place and put this all behind us."

She nodded. "Don't get dead, please. I like my boyfriends living and breathing."

"Got it." He chuckled.

The door opened on his side, and Conner slid out. "Be back as fast as I can. Don't you dare move from this car, or I'll spank your ass so hard you won't be able to sit for a week."

A chill raced up her spine as she grinned at him.

Of course he knew her well enough to realize his threat would only encourage her to jump from the safety of the vehicle just to goad him.

And then the door closed, leaving her in silence.

So many things had happened over the afternoon. She

stared at the strange metal building where intelligence suggested Anton Yenin was located this afternoon. They still didn't have all the pieces together to finish the puzzle, but they were getting close.

Conner had told her everything—finally. He'd been keeping so many things from her under the guise of protecting her from the possible vultures that her head was spinning. He'd even lied about his feelings for her to get her to leave Rafe's house on Monday so she wouldn't be in harm's way.

She'd nearly buckled over as though sucker punched when she realized the entire scene had been staged. He did care for her. He'd been protecting her the only way he knew how—by cutting things off.

"This isn't going to work between us. All we do is fight. It's how we started out." His words rang in her head. She should have realized they made no sense. He loved fighting with her. But she'd been so angry at the time, she believed him. She'd even tossed her own angry four-letter words his way.

The damage could have been irreparable.

It looked like neither Missy nor the esteemed Dr. Chang had been involved in the allegations. That trophy went to Anton Yenin. It made sense once Conner explained it to Sabrina.

The mafia guy wanted Conner to fight for him. And he'd decided to stop at nothing to attain that goal. Probably thought if he got Conner fired, he would have no choice but to fight for money.

He lost the battle. And now Sabrina sat in the back of a squad car while Conner went inside to face Yenin and put an end to this shit story.

~

Conner walked into the makeshift arena and headed straight for the offices with Rider by his side. They'd both been there before and knew the layout. It was well known as a hot spot for underground fighting. Though more often than not, the police had more important things to worry about than trying to catch the side betting of the crowded arena on a fight night.

Lucky for Conner, Rider was on the police force and more than knowledgeable about both the Russian mobster and his dealings. Conner didn't expect any trouble this afternoon. He just wanted to exchange a nice tit for tat with Yenin. And of course, he had plenty of backup sitting out front in the event things went south.

There weren't many people inside. It obviously wasn't a fight night.

Two men stood just inside the building as Conner and Rider entered. They didn't have to introduce themselves. Everyone knew them in the MMA circuit. "We're here to see Yenin."

"He's not available," the shorter guy said with a smirk.

Conner leaned forward. "I wasn't asking, mother fucker. Make him available."

The guy's face fell, and he stood with a growl and stomped slowly toward some stairs to the left. He didn't make it far before Yenin's voice could be heard from upstairs. "It's okay, Boris. Let them in." Yenin turned around and entered through a door without greeting Conner and Rider.

Conner took the stairs at a fast clip, Rider on his heels. When he reached the top, he opened the door he'd seen Anton enter through and was shocked to find a woman sprawled half-naked on Anton's couch.

Even more surprising was that he knew the woman.

"Angelica?" What the hell was his lit student doing in this arena looking half wasted?

Anton stepped from behind his desk and came around to the couch with a smirk on his face. "Oh, that's right. You two know each other." He leaned down and stuck his tongue in Angelica's mouth before she could protest.

She squirmed away from him, but he held her tight.

On second glance, Conner realized she was completely naked. There was a ratty throw blanket covering her vital parts, but as Anton ruthlessly mauled her mouth, the cover slipped down her body, exposing her ample tits.

When Anton finally released her with a chuckle, she scrambled backward on the couch, tugging the throw up to cover her body. Her eyes were bloodshot. She wasn't just drunk. She was strung out on something.

Conner had never seen her like that. In fact, she was usually prompt and ready to learn in his class. He was beyond surprised to see her in this environment. It couldn't be a coincidence. This saga kept getting weirder.

His gaze jerked to Anton. He had more pressing matters to attend to first. Then he would consider what to do with Angelica. Stepping forward, he narrowed his gaze.

"How do I rate a visit from the good professor today? Have you decided to come to your senses and fight for me?" Anton stood in front of Angelica, crossing his arms over his chest and spreading his legs in a defensive stance.

"Not a fucking chance, Yenin. Not even if you manage to get me fired. Which you failed at today." Conner stepped closer. How the hell was he going to get Angelica out of this? He was more confused than he'd been all day. Something wasn't right.

A dozen lightbulbs went off, none of them bright enough to clue him in. He glanced at Angelica again as

Anton rounded behind his desk. "What are you doing here, Angelica," he asked.

She suddenly perked up and plastered a smile on her face, batting her eyes. She stood and sauntered over to Conner. When she reached his side, she leaned into him, wrapping her arms around his middle and setting her head on his chest. "Did you come to rescue me, Conner?"

Conner? Since when did she call him by his first name?

She gazed up at him, her bloodshot eyes blinking.

"Are you responsible for all this?"

"All what?" she asked, her gaze wandering aimlessly to Rider at his other side. Her smile widened. "My oh my, are all your friends as fucking hot and sexy as you?"

"Angelica," Conner demanded. "Did you try to get me fired?"

Anton tipped his head back and roared with laughter.

Conner stared at the man, shrugging Angelica off him and leaving her in Rider's hands. "What, may I ask, is so funny?"

"You." Anton held his gut as though he were unable to stop chuckling at the funniest joke he'd ever heard. "Good God, man, you think this whiney piece of ass is capable of pulling off such a scheme?" His face immediately went serious. "I assumed you were here to take me up on my offer."

"Not a chance in hell, Yenin. I've already said that. Though I do need to thank you for leading me to realize who was fucking with me. I hadn't expected you to stoop so low. I underestimated you."

Anton slammed his hand on his desk, making everyone flinch. "And you'll still be underestimating me if you don't wise up and get on board."

"I've told you repeatedly I won't fight for you, and I mean it."

"Not even if you need the money?" He smirked.

"How did you do it?"

"Do what?" Anton tapped his fingers on his desk. The man was short enough his hands touched the desk while he was standing.

"Frame me." He still hadn't told Anton there was a flaw in his framing. It seemed the man might truly believe Conner was screwing a student. He jerked his gaze to Angelica again where she now leaned on Rider, swaying, her ass hanging out for everyone to see. The blanket was tucked against her front, but she seemed oblivious to the fact her ass hung out. "I suppose you used Angelica to get to me?" A lucky and easy addition to the puzzle.

Anton chuckled again. "She was most helpful filling in the blanks, and so forthcoming with information. It was almost too easy."

"She told you I was dating a student?"

"She even gave me the name of your sweet piece of ass. Sabrina Duluth. How is she in bed anyway? A tiny waif like her? What did you see in her? Can't be much to write home about, as you Americans like to say."

Conner fought the urge to haul off and punch Anton in the nose. It wouldn't do any good, and ten of his private mafia would be on Conner so fast, he wouldn't know what hit him. "You miscalculated, asshole."

Anton tipped his head to one side. "How so?"

"Sabrina isn't a student."

Anton flinched. His gaze went to Angelica. "You bitch."

Angelica's eyes widened. Her mouth fell open. "I never told you any such thing. I have no idea if that skinny bitch is a student or not."

Anton reached down and swiped an arm across his desk, sending the contents flying into the air to land on the floor.

Conner glanced at Angelica. He actually felt sorry for her. She was probably set up. "How did you get messed up with these people, Angelica?"

"Oh, she was easy to reel in," Anton responded. He leaned over his now-clean desk and growled. "This sexy piece of ass was following you everywhere. My men kept seeing her as they trailed you. I sent one of my men to her favorite haunting place, and she was eating out of his hand in no time. Crazy bitches are way too easy these days." He glanced in her direction again, his gaze wandering up and down her naked backside. "Lucky for me, she turned out to be a fine piece of ass too."

"So you lured her into your web and then pumped her for information to get me fired?"

"It wasn't difficult. The bitch was drunk. She told me everything without much inquiry."

"Why, Angelica?"

The girl pouted and dipped her head. She was more sober than she had been when Conner first entered. Maybe she wasn't as strung out as he thought. "I wanted you to notice me. But you only had eyes for that skinny waif Sabrina."

"So you set me up to get me fired? You thought that would help your cause?" He was angry.

She shook her head. "I didn't know anything about getting you fired. I just wanted you to see me."

Conner ran a hand through his hair and took a breath.

"Let's get out of here, Conner. We're done here." Rider's voice broke the lull when he spoke for the first time.

Conner ignored Rider and narrowed his gaze at Anton. "Let's get this clear. You made a mistake when you told Sabrina I was getting fired this morning."

"How? Everyone knew it."

"Nope. Just you."

"You can't prove that."

Conner chuckled this time. "Anton. You're a smart guy. Surely you can tell we outsmarted you this time."

"The email."

"Yep." Conner nodded while Anton realized his mistake. The university had replied to his last email. Thanking him for letting them know about the unethical behavior of their staff member and assuring him action would be taken quickly. They made up a pile of lies about verifying that the woman in the photo was indeed a student and would be firing Dr. Bascott that very morning.

In reality, no meeting had been taking place at all. It was staged. The group was simply gathered in that conference room in hopes to lure in the culprit by making him think Conner had been fired.

Anton played into their hands faster than expected by waiting for Conner at the gym during the meeting. Sabrina's involvement was unexpected.

Conner cringed to think she had endured a conversation that morning with Yenin.

The dean and the fake group meeting in the conference room had done so in hopes of flushing out the culprit, assuming it might take a while for the accuser to slip up and rat himself out with information only he or she was privy to—that Conner had been fired.

They hadn't expected Sabrina to storm in. They hadn't expected a lot of things. They for sure hadn't expected to put the matter to rest so swiftly. That was just luck.

Anton Yenin had opened his mouth too quickly and stuffed his entire shoe down his throat.

The Russian opened his mouth again now, but no sound came out.

"Ah. So finally you have nothing to say. Listen, asshole. You've been tailing my ass for months. Obviously you've had enough spies to know my every move, including when I took a shit and who I spoke to. You've terrorized my girlfriend. I want this to stop. I am not coming to fight for you. I want every copy of the pictures you took right now, and I don't want to see your face again."

"Why would I do that?" Anton hedged.

"Because this place is surrounded with SWAT as we speak. So, unless you want me to give the word and arrest everyone inside, including you, for conspiracy, you'll do as I say."

Anton hesitated for several seconds and then turned toward a safe on the wall behind him and twisted the dial several times until it opened.

Conner ignored the piles of money inside and concentrated on the jump drive the man handed him as he turned back around. "That's all of it? There are no other copies?"

Anton shook his head. "I'm a man of my word."

Conner chuckled. "Right." He leaned forward, putting his own hands on Anton's desk. Conner was almost a foot taller than the man. "Do not piss me off again. Do you understand?"

Anton nodded, his gaze angry.

Conner turned around and left the office, pocketing the jump drive.

Rider held the door open, Angelica now covered in the blanket at his side.

They didn't say a word as they left the makeshift arena and stepped out into the fresh air of the Vegas afternoon sun.

Conner turned toward Rider. "Thanks, man. You got this?" He nodded at Angelica. The last thing he wanted to do was deal with her. The police could handle her. They would want to question her extensively. Hopefully they would shake her up and scare her straight. Conner doubted she'd ever been in as much trouble as she was today.

"Yep," Rider confirmed.

Conner hesitated and turned back to Angelica. "How long have you been following me?"

She shrugged.

"Why?"

"I wanted you to ask me out," she mumbled, lowering her gaze.

"You're a student." He ran a hand through his hair. Obviously she wasn't playing with a full deck. "Did you key Sabrina's car?"

She ducked her head farther. That was all the answer he needed.

CHAPTER 23

Sabrina turned onto her back and stared up at the ceiling with a sigh. She still couldn't believe Conner had gone to such lengths to keep her name out of his problems with the university. She wanted to throttle him, even though he explained his reasoning—that once someone is accused of something, it never goes away. Some people would always believe she'd broken the rules.

Never mind he was willing to lose his job over it. Stupid man.

Nope. All he cared about was salvaging her reputation. And the only way he knew to ensure that was to refuse to tell the dean who was in the pictures. There had been no guarantee her coming forward would exonerate him anyway. It could just as easily have been too suspicious for the dean to believe. In which case, Sabrina would be tainted as the evil student who fucked the professor, and Conner still would have been fired.

She thought he was crazy.

The water shut off in the bathroom, and she turned her

face to watch Conner saunter in with a towel wrapped around his body.

Sabrina had already showered before him. She'd headed straight for the bathroom and stripped out of her clothes the second they returned to his house while Conner had returned several phone calls to The Fight Club and Joe.

When he'd finally entered the bedroom, she was resting naked on his bed, staring at him coyly on her side, her head propped on one hand.

Conner's eyes had gone wide, and a genuine smile had spread across his face for the first time that day. He held up one finger and padded into the bathroom.

That was three minutes ago. Now, a dripping male specimen twice her size with a body to die for sauntered toward her, dropping the towel on the floor as he did.

When he reached the bed, he lowered his gaze to the floor and spoke in a voice she knew he saved for quoting literature.

"...For what is not connected with her to me? And what does not recall her? I cannot look down to this floor, but her features are shaped in the flags! In every cloud, in every tree—filling the air at night, and caught by glimpses in every object by day—I am surrounded with her image! The most ordinary faces of men and women—my own features—mock me with a resemblance. The entire world is a dreadful collection of memoranda that she did exist, and that I have lost her!"

She giggled. "Is *Jane Eyre* all you ever quote?"

He lifted his gaze and gave her another good one.

"'I was wrong to deceive you. I see that now, it was cowardly. I should have appealed to your spirit as I do now.'"

Sabrina flushed. She wanted him.

And she got her wish. He landed over her, grabbing her hands to hold them over her head as he smothered her with his body.

He lowered his face without a word and took her mouth in a kiss that scrambled her brain.

Sabrina couldn't move a muscle. She was trapped. And she was not sorry. She was right where she wanted to be.

When he lifted his mouth off hers, it was to look her in the eye. His gaze was intense. "I missed you."

"I missed you too."

"I never want to fight like that again."

She smiled. "What fun would that be?"

He lifted one brow. "I'm going to spank your ass. You realize that, right?"

"I figured." She bit her lower lip, not wanting him to realize how many times today she'd thought of bending over his knee when they were finally alone. He would be furious with her for so many reasons.

And she needed the intensity of a spanking to get her over the stress of living without him for the last week.

He hesitated, seeming to read her expression. And then he lifted off her and twisted to sit so his back leaned against the headboard, dragging her across his lap.

She moaned as he situated her.

His hand landed on her ass and rubbed. "You're supposed to be nervous and reverent," he chided. "Not so aroused by the prospect of my hand swatting your ass that you moan before I've begun."

"Sorry, Sir." She fought the urge to squirm. Everything he did aroused her. She was desperate for his touch. His hand on her ass. His cock inside her. His mouth wrapped around her breast. Anything. Everything.

Conner held her lower back steady while he stroked her ass with his other hand. He leaned to one side and reached for the bedside table.

She heard the drawer open, and then he righted himself.

She didn't look over her shoulder. The suspense of whatever he had planned was enough.

A pop sounded, alerting her to what had to be lube. And then she flinched as a line of the cool liquid landed on her crack.

"I'm going to take you here tonight, baby."

She gritted her teeth. Was that more than she bargained for?

No. She could do it.

She trusted him. He would be gentle when needed.

One finger landed on her tight hole and circled the entrance several times before pushing inside.

Sabrina squeezed her ass cheeks involuntarily.

"Relax, baby. Just feel. I'm going to plug this tight hole while I spank you. Afterward, I'm going to fuck you so hard, you won't be able to speak."

"Yes, Sir." Her voice was deep, breathy. Someone else's.

Conner removed his finger and replaced it with the head of a plug. Immediately she knew it was larger than the last one he'd used.

She braced herself, holding her breath while she tried to relax her ass.

With a few twists, the plug slipped inside her, filling her fuller than anything she'd ever experienced.

"Conner…"

"You're okay, baby. Just breathe."

She did as he said, taking a long deep inhale and then letting it out.

"Good girl." Without warning, he spanked her hard, right beneath the plug, so low on her ass that his hand made contact with her thighs as well.

It smarted. But her pussy immediately grew so wet she knew she was dripping onto the bed.

"Spread your legs wider, baby." He nudged her thighs as he spoke.

She complied, exposing herself to his palm.

Conner slapped her again. Higher this time, on one cheek.

She flinched, but it wasn't too bad.

Then a series of swats landed on her, back and forth, alternating cheeks. The heat rose, telling her how pink her ass would be if she could see it.

After massaging her ass for several seconds, he spanked her again. Lower this time, at the V of her legs. And then even lower, covering her thighs with his palm.

Sabrina moaned. She was close to coming. She'd been submissive for a long time. She'd done many spanking scenes with many Doms. None had made her come without touching her pussy.

"Oh, baby. That's so hot. You're so aroused."

She moaned in response and didn't move a muscle. She was afraid if she squirmed against his thigh, she would come.

"My girl needs to come so bad."

Would he let her?

The last time he'd spanked her, he'd left her wanting all night long. Surely he wouldn't do that again this time. They needed each other. She needed him…

Suddenly Conner lifted his thighs several inches, forcing Sabrina's ass higher. "Legs wider."

She spread them again, as far as she could manage.

He spanked her at the juncture of her pussy and her ass.

Sabrina squealed. She was so close.

And then he shocked her, his next swat landing solidly over her pussy. Hard.

She came so fast, she had no warning. She lifted her face off the bed, bracing herself on her forearms in disbelief as her orgasm slammed into her. Wave after wave with no direct contact to any part of Conner. His hand had immediately disappeared after that last slap.

"God, that's beautiful," he whispered. "I'll never get enough of watching you come. But watching you come while lying over my knees, your ass a lovely shade of pink, and no contact with your pussy? That's priceless."

Every word he uttered was reverent.

Before she caught her breath, he flipped her over and landed on top of her, snuggling between her legs and forcing them wide. He gripped her hands and held them over her head once again.

"You're mine, Sabrina."

"Yes." She couldn't breathe or even see clearly.

"We won't go through another week like that."

"No," she agreed.

"I'm going to fuck you now. Have you been taking your pill?"

"Of course." She groaned at the thought.

"May I?"

"Please, Sir. God, yes." She wanted nothing more than to have him inside her without a condom.

Before she finished her thought, he thrust into her so deep she arched off the bed on a groan, her head tipping back to expose her neck.

She wanted to wrap her arms around his middle. But a tug proved he wasn't going to relent. He held her firmly.

He stared into her eyes before pulling slowly out of her and slamming back in. His cock felt huge rubbing against the plug. So full.

Sabrina closed her eyes and let herself feel. Every part of her was sensitized as he stroked through her again. Her arousal rose once again, another orgasm threatening to tip her over the edge so soon after the first.

"Don't come yet, Sabrina."

A deep groan escaped her lips. How was she going to hold back? Every stroke felt like heaven. She'd missed his cock so much.

"Baby, look at me."

She blinked her eyes open.

"Don't come," he commanded again.

"I'm trying, Sir. But…"

He shook his head. "Do better than that."

She gritted her teeth, pursing her lips against the rising need.

Conner fucked her pussy harder, faster. He wasn't helping.

Suddenly, he was gone. In a quick motion, he flipped her over and dragged her to her knees. The plug was pulled out in the next instant, his cock resting at her entrance, more lube dripping onto her crack. Conner gripped her hips and held her steady. "Ready, baby?" His voice was hoarse as though he'd been screaming all evening.

She nodded into the mattress, resting on her forearms. She expected him to thrust into her, but he surprised her, easing his cock slowly into her ass.

Oh God. So full. So tight. Her pussy gripped at nothing.

After several agonizingly slow seconds, he was fully seated. "You okay, baby?"

"Yes, Sir."

He reached his arm around her middle and pushed several fingers into her pussy. "Oh yeah. That's it. I can feel your walls clenching around my fingers. You need to come so badly, don't you, baby?"

"Yes, Sir," she muttered.

He withdrew his cock most of the way out and then pushed back into her ass. A deep moan escaped his lips.

Sabrina smiled. Thank God she wasn't the only one affected by this. "Sir…" She was going to come.

Conner let loose, fucking her ass in rhythm with his fingers in her pussy.

It felt so good. Too good. Better than good. She rocked into his thrusts, holding her breath to keep the orgasm at bay.

"Now, baby. Come for me."

That was all she needed. Both her pussy and her ass contracted, milking him in both holes at once. The orgasm was all-consuming. Her entire body participated. Her arms shook as she rode the waves of bliss.

And then Conner came, pushing himself deep inside her tight rear as he roared his release. When he was finished, he eased her onto the bed, slipping out of her to land at her side. He still covered most of her body, one arm wrapped around her back, one leg covering both of hers.

She faced him, unable to lift her head. His lips landed on hers in a gentle kiss. "I love you."

Her heart overflowed. "I love you, too, Conner." She couldn't move more than her lips. He'd rendered her useless.

His smile broadened. "Do you think we can cut down on the verbal barbs?"

"Probably not." She smiled back.

His eyes wrinkled with mirth. "Good. 'Cause life would be awfully boring without you challenging me at least once a day."

EPILOGUE

Six months later...

Sabrina rounded the corner into her bedroom, a fresh roll of packing tape in her hand.

She leaned against the doorframe when she saw Conner lounging on her bed, his back against the headboard. "What are you doing? That doesn't look like packing to me." She padded forward. He had a box in front of him. She recognized it as one she'd kept under the bed. It was open.

Conner was thumbing through some pages he'd lifted out of it. "Jesus, baby. This is amazing." He didn't look at her as he spoke. His gaze was riveted to the paper he held.

Sabrina swallowed. "Conner, that's very personal. I don't think I want you reading my work." She reached out to swipe the pages from his hand.

Conner jerked out of her grasp. "Why are you hiding this?"

She narrowed her gaze at him. "I told you. I'm not

ready. My work isn't that good. Those pages are old. I wrote that years ago. Let it go."

He turned to meet her gaze. "Baby, you *are* ready. This is better than any of the ten thousand books I've personally packed up all over your house. I suppose your computer is filled with more work you've written recently."

She rolled her eyes. "And I also told you it's a gamble. It takes time to write a good book, and time is money. I have a job I can't do while I'm devoting myself to writing."

He jumped off the bed so fast, she blinked. The next thing she knew she was lying on her back on top of several papers with Conner hovering over her, straddling her waist.

She squirmed, but he had her pinned. He grabbed both wrists and then lifted one and twisted it so he held her hand in front of her face. "See that ring?"

She rolled her eyes again.

"Yeah. I put that there for a reason. It's a done deal. Your house is sold. Your million books are about to go in the moving van. You're mine." He grinned. He was super proud of himself. "Now, the way I see it, you don't have a mortgage anymore. No bills. I've managed for fifteen years on my salary. I bet adding your tiny little mouth to feed won't break me."

She didn't move.

"What do you say? Give it a shot. Yeah? What do you have to lose?"

"My dignity?"

He lowered his face and kissed her lips, holding her hands above her head. "You're a fantastic writer."

"How long were you lying here reading through my stuff?" She felt a flush run up her cheeks. She was going to hyperventilate.

"Long enough."

"Conner…" There was one more detail he didn't know. She'd been reluctant to tell him. She bit her lower lip. "We need my salary."

He narrowed his gaze. "Bullshit. You're scared. When I asked you to marry me, I thought I was marrying a feisty woman in jeans with a dirty mouth. What happened to her?"

"She's pregnant."

The long silent pause was deafening.

She watched his face as he blinked several times.

Shit. Would he be mad? They weren't even married yet. Hell, they'd only been engaged a few weeks. He'd badgered her to sell her house and move in with him for months. Sabrina had hedged. It was a huge step. She worried about not having her own private space where she didn't have to submit to him.

Finally Conner had weaseled that concern out of her. He'd turned one of his guest rooms into an office and sat her down inside the wonderful inviting space. "No submitting in this room. I promise. It's your domain. I won't ask anything of you when you're in here. Consider it a safe room."

When she'd woken up the next morning in his arms, she found him kissing each of her fingers. It took her a moment to realize there was a ring on her hand. He'd slipped it on in the night.

Sabrina bolted up in bed and lifted her hand to her face. "Conner. Oh my God."

He smiled. "You like it?"

She glared at him. "Usually men ask first and then put a ring on."

He shrugged. "I figured this way it would be too late for you to say *no*."

She swatted him with her other hand, still staring at the enormous rock.

"Well?"

"Well, what?" she teased.

"Will you marry me, Sabrina?"

She hesitated, but only for the satisfaction of making him squirm. When it appeared he might faint—his face was so white—she put him out of his misery. "Yes."

Now, she stared at that same man with that same white face once again. If he fainted on her, he would crush her with his weight. "Conner?" she whispered. *Shit.*

"Are you sure?" he finally asked, licking his lips. He wiggled himself lower down her body and off her waist until he straddled her hips instead. His gaze roamed down to her belly.

"Yes." She held her breath, waiting for him to catch up to her. She'd known for a few days. He deserved a moment.

They'd talked about having kids. It had worried her. Conner insisted he wanted them. But they hadn't discussed when. Obviously now wasn't exactly the plan.

Finally, he released her wrists and smoothed his hands down her arms until he gripped her waist with his huge palms. He wormed his way down her body until he was flat, his face hovering over her belly.

Sabrina couldn't breathe. She hadn't planned to tell him like this. She knew when it happened. Damn antibiotic she'd taken last month…

Conner eased his palms under her shirt and pushed it up to her bra. He set his lips on her bare belly and kissed it reverently. "Best news ever."

She exhaled. Tears escaped the corners of her eyes.

The hottest man alive loved her. He wasn't mad. He lifted his gaze to her. "That gives you nine months."

"Nine months for what?"

"To finish that book you're writing before we never get enough sleep again." He grinned.

"Conner." She groaned. He wouldn't leave it alone.

"Don't sass me, woman. I don't care if you are pregnant. I can still take you over my knee."

She giggled. He was so ridiculous sometimes. She decided to goad him. "You still haven't used that flogger on me. Maybe if I'm extra naughty. Hmm." She bit her lip while she pondered the idea. He was still reluctant to use the flogger, saying she was too important to him to risk her emotional ability to handle that level of dominance.

"You're kidding, right?" He narrowed his gaze. "No way in hell I'm flogging my pregnant wife." He shook his head. He was getting ahead of himself calling her his wife, but she figured with this new information he was liable to drag her to the justice of the peace that very afternoon.

Besides, the word sounded awesome coming from his lips. *Wife*.

He steered the conversation back to her writing. "You'll write the book and get a publisher before that baby comes, or I'll withhold sex for months until you do."

"You wouldn't dare." Her eyes widened.

He nodded. "In fact, it can be an incentive. If you don't meet a daily word count, I don't fuck you."

Her mouth fell open. "You can't do that."

"Watch me." His head dipped again to nuzzle her belly. "So happy," he muttered.

How had her world gotten so perfect so fast? She wove her hand into his hair. "I love you."

"Love you too, baby." And then his tongue was on her, inching its way south. So much for packing…

AUTHOR'S NOTE

I hope you've enjoyed *Want* from The Fight Club series. Please enjoy the following excerpt from *Lust*, the next book in the series.

LUST

THE FIGHT CLUB, BOOK SIX

Zane swung into the passenger side of the ambulance and somehow managed to shut the door and buckle himself in before jerking his phone out and pressing speed dial for Rider.

Vance drove. He turned on the siren before they pulled away from the fire station and headed west. "Rider called this in?" Vance glanced at Zane, who nodded as he listened to the phone ring on the other end.

"Come on. Come on. Pick up."

"Zane."

Zane exhaled briefly before speaking. "Rider. You hurt? Emily?"

"No. No. We're both fine. Called this in from my neighbor's house. Two doors to the left. You on the call?"

"Yep. Be there in a few minutes. What's the situation?"

"Emily went outside to sit on the patio and heard screaming. She yelled for me, and I ran in the direction of the noise. Her name's Abby. She just moved in about a month ago. We've only met a few times. I think Emily has talked to her more than that."

"Dude."

"Yes?"

"What's Abby's problem?"

"Shit. Right." There was a pause, and then Rider lowered his voice. "She's trapped under her back patio."

"Come again?"

Rider's voice grew more muffled. "Apparently there were kittens under the patio whining. Abby crawled halfway under to rescue them." He was practically whispering.

"Rider? What the hell are you not saying? I can barely hear you. Is it a secret that your neighbor is stuck?"

"Fuck. Man. I'm trying not to chuckle," he mumbled. "It's not funny. A piece of the porch slipped and pinned her underneath."

"And this is funny how?" Zane held on to the handle above the door as Vance rounded a corner.

Rider cleared his throat. He sounded more serious when he spoke again. "Uh. Well…"

"Never fucking mind, dude. We're pulling in. Be back there in a second." Zane ended the call and dropped the cell next to him in the console.

"What was that about?" Vance asked as they jumped from the ambulance and made their usual fast-paced walk to the back of the truck to grab their packs.

The Vegas heat was already stifling this morning. Zane felt the hot sun burning the back of his neck. "Not a fucking clue. Some woman is trapped under her porch. Not sure what Rider was mumbling about, but somehow he finds this humorous."

Vance tipped his head and grinned. "You never know. I've only been with the department six months myself, but Lord have I already seen my share of weirdness." Vance heaved his pack higher up on his shoulder as they both rounded the side of the house.

The first person Zane saw was Emily, Rider's fiancée. She was kneeling next to the steps of the back porch, leaning forward.

Rider grabbed Zane's attention next. He jogged into Zane's line of sight. "You're gonna need some tools to extract her. I think there's a nail jabbing her."

Zane nodded, furrowing his brow as he rounded the steps and came around Emily. And then he hesitated. *Jesus.*

Whoever Abby was, she had the best fucking set of legs he'd ever seen, and the finest ass too, made all the more obvious by the fact that she wore cut-off jeans that were short enough he could see the rounded globes of her amazing ass peeking out from underneath.

And that was all he could see because the rest of her was hidden under the porch.

Vance didn't seem nearly as affected. He immediately kneeled at Abby's other side and set a hand on her thigh.

Zane gritted his teeth. For some fucked-up reason that made not one lick of sense, he didn't like Vance fondling the sexy legs. He felt the irrational urge to swat Vance away and take his spot next to the sweetest ass he'd ever seen.

A slightly repressed chuckle to his right made Zane whip his gaze to find Rider staring at him, his lips pursed and his eyes dancing with mirth.

The man was right. This was not a laughing matter, but holy mother of God, Rider knew Zane well. He'd clearly been trying to find a tactful way of warning Zane about Miss Sexy Legs and hadn't managed to get the words out before Zane arrived.

Vance's voice jerked Zane back to face the situation. "I think we need some tools, Zane. Call for backup."

Zane didn't like the sound of that. He rushed forward, ignoring the request and kneeling on the ground behind Miss Legs, intent on figuring out what on earth had her so stuck they needed more equipment.

Emily leaned out of his way as Zane placed one hand on the ground beside Abby's hip and lowered his face to peer under the porch.

Fuck.

The first thing he noticed was the board that had slipped and fallen on her ass just below her waist. The second thing he noticed was the nail sticking out the top of the board, rusted and crooked. If that nail was as long as he suspected, a good portion of it was currently puncturing her ass.

And then he heard her voice for the first time. She sniffled and then spoke softly. "Can you lift it off?"

Zane twisted his gaze to Vance, who raised his eyebrows and stood. "Okay, then. I'll call it in. *You* talk to the woman."

"Abby," a tiny voice informed them.

As Vance moved to step back a few paces, Zane took the spot he vacated. "Abby. Ma'am. My name's Zane. I'm a medic with the fire department. We're working on it. Hang tight, okay?"

"Zane..." It sounded as though she was trying his name out on her lips.

He leaned closer, trying to get a better look at her. But it was too dark under the steps and all he could see was a mass of black hair. "I'm right here, Abby. Hold on, hon."

"I'm scared. And dirty. And embarrassed."

Zane chuckled low. "I'm sure you are. Don't worry. Nothing to be embarrassed about. Shit happens." He touched the board lying across her back and started to lift it. It barely budged.

Abby squealed. "God. Stop. Oh my God." Her legs tensed; her toes, tucked in an old pair of sneakers, curled under to brace herself.

Zane released the board slowly. *Shit.* "Okay. Okay. I won't touch it again." He shifted his gaze to follow the length of the board. It had dislodged from the bottom of the porch but remained wedged tight on one end. The only lucky aspect of this situation was that it had stopped short of putting all of its weight on Abby. It was long and heavy.

"It hurts so bad." She began to cry.

Her sobbing tore a hole in Zane, and he tried to shake the irrationality of the way he felt about this woman he'd never seen. Fine legs and a fantastic ass, albeit an impaled one, were not usually the only criteria he used to select a woman. A serious case of pure lust.

Sirens wailed again. He knew they were getting close. "There's a fire truck almost here, baby. They have more tools than the ambulance." He leaned in, squeezing himself a few inches under the porch alongside her, telling himself she needed the moral support. And why the hell was he assigning her endearing nicknames? *Baby? Jesus.*

A small hand, covered in dirt, wormed its way toward him and grabbed his as he reached closer to brush her hair back. He still couldn't see her face, but he felt the wetness of her tears running down her cheeks. "It hurts, Zane."

"I know, baby. We're gonna get you out of this. I promise." *The nail must be deep.*

He thought she nodded as she gripped his hand tighter. Her fingers dug into his palm. He didn't give a fuck.

She rested her cheek on her other arm bent under her head. "I've never been so humiliated in my life."

Zane stroked the back of her hand with his thumb. It was all he could do to soothe her. "You're going to be fine. Think about something else." He glanced around in the dark and spotted a flashlight next to her. It wasn't on. He needed to talk to her to keep her calm. "Emily said you were looking for kittens. Where are they?"

She sniffled. "Damn things ran out as soon as I wiggled under here and got stuck."

He chuckled at her cussing. She was feisty. He liked feisty. *What are you thinking, man? Who cares if she's feisty?* "Figures. Squirrelly little things. Can't trust them to stay still for one minute," he teased.

"Are you making fun of me?" She winced. "Never mind. I'd make fun of me too."

Zane reached for the flashlight with his free hand.

"Batteries are dead," she muttered.

"Figures."

"Yeah. I'm not having a good day. Better watch out. The house might fall on you." She didn't laugh. In fact she winced again. At least he'd managed to keep her mind off her problem for a few minutes.

Voices behind Zane told him the cavalry had arrived. He twisted his head an inch to see better, but Abby gripped him harder. "Don't leave. I'm scared."

"Not going anywhere, baby," he whispered, holding her firmly. "I've got you."

Two men from the station moved closer. He watched their feet as they shuffled forward to assess the situation.

Zane spoke to them from his semi-hidden location. "There must be a nail sticking out the other side of that board. She's pinned pretty good."

"Got it." That voice belonged to Gavin. That meant the other legs were undoubtedly Troy's. Good men. They would get her out of this mess, but Zane's chest actually hurt for the pain she would endure as though she were his own wife. He stopped breathing for a second at the absurdity of that thought.

The men discussed their options for several moments and then leaned in closer. Troy spoke. "Gonna have to hoist this board off her. We'll use a jack. Zane, can you hold her steady when we're ready?"

"Yep." He hated every bit of this. Usually he could remain completely disassociated when on a call. Always. Not usually. He was trained to separate his emotions while at work.

Not this time. Not this woman. Not Abby.

She whimpered again. "What's he talking about?" she mumbled.

Zane inched farther under the porch. He was almost in the same predicament as she was now, his back grazing against the underside of the wood. His face was nearly level with hers, though he couldn't see her features clearly. Her hair was a tangled mess all around her, long thick locks blocking his view, concealing her further in the darkness. He could barely make out her lips, and only because she licked them. "They're going to use a jack, kind of like a car jack, to lift the porch off you."

She sucked in a breath. "That's gonna hurt like a mother fucker."

Zane chuckled. "Yes it is, but the alternative is spending the rest of your life under this porch in the dark waiting for the rusty nail to kill you slowly."

She almost giggled, her body shaking as she took in his words. "Don't make me laugh. That hurts even more."

"Sorry, baby." He stroked her hand again. "I'm going to let go of your hand and brace your legs now."

She gripped harder. "Not sure I like that idea."

"It's not my first choice for this morning either, baby."

She released his grip, curling her hand into a fist and tucking it under her chest. She took a deep breath. "Zane."

"Yeah."

"I'm really, really stuck. It feels like a ten-inch nail is running into my ass."

"I know. And we're going to get you out from under here. And it's going to hurt. And then I'm going to take you to the hospital and they will fix you up."

"Ready?" Gavin asked from above.

Zane wiggled his hand out from under the porch and gripped Abby's thigh right below her ass cheek. He held her tight.

She tensed, every muscle under his hand firming. "Shit."

"You okay, Abby? They're going to start lifting now."

"Mmm hmm. Too bad the most action I've had with a man in months is beneath my back porch with a nail impaling my ass, but sure. Go for it."

Zane chuckled. He held her tighter, gripping her thigh and biting his cheek to stave off his ridiculous reaction to her sexy ass. Her fucking perfect sexy ass. Firm. Smooth. An excellent handful. *And impaled with a rusty nail, you asshole.*

Abby screamed as the jack lifted the porch. Her body jerked, but Zane held her firmly in his grip, his fingers digging in to her thigh, oh so precariously close to her pussy.

"Son of a bitch," she yelled. "Just fucking do it already."

"Can you move any faster?" Zane twisted his face to shout.

Troy leaned over. "Trying."

And then the jack stopped a few inches above her ass, and Gavin spoke again. "That's all we can do. We're going to have to cut the nail. It's embedded deep."

Abby squealed. "What did he say?"

Zane held her hand tighter and wiggled his other arm back under the porch to brush her hair off her face again.

"They have special tools to cut through the nail, Abby. It's gonna be okay."

She shook her head. "No. God. No no no."

He held her face in his hand. "It's the only way. Normal procedure. Without knowing how deep that nail is, we need to transport you to the hospital without removing it. Let them handle it."

"Oh God." Her voice squeaked with renewed panic. "Can't they just fucking pull it out?"

"I wish they could, baby." He brushed tears from her cheek. He couldn't see her face, but he could feel her fear with his fingers. Her lips were pursed as she set her other cheek on the ground in defeat.

A loud noise filled the momentary silence.

Abby stiffened.

"Can you hold her steady again, Zane?" Gavin asked.

Zane reluctantly released her face to maneuver his hand back down to her thigh and hold her steady.

She tensed every muscle in her body, her thigh and ass stiff beneath his grip as the noise grew closer.

"Quicker, Gavin," Zane yelled.

"On it," Gavin responded.

Zane gritted his teeth and held his breath alongside Abby as the saw did its work, carefully cutting through the nail between the board and Abby's butt.

Suddenly the noisy saw disappeared, the board lifted off several inches, and the light of day filtered under the porch.

Abby yelped and then she squirmed. "Oh God. Get me the fuck out of here."

Zane scooted back, keeping his face low to make sure she was truly cleared, and then he grabbed her by the hips and dragged her out from under the house slowly, careful not to let the nail become embedded any worse.

"Shit. Shit shit shit," she screamed.

As soon as she was clear, still lying on her stomach, Zane shouted instructions. "Clean gauze. Saline. Hurry." He leaned down to speak directly to Abby's ear, covered in her hair. "Hold still, baby. Let me secure the site and get a gurney."

"'K." Her voice was soft, but her breathing was heavy.

Zane took several items from his partners as they were handed to him. Vance kneeled on Abby's other side. He already wore a pair of sterile gloves, but he only held Abby steady as Zane put his own on. Bless Vance for whatever possessed him to realize this was Zane's gig. Zane didn't even look up to make eye contact with his partner.

Abby's shorts were torn. He carefully lifted the denim over the nail and tugged her low-riding shorts down a few inches, revealing the thick rusty nail and angry puncture at the top of her right cheek, oozing blood. He grabbed the bottle of saline that landed in his hand and poured it over the wound.

Abby flinched, but she didn't scream again.

Thank God. If he heard her make that sound one more time, he would surely melt. He would gladly go the rest of his life never hearing that fear and pain coming from Abby's lips again.

Next, he grabbed the offered gauze and draped it gently around the wound.

"Shit," she muttered, but not as forcefully this time.

"Hang on, baby." He taped the gauze into place across her lower back and butt cheek and then moved a few inches away from Abby for the first time since this entire fiasco began. "Gonna lift you onto a board now, Abby."

"'K."

Vance stuck the stiff board up against Abby's side. Zane

tucked his fingers under her hip and shoulder while Vance did the same on the other side.

"One, two, three," Vance said. Together they eased her from the ground to the board, leaving her on her belly.

Abby whimpered again, but she didn't cry out.

Zane mirrored Vance as they lifted the board onto the gurney and then hoisted it from ground level to his waist. He brushed her hair from her face. Her hands were balled up under her chest as he tucked a lock of thick black hair behind her ear. Tears smeared her cheek. Mascara ran down her face.

And he'd never seen anyone more beautiful. She took his breath away. Huge blue eyes blinked up at him. She licked her full pink lips and gave him a smile. "Thanks," she whispered. She wiggled out a hand and grabbed his where it hovered at her ear.

"Any time." He smiled down at her but forced himself to stand straighter.

Vance started pushing the gurney. Zane took the other end. As they wheeled her up the slight incline toward the side of the house, Zane caught Rider's gaze for the first time since he'd arrived on the scene.

Rider's brow was furrowed in natural concern, but his lips were tipped up at the corners. The bastard was smirking. He wrapped his arm around Emily and held her to his side. Zane watched as he kissed his fiancée's forehead and pulled her tight. It was a natural reaction anyone had after something intense made them grateful for their unblemished lives.

As Rider set his cheek against Emily's head, he smiled at Zane and lifted his brows.

How did the damn man know him so well?

Zane turned his gaze back to the woman he was hauling around the house. He wanted to stroke his fingers through her thick hair and kiss her temple the way Rider had done to Emily. That wasn't even close to reasonable or possible, however.

And he needed to get his head out of his ass. He didn't know this woman. Just because her butt was fucking fantastic and she had the nicest legs he'd ever set eyes on didn't mean he should race out and buy her a ring.

Hell, he'd probably never see her again after he dropped her at the hospital. Whatever tone he'd heard in her voice and whatever look he'd thought he'd seen in her eyes, both were a result of her stress and fear. To think this woman had even one tiny thought toward him romantically was ridiculous.

ALSO BY BECCA JAMESON

Canyon Springs:

Caleb's Mate

Hunter's Mate

Corked and Tapped:

Volume One: Friday Night

Volume Two: Company Party

Volume Three: The Holidays

Surrender:

Raising Lucy

Teaching Abby

Leaving Roman

Project DEEP:

Reviving Emily

Reviving Trish

Reviving Dade

Reviving Zeke

Reviving Graham

Reviving Bianca

Reviving Olivia

Project DEEP Box Set One

Project DEEP Box Set Two

SEALs in Paradise:

Hot SEAL, Red Wine

Hot SEAL, Australian Nights

Hot SEAL, Cold Feet

Dark Falls:

Dark Nightmares

Club Zodiac:

Training Sasha

Obeying Rowen

Collaring Brooke

Mastering Rayne

Trusting Aaron

Claiming London

Sharing Charlotte

Taming Rex

Tempting Elizabeth

Club Zodiac Box Set One

Club Zodiac Box Set Two

The Art of Kink:

Pose

Paint

Sculpt

Arcadian Bears:

Grizzly Mountain

Grizzly Beginning

Grizzly Secret

Grizzly Promise

Grizzly Survival

Grizzly Perfection

Arcadian Bears Box Set One

Arcadian Bears Box Set Two

Sleeper SEALs:

Saving Zola

Spring Training:

Catching Zia

Catching Lily

Catching Ava

Spring Training Box Set

The Underground series:

Force

Clinch

Guard

Submit

Thrust

Torque

The Underground Box Set One

The Underground Box Set Two

Saving Sofia (Special Forces: Operations Alpha)

Wolf Masters series:

Kara's Wolves

Lindsey's Wolves

Jessica's Wolves

Alyssa's Wolves

Tessa's Wolf

Rebecca's Wolves

Melinda's Wolves

Laurie's Wolves

Amanda's Wolves

Sharon's Wolves

Wolf Masters Box Set One

Wolf Masters Box Set Two

Claiming Her series:

The Rules

The Game

The Prize

Emergence series:

Bound to be Taken

Bound to be Tamed

Bound to be Tested

Bound to be Tempted

Emergence Box Set

The Fight Club series:

Come

Perv

Need

Hers

Want

Lust

The Fight Club Box Set One

The Fight Club Box Set Two

Wolf Gatherings series:

Tarnished

Dominated

Completed

Redeemed

Abandoned

Betrayed

Wolf Gatherings Box Set One

Wolf Gathering Box Set Two

Durham Wolves series:

Rescue in the Smokies

Fire in the Smokies

Freedom in the Smokies

Stand Alone Books:

Blind with Love

Guarding the Truth

Out of the Smoke

Abducting His Mate

Three's a Cruise

Wolf Trinity

Frostbitten

A Princess for Cale/A Princess for Cain

ABOUT THE AUTHOR

Becca Jameson is a USA Today best-selling author of over 90 books. She is most well-known for her Wolf Masters series and her Fight Club series. She currently lives in Houston, Texas, with her husband and her Goldendoodle. Two grown kids pop in every once in a while too! She is loving this journey and has dabbled in a variety of genres, including paranormal, sports romance, military, and BDSM.

A total night owl, Becca writes late at night, sequestering herself in her office with a glass of red wine and a bar of dark chocolate, her fingers flying across the keyboard as her characters weave their own stories.

During the day--which never starts before ten in the morning!--she can be found jogging, running errands, or reading in her favorite hammock chair!

…*where Alphas dominate*…

Becca's Newsletter Sign-up:
http://beccajameson.com/newsletter-sign-up

Join my Facebook fan group, Becca's Bibliomaniacs, for the most up-to-date information, random excerpts while I work, giveaways, and fun release parties!

Facebook Fan Group:
https://www.facebook.com/groups/BeccasBibliomaniacs/

Contact Becca:
www.beccajameson.com
beccajameson4@aol.com

facebook.com/becca.jameson.18
twitter.com/beccajameson
instagram.com/becca.jameson
bookbub.com/authors/becca-jameson
goodreads.com/beccajameson
amazon.com/author/beccajameson

Printed in Great Britain
by Amazon

21929765R00175